─────────────── ★ ───────────────

The package arrived at my desk in the Friday mail. No return address, and a San Francisco postmark.

I thumbed through the mail, stopping to poke at the bulky envelope. The contents felt lumpy yet squishy through the padding. With interest, I pulled off the mailing tape and opened an end of the envelope. A ripe odor of raw poultry seeped out.

What seemed to be a quartet of small, plucked, headless game birds were pressed side-by-side in the plastic; they were lapped by watery, blood-tinged liquid.

It was obvious now why the envelope was wet. The other end of the plastic bag had been clipped off at one corner, and a wide strip of white paper inserted over the birds' chests. There was just one word lettered, in neat though runny black letters, on the paper. *Revenge,* it said.

─────────────── ★ ───────────────

Previously published Worldwide Mystery title by
CYNTHIA LAWRENCE

DEATH TO DONUTS!
(In A Feast of Crime)

CHILL
BEFORE
SERVING

CYNTHIA P. LAWRENCE

W🌐RLDWIDE®

TORONTO • NEW YORK • LONDON
AMSTERDAM • PARIS • SYDNEY • HAMBURG
STOCKHOLM • ATHENS • TOKYO • MILAN
MADRID • WARSAW • BUDAPEST • AUCKLAND

Recycling programs
for this product may
not exist in your area.

CHILL BEFORE SERVING

A Worldwide Mystery/September 2012

First published by iUniverse, Inc.

ISBN-13: 978-0-373-63712-6

For Robyn Gair,
who died too young.

PROLOGUE

SIXTY TINY HEADLESS BIRDS lay in the dark. They were lined up in neat rows in trays, their breasts stiff with cold. The steel door of the meat locker opened. The intruder stepped in and switched on the bare overhead light. Swirls of refrigerated air turned quick breaths into vagrant puffs. Silently the heavy door swung closed.

Outside the meat locker, the kitchen and the restaurant, it was night. The intruder had dressed for invisibility as well as warmth: black wool pullover, black watch cap over the ears, black pants, socks, tennies, thin black leather gloves. One hand carried a small satchel which was hurriedly placed on a steel utility table.

The satchel yielded a large hypodermic and a bottle filled with clear liquid. Quickly the intruder filled the needle, softly singing a nursery rhyme, more to keep sensitive teeth from chattering than for a need of self-expression. When the pie was opened, went the rhyme, the birds began to sing. Efficiently, a glove-clad hand pinched each bird's breast while the other hand plunged a nee-

dle under the skin. Wasn't that a lovely dish to set before the king.

It took no more than ten minutes to inject all sixty birds. The intruder dropped the hypodermic into the satchel, snapped the bag shut and left the meat locker, remembering to switch off the ceiling light. Only the birds had been disturbed and they were too dead to squawk.

ONE

I WAS GETTING very tired of eating chocolate truffles, even the hazelnut kind. Next aisle over, a sliver of Parma ham tempted me. And a cube of pistachio-studded pate.

It was close to lunchtime and though the San Francisco breezes were whistling to me outside, my feet in their thin-soled pumps reminded me that I'd already covered a few acres of the convention center. Another wisp of ham, a soupcon of honey mustard and a crust of the local sourdough would do nicely for lunch. A woman wearing big hoop earrings and a monk's robe thrust a paper cup of Double Delight Mint Mocha Cappuccino into my accepting hand.

A willing captive of that temple of tidbits, the annual Fancy Food Show, I roamed in search of the new and trendy. I'd flown up from L.A. early that morning to meet my partner and boss Nick, master pizza maker and Westwood restaurateur. As junior partner, my job is to run the catering department at Dellacasa's. I don't cook or carve ice swans. I manage, and shlepp, create menus and theme parties, calm the clients and send out the bills.

Once a year, Nick and I go to the Show. We greet old and new suppliers and sample our way through the aisles of Oregon jams and French Bries, Swiss chocolates and Thai peanut sauces.

I'd noted earlier that sausages were this year's stars. At a dozen booths, a variety of plump wieners sizzled on portable grills. I'd stopped at a few, sampling chunks of pork-with-port wine, herbed turkey, smoked apple sausage, kielbasa, even tofu pups. Meanwhile, I searched for Nick, up one crowded aisle and down another. Stopping at yet another sausage demo, transfixed by the man behind the grill.

He had a knife in his hand and an attitude. His name, I would learn soon after this first encounter, was Polley. No alarm bells went off as I watched him, but it really didn't matter. It was not in my power to change the events which were about to shake up my snug little world.

The sausage man was, at a guess, late forty-something. Small and wiry. His eyes, when he looked up, were green and unnervingly direct. There were squint lines at the corners, as if he'd habitually had a cigarette dangling from his lips, and still missed the curl of smoke. Black hair combed severely back. Hawk-like nose. A cool half-smile. Powerful hands that mesmerized the small crowd that had gathered to watch him.

It wasn't that he turned the four sausages on the

grill; he lifted and slapped them down until they hissed and squirmed. His fork carried them to a chopping block. With deft, gleaming strokes of a chef's knife he slashed each sausage on the bias into precision-cut pieces and stabbed each piece with a toothpick.

There was applause from his audience. He nodded, as if taking a deserved bow. Green eyes surveyed the crowd, stopping at me.

"Ah, pretty lady," he said, the intimacy in his voice pulling at me, "what can I offer you? Everything in this booth is delicious."

There were a few titters from his audience. I'd already sampled enough goodies to have lost my appetite and, besides, he'd annoyed me. Politely, I shook my head, no.

No? One thick black eyebrow lifted. The cajoling voice changed to real or mock indignation.

"Lady," he said, "you don't know what you're missing!"

This one-sided exchange had some spectators applauding. I could feel the color rising in my face. I turned away and walked straight into—Nick!

"Catherine, don't go. I want you to meet someone."

He called out, "Bravo, Polley, bravo!"

The sausage demonstrator looked in Nick's direction. A broad smile lit his face. He edged out of the cramped stall and walked up to Nick, who was a good head taller. Like a boxer, but gently, he jabbed Nick's arm.

"Nick Dellacasa. I didn't recognize you without a pepperoni in your hand."

Nick grinned. "You should see the restaurant now, Polley. We out-fancy anything you call Italian up here."

I uttered a discreet *ahem*.

"Ah, Catherine," said Nick. "I saw you standing here and came over. And, look who else I found. Cat, I'd like you to meet Polley Arbusto." Emphatically, as if he expected me to disagree, he added, "The greatest chef on the entire West Coast."

"That's kind of you," said Polley.

Nick went on. "Polley, this is Catherine Deean, my catering partner. Friend to me and Rosie. *And,* godmother to my two boys."

We shook hands. He had a firm, no-nonsense handshake. A courteous smile for me, because I was Nick's friend. But the green eyes appraised me. What was I *really* to Nick? they asked. I was glad my suit was a sedate knee-length.

I couldn't pin it down, but somewhere I'd heard his name. Maybe Nick and Rosie had talked about him. No, there was more to it, I felt sure. Something about Polley made me uneasy.

After nibbling all day like a depraved mouse, all I wanted for dinner was comfort food: a gummy grilled American cheese sandwich and equally bland soup in the hotel coffee shop. Followed by the local TV news and CNN in my hotel room. It didn't always happen that Nick and I dined together on a short trip like this. Nick had old buddies from the year he'd lived and worked in San Francisco, as well as suppliers who were happy to carry him off to wine, dine and talk shop. This time Nick drew me aside to tell me he and Polley were having dinner in Chinatown. Nick was in high spirits, his strong face flushed and eager, like a kid who's been offered a second ride on the Cyclone.

"You don't mind, Cat, if just us two paisanos get together and do some catching up over dinner?"

I assured him that I'd gotten up so early to catch my flight, all I wanted was a warm bath and the new issue of *Gourmet.* Later on at the hotel, I had tried to call my reporter friend, Nate Greene, at the *Post-Ledger* but he was out of town on assignment. So there was ample time to think about Polley.

Why, for starters, was the greatest chef on the West Coast working for a few bucks an hour as a demonstrator at the Fancy Food Show? It didn't seem that he was there to represent a restaurant. The only sign at the booth said, "Le Figlie Sausages," an excellent national brand.

Why, a minor puzzlement, was Nick choosing to have dinner in *Chinatown?* Nick was a fervent believer in Italian/California cuisine, with its woodburning pizza ovens, the deifying of the roasted red pepper and the oddball greens, the grilled meats and Chardonnay sauces. A restaurant tour of the city with Nick became a blur of pastas, purees and undercooked veggies. What an evolvement from Nick's original Sicilian pizzeria in Brooklyn!

It was also obvious that Polley had an appetite for women—*for heavensakes, so what?* I was tired, that was certain, and reading sinister secrets into the glance of a man I'd met for ten minutes, a talented man, a friend of Nick's—and I adored Nick.

Time for bed. Tomorrow, before our plane to L.A. left at noon, I was to interview two local chefs for a temporary opening in my catering department at Dellacasa's.

I had just drifted off when the phone rang.

"Cat?" said Nick. "Did I wake you?"

"No, not at all. How was your dinner?"

Nick sounded excited, a little drunk.

"Wonderful, just wonderful. Listen, Cat, early tomorrow, you might as well cancel those two appointments."

"Oh?"

A pause, then, "Polley's agreed to come and cook for us."

"Oh."

"It's okay, Cat, he's the best. Trust me."

"Of course I do. But you told me you haven't seen him in a long time." And, after all, catering was my department. "Where's he been cooking lately?"

A trifle defensively: "Well, he hasn't. He got himself into a little trouble up here, and he needs to make a fresh start. Listen, I'll tell you all about it on the plane. Don't worry. Get a good night's sleep. I'll see you at the airport."

"Uh, Nick, what kind of—?"

I could hear Polley's voice, muffled, in the background.

"I've gotta go. Polley's brought his car around and there's no place to park. We're going to some joint near the Presidio for a nightcap." A chuckle.

"Sure, Nick. I'll meet you at the airport."

I cradled the phone. How could I be hungry again? In my carryall was a goldfoil sample box of two bittersweet chocolate truffles topped with candy leaves. Fumbling in the dark, I dug it out, thoughtfully demolished the chocolates, rejected brushing my teeth a second time, punched up the bed pillows and fell asleep.

TWO

AT THE GATE, Nick looked about as wobbly as an aspic in an earthquake. He'd avoided questions on Polley's troubles during the hour plane ride to L.A. In truth, he was dreadfully hungover. With quavering hand, he'd accepted a plastic glass of Bloody Mary mix, sipped, then slept with little hiccuping snores until we landed.

I had never seen Nick that strung out. As Italian chef, businessman, proud husband and father, he is a man of moderation and good humor. Not that I couldn't imagine a younger, wilder Nick. The surprise was that he'd been so easily led around now. How much nostalgia, how many martinis before Polley got a new job?

Our cars were parked at the airport. Nick drove home for a further nap before the dinner hour at Dellacasa's. I went directly to the restaurant. Mario, our catering chef, had taken a late lunch; my news would have to wait. Nick's wife, the serene and lovely Rosie, was paying bills in the back office. I said casually that Nick had hired a temporary chef. At the mention of Polley's name, Rosie's shining brown eyes turned black and opaque; she clutched her desk as if she was determined to break off an edge.

"Did he?" said Rosie, and that was all she said before marching grimly off to a meeting with our paper goods supplier. I ran up the stairs to my little office and called Nate Greene.

"Nate? Cat Deean."

"Hi, gorgeous girl, where are you?"

It's always a pleasure to hear Nate Greene's voice. He still has the warmth that many reporters lose along with their illusions about goodness, justice and the chances of the Dodgers.

"I'm back in L.A."

"Yeh, your message was waiting for me this morning. Sorry I missed you. I was in Sacramento covering a hearing on pesticide residues in food. Scary stuff. But let's talk about something more pleasant. I saw in the columns that you catered a dinner for Ronald Wesley." Ronald is a director and a multi-Oscar winner.

"Oh, that was a few months ago," I said.

"Well?"

"Well, what?"

"You're up there with the star makers. Has fame gone to your head? Have you turned blonde and acquired a pair of Rottweilers?"

"No to everything," I said, smiling at the phone. "I'm still humble and brunette, and when I come home from work after midnight I'm not about to walk any pet that's tamer than a starved wolf.

"But Nate—"

"Yes?"

"Yesterday's phone call was strictly social. Today I need a favor. Some information, actually."

Nate has been generous with information and favors since we met in a World Lit class at UCLA. Sometimes I wish that we had fallen in love back then, but we were two gentle adolescents searching for our passionate opposites. After our senior year, Nate left for graduate school at Berkeley. Too bad.

"You've come to the right desk, ma'am. The secret of a perfect souffle is whipping the egg whites into a mad froth…"

A weak heh-heh from me and he stopped. "Okay, Cat, what's up?"

"I need to know about a chef up your way, name of Polley Arbusto. Could you look him up and see if he's in your newspaper files? Or ask your restaurant critic. I mean, where Polley worked, what kind of reputation he has. And, some reason why he'd want to leave town." I paused reflectively. "Maybe money, or an ex-wife, or a jealous girlfriend."

Nate was saying, "Polley Arbusto? Polley? Oh, wow, you mean HIPPOLYTUS ARBUSTO!"

"You know him?"

"Listen, everyone in the Bay Area knows him. He's dropped out of sight since his release. His restaurant has a new name, new owners. I thought Arbusto had left town."

I could hear the reporter's instinct take over. "What's your connection with him, Cat."

"I just met him yesterday, but he's an old friend of my boss. Nick's hired him. What do you mean, *release?* Was he in jail?"

"Just overnight, I believe. For questioning. But the cops couldn't make anything stick, so they had to let him go."

My skin began to prickle. Probably the March winds.

"Questioned about what?"

"Sorry, I didn't say, did I? It was murder most foul. Or, as more than one of our antic journalists said, murder most F-O-W-L."

Fowl murder? "I give up. What's the joke?"

"No joke. There's quite a bit of feeling up here that Arbusto poisoned the quails he served at his own restaurant."

Oh, swell.

"Do you believe it?" I asked.

Nate avoided a direct answer.

"Proof, one must have proof. Arbusto was nearly arrested for murder but there wasn't any solid physical evidence—except, of course, that he prepared the meal. Anyway he walked. Lots of people have it in for him, though. Including most of the gay community up here."

"He's anti-gay? In San Francisco?" I kicked off my shoes and slumped in my chair.

"Depends to whom you're talking. Arbusto's got a loud mouth and a quick temper. In fact, the dinner was to be a peace offering to a gay activist. So, guess who died? The guest of honor!"

It was definitely cold in my office. "I'll admit," I said, "I didn't hear the Hallelujah Chorus when we met, but I can't believe he's nutty enough to murder someone in his own restaurant."

"That's how the police saw it, too." said Nate. "Listen, I'd love to keep talking but I'm on deadline. If you have a fax I'll send you some of the stories about the murder. Give me a couple of hours. We can talk later or tomorrow after you've read them."

I gave him Dellacasa's fax number, thanked him and hung up.

How did we ever get along without the fax? Now the customer who orders take-out on our $6.99 meatball sandwich and a Diet Pepsi no longer needs to interact with a human voice.

Thanks to Small Electronics, my friendship with Nate hummed along by fax, phone and voice mail. Yet I'd never even called him for drinks on my occasional trips to San Francisco.

Well, for five years I'd been married to Gil. Last year, during the divorce, I'd put on ten pounds from a big helping of aggravation. Disaster on my

five-foot-four frame. Awful memories of being
a chunky teen. I'd also given up Mr. Joseph and
endured cheap, bad haircuts (Frank's Fun Salon)
while I paid off my lawyer.

On client days I'd hid under a loose black silk
jacket and wide-brimmed straw hat, and I looked
passable. But about as desirable as a day-old
doughnut. Now I was finally back in shape and,
maybe, it was time to take a chance with a trusted
old friend.

As promised, Nate sent the newspaper's clippings about Polley and the restaurant murder. After
reading through them it seemed to me that Nick
had left part of his brain in San Francisco.

I'd asked Winona, our hostess and guardian of
the fax machine, to be sure that Rosie and Nick
didn't see the articles. Winona is a student in the
Theater Arts program at UCLA. She has long pale
hair and smells faintly of lemon verbena. She called
my office.

"They've arrived," she said in deep, conspira-
torial tones. I hurried down the stairs, put finger
to my lips to signify secrecy and took the curling
sheets of paper.

Nate had sent copies of two stories. Both were
datelined last August. I understood now why I'd
missed an occurrence that must have caused shud-
ders throughout the restaurant business. August
had been my post-divorce European fling, nearly

a month of reestablishing my identity as a happy, resourceful single woman, traveling alone but not lonely. Most of the time I believed it. Once back home, memory told me, I'd seen follow-up articles in the trades. Not that I'd paid much attention. In the category of bizarre crimes, my town will always outperform San Francisco. Now I eagerly arranged the stories by dateline, beginning with the news of the murder.

PERRY FRAMBOISE COLLAPSES, DIES IN RESTAURANT

GAY ACTIVIST IS STRICKEN DURING AIDS BENEFIT DINNER. POLICE SUSPECT POISONING AS OTHER GUESTS BECOME ILL, ARE HOSPITALIZED.

BY PEGGY C. MEADE
STAFF WRITER

SAN FRANCISCO–A peacemaking dinner at a trendy downtown restaurant turned deadly last night for guest of honor Perry Framboise. The prominent gay activist, 45, collapsed at the head table as dessert was being served, and died within minutes. Twenty-four other guests became ill as they waited to be questioned by police, and were rushed to area hospitals.

A dinner guest, Dr. Frank Milch, administered first aid as the stricken Framboise lay on the restaurant floor. "He went into convulsions and then lapsed into a coma. Death came within minutes," Dr. Milch later told reporters who had gathered outside Arbusto's, the Stockton Street restaurant where the benefit was held.

Paramedics who had been called when Framboise became ill remained on the scene with Dr. Milch as other diners began to complain of blurred vision, thirst and fever.

More ambulances were dispatched. Stockton Street at 10 p.m. became a traffic nightmare of sirens and flashing lights as vehicles from the police, medical examiner and paramedics jockeyed for parking space. Police cordoned off the block to regular traffic.

At an impromptu press conference, Inspector Alvin Howard stated, "Dr. Milch told us and the restaurant owner, Mr. Arbusto, has confirmed, that only two guests did not become ill. Those were Dr. Milch and another guest, both vegetarians, who had vegetable plates instead of the game birds course.

"It's too early at this point," added Inspector Howard, "to know whether we're talking about food poisoning or something more deliberate. The medical examiner tells me it will be several days before we have that information."

The twenty-four guests who became ill were given hospital emergency room treatment. Twenty-three were released later that night. One, an AIDS patient, was kept at an area hospital for observation.

In an interview with Hippolytus Arbusto, chef and owner of the popular Arbusto's, the restaurateur said, "This is a terrible tragedy. I don't know how it happened. Everything I prepare is from fresh and wholesome ingredients. Mr. Framboise had a double helping of my quails. He was a big, heavy man. Maybe he ate too much, sometimes people like him don't take care of themselves too well. I was trying to show my goodwill, and look what happened."

The dinner at Arbusto's was a peacemaking gesture to Framboise and the gay and lesbian community. Framboise and other activists had recently picketed Arbusto's after the owner insisted that two gay diners leave.

"It wasn't a matter of civil rights for gays," said Arbusto after the incident. "Those two fellows were making out at one of my front tables. Some other guests were embarrassed. I would have kicked out a man and a woman if they had behaved that way."

Framboise had called off the pickets after a spokesman for Arbusto agreed to hold a benefit dinner to raise funds for AIDS research, with the restaurant picking up the tab. It was last night's dinner to help save lives that turned deadly.

Well! Polley Arbusto, murderer or not, seemed to specialize in cooking his own goose. How could Nick…?

I turned to the second story and learned more indigestible facts about our new chef.

POISON KILLED FRAMBOISE SAYS CRIME LAB

CROWDS OF MOURNERS LIGHT CANDLES OUTSIDE ARBUSTO'S AS RESTAURANT OWNER IS QUESTIONED BY POLICE THEN RELEASED.

BY PEGGY C. MEADE
STAFF WRITER

SAN FRANCISCO–A defiant Hippolytus Arbusto returned last night to Stockton Street to be greeted by a candlelight vigil outside his darkened restaurant.

Arbusto was released by the police after questioning in the Sunday night death of gay activist Perry Framboise. He declined to answer questions from waiting reporters, stating only that his kitchen should be above suspicion. The chef is noted for his creative use of fresh, locally grown and raised foods.

A spokesman for the medical examiner's office confirmed late Monday that poisoning is suspected in the restaurant death of Framboise and the illnesses of twenty-four other diners during the private AIDS benefit dinner. Toxicology tests are still being conducted, said the spokesman.

Although Arbusto parked his car at the rear, the restaurant's chef and owner made a point of shouldering his way through the crowd to the front. Floral offerings left during the day, from a single rose to bouquets and a massive black-leaved wreath, filled the entranceway in front of the carved oak and beveled glass door. Arbusto stepped over the flowers and unlocked the door. He shook his head and called, "You're after the wrong man. I'll be open again for business tomorrow." From the crowd came loud and angry retorts. Arbusto listened to the shouts, seemed surprised and then slipped inside the restaurant.

Framboise's friends and sympathizers had been gathering since dusk to light candles and mourn. Police later estimated that, by dark, several hundred people filled the street. It was closed to traffic on Sunday after Framboise died and other diners who became ill were taken away in ambulances. At 6 p.m. last night the block was once again cordoned off.

Homicide Inspector Alvin Howard said, "We respect this great emotional tribute, but we can't keep the street tied up indefinitely. Mr. Framboise's business associate, Blaine Shepherd, tells me that the candlelight vigil will end tonight, and that a memorial service will be announced in the near future."

He noted that an investigation will continue as the police wait for the medical examiner's report.

I folded the stories, stuffed them into an envelope and tucked it into the back of a desk drawer. It was time to check supplies for tonight's birthday party in Bel Air. Mario would be serving up, in that gated bastion of good living, California peasant fare. All vegetarian. Spinach lasagna. Eggplant alla parmigiana. Artichoke frittata. The marbled steak is an endangered species locally.

I wondered what Polley would prepare when he took over the catering kitchen. And if he had a secret ingredient for his quails. Since I was talking myself into paranoia, I wondered if Polley would assume that I was one of his job perks. Just as unsettling, I'd seen how easily he wielded a wickedly sharp chef's knife. Was he as volatile as the newspaper stories implied? My esteemed relative, Aunt Sadie, often says: when life hands you a lemon, make lemonade. I'd have to ask her what to do about a lemon who possibly might want to squeeze back.

THREE

NEXT MORNING I TRIED to sleep late but a political pollster phoned and woke me shortly after nine a.m. She wanted to know how I felt about the candidates for State Assembly. Was crime or unemployment uppermost in my mind. Was I gay or straight; Anglo, Asian-American, Afro-American, Native American or Latino.

I was undecided, I told her, about almost everything. After all, life's events were so unexpected, how could a thinking person offer certainties? She thanked me warily and hung up.

I yawned, poured my papaya juice, ground some Brazil Santos whole beans and started the coffee, searched in the refrigerator for a slice of whole wheat bread for the toaster and remembered, once again, that I had no toaster.

A divorce can free you of the burden of worldly goods. Our parting was friendly and, since I'd asked to end the marriage, and Gil really was hurt, I was extremely generous (to my mind).

He took the toaster and the omelet pan; I got the coffee grinder and the Cuisinart. I kept grandmother's mission oak dining table. We split the six rush-bottomed dining room chairs we'd found at an auction one serendipitous Saturday in Pasadena. It's a crisis if I want to invite more than two friends for dinner.

What was that burnt smell overpowering the aroma of my fresh-brewed coffee? The bread I'd slipped under the broiler had become a blackened ruin. Damn it, Cat, you don't need to be coupled to buy a toaster; Macy's will allow you to take home a new Sunbeam even if it isn't a wedding gift.

I sacrificed another slice of whole wheat, scraped it, and opened a jar of grapefruit marmalade. First day off, hit the housewares department; buy a toaster. An omelet pan. A whisk. I'd agreed to let Gil have the apartment with a view of Redondo Beach, no regrets, it was such a long commute to Dellacasa's. My new apartment was an upper one bedroom with balcony, on the fringes of Beverly Hills. A bowl of vanilla pudding has more character. But I'd wanted to move in a hurry, and it was available.

I poked an arm outside the front door of my apartment, retrieved my newspaper and turned to the daily horoscope. "Powerhouse day," it said, "you'll exude personal magnetism, sensuality. Also a good day to sharpen tools."

I exuded the usual irritability I carried around when I hadn't had enough sleep. It was after midnight yesterday when Mario, my crew and I had packed up and left the Bel Air party. We'd said almost wistful goodnights as Mario walked me to my car before driving the catering van back to Dellacasa's. Oh, in the past we've had a few rousing kitchen quarrels: his creative flights vs. my need to control costs, but over the past two years we've evolved into a team.

Last night was one of our smoother collaborations. The host had known Nick since the early life in Brooklyn. Not long after Nick and Rosie moved to L.A. and opened a Sicilian-style *trattoria,* young Ciccio Bosco followed, with his widowed mother, Sarafino, and the three maiden daughters, Teresa, Maria and Mimi.

As time went on, Ciccio, once voted the sexiest dancer in the Lafayette High School senior class, became a dance studio instructor. In the cha-cha-cha-crazed '60s, he opened the first of what became a profitable chain of studios. Along the way, he grew sideburns, slicked back his black hair, and glided his tall, taut body into his new identity as Carlos, The Tango Teacher.

When salsa hit the dance floor, Carlos became rich. He turned vegetarian, switched from Chianti to obscure Italian mineral waters, and bought the Bel Air house with its separate wing for his mother and the maiden daughters.

Sarafino, in black, sat with her usual scowl in the corner of the Italian Provincial living room, banned from the kitchen, forbidden to cook her justly famous Fried Calf's Brains, cast aside by her only son for a *catered* birthday dinner, oh! the shame of it.

The three maidens who, unfortunately, had inherited their mother's moustache, and a shyness all their own, could not console Sarafina.

The twenty guests: cousins, uncles, dance studio managers, paid their respects and received rigid nods in return. But she brightened when Nick and Rosie stopped by with a gift after Dellacasa's closed for the night, and even accepted a sliver of our rum-soaked, whipped cream-topped orange chocolate birthday cake.

I enjoyed the melodrama. Caterers are, after all, witnesses to peak moments in other people's lives. We can tell (though we don't) which uncle raided the punch; what cousin wiped out the petits fours; whose husband hid under the stairs with a bridesmaid. Admittedly, sharing other people's celebrations can make me lazy about—in that glib cliche—getting a life. A life? Today, I'd be lucky to get through one afternoon appointment while projecting personal magnetism and sensuality.

I could blame it all on Mario's coming departure.

Despite his name, Mario is not Italian, he's black (Afro-Caribbean-American, to be PC), born into the large Belize community in L.A. He's been our catering chef for two years, hired from the culinary arts program at a downtown trade school. But Mario wants to be a world-famous French chef.

Nick has known from the start that someday Mario would go to France to serve his apprenticeship. He finally was accepted at L'Auberge du Griffon, a country inn near Lyon, with help from Nick's cousin, Nello, a pastry chef at the Majestic in Cannes.

Nick has given Mario a six-month leave of absence; past that, he must decide whether to stay on for the slow climb to four-star glory in France or be king of his own catering kitchen in Westwood. Meantime, Dellacasa's would bring in a temporary catering chef.

Enter Hippolytus Arbusto.

Sexist, probably. Manipulative enough to undermine me to Nick, I think so. A murderer? I couldn't quite convince myself.

I wasn't naive. I'd learned painfully that violence was not only as American as apple pie, it could be downright down home. Once, a neighbor on a rampage nearly sent me to that Party Without End where the cheese straws never wilt, and neither the champagne nor your aching arches ever go flat.

That episode was behind me. The nightmares were over. I was ready again to trust humankind.

Hah! I see myself now rather like a live lobster floating in a warm bath, lazily waving a claw and wondering why the water was beginning to bubble.

But the sky that morning was clear and smogless, and the sun was its conventional shining self. I reached for my briefcase.

My appointment today was with the Vignolo family and their wedding consultant. I needed a final okay on the menu, a look at the grounds for the garden ceremony and reception. Then check out electric outlets, decide where to place the serving tables. It was simpler to go directly from my apartment to the Brentwood house. Mario could meet me there. I phoned him at Dellacasa's.

"Hi, Cat. Super party last night, wasn't it?"

I agreed and explained the reason for my call.

"Hmmmn," said Mario, "let me think."

"Are you busy?"

"It's not that. I came in about half an hour ago and Nick wanted to talk to me first thing. Guess what, Cat?"

"You're not going to France? You're buying a Taco Bell franchise?"

"Better than that! My replacement can start right away, next Monday. Mr. Arbusto phoned Nick and told him he'd be in L.A. later this week. Nick says to spend a couple of days showing him the kitchen and going over our recipes, and then I can leave. But, heck, he'll probably have his own ideas."

"I hadn't thought of that," I said, thinking now of having to renegotiate menus, possibly reprinting all of our folders.

"How great for you," said Mario, "to work with the best."

"I suppose," I said, buoyed up a bit by his enthusiasm. But I added, "The poisonings in San Francisco. They don't bother you?"

"Nick told me that the fellow who was killed had made some enemies. Mr. Arbusto thinks it was just bad timing that it happened at his restaurant.

"Honestly, Cat, he is one of the most creative chefs on the West Coast. You have to believe in him."

"All right, I'll try. What about this afternoon?"

"Sure, I'll meet you. It's important that Mr. Arbusto knows I left everything in good condition."

I was about to hang up when Mario said, "Wait. Rosie's here. She wants to speak with you."

Rosie said, "Catherine. Don't worry. Nick is a good man but he acts like an old Sicilian sometimes, like everyone in the world is a blood relative. Let Polley lay a finger on you or Winona, and he can take his *pastafazool* back to San Francisco."

A long pause, as if she was deciding what else I should know.

"Rosie, are you still there?"

"Sure. Well, that's what I wanted to tell you."

I thanked her and she hung up. The phone rang again.

"Hi, it's Nate. I called Dellacasa's and they said

you were still at home. Probably better. You may want to keep this quiet."

"What? What have you heard?"

"Well, I talked to the chef at a restaurant where I'm one of the regulars. Asked him about Arbusto. He had plenty to say about a little incident that was hushed up."

"An incident?" Might be bad news for Nick.

"Look, there's a lot of pressure in becoming a top chef. I'm surprised more of them don't go over the edge.

"Anyway, a couple of years ago, Arbusto got into a fist fight with a pastry chef named Armand who supplied some of the cakes and tarts and all that for the restaurant. Arbusto smashed his fist into the chef's nose and broke it."

"Who started the fight?"

"Don't know. But Arbusto paid the hospital bills and made Armand his exclusive purveyor of dessert baked goods."

I frowned at the phone. "In return for dropping a lawsuit."

"You got it, gorgeous. Have to rush. Talk to you soon."

Powerhouse day, hmm? It was warm for March, but I clad myself in my red wool power suit and drove towards Brentwood, so distracted I took a wrong turn and ended up in Santa Monica.

FOUR

POLLEY STOOD IN the center of his new workplace. Green eyes checked out my leg-baring tight black skirt, a fashion mistake I wore only when I had no client appointments. Damn it, Polley!

He glanced at the clock on the kitchen wall. It read: 9:32.

Don't be defensive. I said flatly, "Book signing and dessert-and-coffee reception last night. Big success."

A self-deprecating sigh. "Training and habit, I'm always up around dawn, no matter what time I get to bed.

"Women have a different sense of time," he continued. I knew what was coming.

"I'm one of the last holdouts," said Polley, "like the old sea captains. A woman aboard is considered bad luck, a jinx!"

"You don't believe that old nonsense, honestly, Polley?"

He flicked an imaginary spot off the sleeve of his immaculate chef's whites.

"I can be a mean bastard when I'm cooking. A guy in my crew might want to pound a skillet on my head. But he'll *leap* when I order him. A woman, now, she'll sulk and drop the soup ladle. Why?"

He was waiting for me to pick up the challenge. I declined. My answer was a non-committal shrug. He took it as a sign of agreement; as if I'd flattened my ears, folded my paws and recognized him as the Alpha dog of Dellacasa's catering kitchen.

"Don't be afraid of me, Catherine. I know I have a reputation for horrible character flaws. But I'm not totally a bad fellow."

I made polite, insincere sounds of denial. "No, no," said Polley, "I want to get this out in the open. I'm not the kind of man that people love. My children, they ignore Father's Day. Not even an ugly tie, for which I'm grateful. My girlfriend? I left San Francisco two days ago. She's probably found a new man by now. I don't inspire faithfulness."

I was surprised that he'd said so much, and quite sure I didn't want to be his confidante.

"It's all right, Catherine," he said with shoulders hunched, hands jammed into pants pockets, holding himself close and protective. "I'll probably never tell you anything this personal again. But I'd like you to understand. Nick says you're bright and capable. Maybe he went overboard in doing me a favor, but I hope you'll trust him. I can be a tyrant in the kitchen, I have a temper, but I'm not a murderer and I am a hell of a good chef.

"Nick and Rosie think the world of you. So let's make Dellacasa's clients happy. I'll create the beautiful food and you'll serve it."

He beamed, inviting me to really, really like him. "We'll share the applause. We'll be a team. How about it, Catherine?"

Polley extended his hand. What the hell, I shook it. After all, with the police in San Francisco still breathing down his neck, he had more to lose than I did.

Well, everyone said he was a great chef. Maybe, like separating an egg yolk from the white, he could keep his ego and his cooking apart. If so, we could all get along for a few months.

Unless he was a murderer. I wondered if he'd shook Perry Framboise's hand as he greeted him before the fatal dinner. As I'd just seen, Polley could go from crass to charming in seconds. Perhaps he could kill that smoothly. If he asked me to sample his brandied apricot crepes, should I worry? I'd heard his desserts were to die for. Well, there were worse ways to go.

"Call me Cat," I said.

THE PHONE in my office was ringing as I entered.

"Catherine? It's Benny, you got a minute?"

I recognized the gravelly voice of Benny Lombardo, our longtime cheese supplier.

"Sure, Benny. I've been meaning to call and

order more of that new Pecorino. Mario likes it because it's less salty than most. But maybe I'll wait. Mario's going on leave of absence."

"That's why I'm calling, Catherine. I just heard Polley Arbusto is coming to work for you and Nick. I didn't want to talk to Nick, he wouldn't listen, but I thought I should warn you."

"It's okay, Benny, I'm a good listener. Warn me about what?"

"Well, last year, Arbusto attacked one of his suppliers."

"Oh, I know about it," I said, relieved he didn't have worse news. "It was that pastry chef, Armand somebody."

"No," said Benny firmly. "The pastry guy was *two* years ago. You remember my uncle Dominic in San Leandro, the one who makes the good Mozzarella? Well, some winery threw a party at a hotel in San Francisco. Maybe Uncle Dominic and Arbusto both got drunk. Anyway, they got into a fight in the parking lot."

"Who started it?"

"My uncle says it was Arbusto, but who knows? Uncle got a split lip and gave Arbusto a black eye, so it wasn't knives or guns or anything like that. But Arbusto's got a real mean temper. You got to watch out, Catherine, for you and Nick."

There was concern in Benny's hoarse, Jimmy Durante-like voice.

"Thanks for telling me, Benny. So far, Polley's been nice."

"That can change, Catherine. Take care."

"Sucker," said my best friend Marcy, her face wreathed in steam. I shifted defensively on the wooden slats of the steamroom and leaned back, letting the hot, moist air seek out and attack any impurities lurking in my pores.

"Am I supposed to picket?" I asked rationally. "After all, Dellacasa's belongs to Nick and Rosie. I just get a very minor percentage of the profits on my catering operation, and Nick didn't even have to offer me that. What happened is," I said, droplets of sweat blurring my eyes, "Nick just saw an opportunity to bring in someone topnotch on short notice and he took it."

"Topnotch?" Marcy stretched out long, trim legs, patted her face with a towel and slapped the fabric on the wet slats. Splat!

"He's practically on the lam from a murder charge, seemingly can't get a real job in San Francisco, beats up his suppliers, and now he's your partner. *Has* Nick discussed any of it with you?"

"Well, no. He just shuffled his feet and said something about giving it time and Polley and I would get along as nice as meatballs and spaghetti."

Marcy snickered. "Which one of you is the meatball, kiddo? Speaking of which, it's dinnertime, we've exercised and sweated. Now can we eat? And, by the way, is he sexy?"

"He might appeal to the foodies. Give some women a perfect chocolate souffle and they'd strip right in the kitchen."

"Gosh, a *warm* chocolate souffle, runny in the middle?"

"Shush. Besides, he has a girlfriend. She's driving down from San Francisco this weekend. We're closing the restaurant early on Monday and having Mario's farewell party. She'll be at the party."

The door to the steamroom opened. Two towel-clad figures entered, sat and went limp. In the hazy light they looked like ghosts waiting for assignment. I lowered my voice.

"Polley said she probably wasn't faithful. Could be his subtle way of telling me he's available."

Marcy stood, a slim figure of damp hauteur. "I need to buy pantyhose. How about the Food Court at the mall? You always like the Chinese combo plate and I can eat Mexican."

"Heavy on the calories and no class. Perfect. It'll prepare me for six months of Hummingbird Livers with Pureed Nasturtiums."

"Just don't drop your soup ladle on his foot, promise me."

FIVE

THE PACKAGE ARRIVED at my desk in the Friday mail. A standard 10-1/2 x 16 padded envelope, the kind sold at any post office or stationers. Addressed in neat letters with a black felt-tip pen:

CATERING DEPARTMENT, DELLACASA'S, and the address. No return address, and a San Francisco postmark.

I was on the phone at the time, checking on delivery of a dozen ricotta cheesecakes for the Compassionate Matrons of Messina awards banquet. On hold, I thumbed through the mail, stopping to poke at the bulky envelope. The contents felt lumpy yet squishy through the padding. With interest, I pulled off the mailing tape and opened an end of the envelope. A ripe odor of raw poultry seeped out.

Pulling the mouth of the envelope wider, I saw a heat-sealed clear plastic bag inside. What seemed to be a quartet of small, plucked, headless game birds were pressed side-by-side in the plastic; they were lapped by watery, blood-tinged liquid. The inside of the padded envelope was gummy with fluid that had leaked from the bag. I reached for the Kleenex on my desk and, clutching a wad of tissues, gingerly pulled out the soggy bag, holding it over my wastebasket.

It was obvious now why the envelope was wet. The other end of the plastic bag had been clipped off at one corner, and a wide strip of white paper inserted over the birds' chests. There was just one word lettered, in neat though runny black letters, on the paper. REVENGE, it said.

I found a small cardboard carton, dumped in the envelope and its contents, and placed the smelly mess on my desk for closer examination.

The birds had obviously been beheaded at a processing plant before packing, but their identity was no mystery. Printed on the front of the plastic bag were the words, "Premium Quails. Four per package." Total weight and preparation tips were underneath. I doubted if the white slip of paper came from the plant.

REVENGE, it read. For Perry Framboise's death? To reaffirm Polley's guilt? REVENGE. Was the message a reminder of a past crime or a warning for the future?

It occurred to me that I'd gotten some bloody liquid on my hands. Unlikely, I told myself, but what if these quails were also poisoned? I hurried to the bathroom and scrubbed. I scrubbed each hand with the zeal of a road company Lady Macbeth.

Back in my office I stared again at the ripped mailing envelope. This time, the message stared back: it hadn't been sent to *Polley*. The package was addressed to the Catering Department at Dellacasa's: a to-whom-it-may-concern statement.

I was annoyed at the sender. A few more words would have been helpful. Was this revenge meant for Polley? Or for everyone who'd welcomed him here? Shows you how poor communication can create problems. This one, I decided, I'd better share with Nick.

He'd been in downtown L.A. since dawn, along with Mario and Polley, buying at the wholesale food markets. They had stopped for breakfast with the owner of Organicrop Farms. The other two were still shopping. Nick drove up to the restaurant's back door just as I came downstairs to see him.

His venerable station wagon was piled with cartons. Peeking in, I could see Swiss chard, cantaloupes, artichokes, sniff the loamy wealth of California's farmlands. Jose and Damien left their kitchen chores to unload the wagon, Nick himself bearing a carton of plump, ice-packed shrimp.

"Cat!" he said enthusiastically. "One of these days, soon, you should go down to the markets with Polley. That fellow is going to get me out of my rut yet."

I lifted an eyebrow, offered a reality check.

"I didn't realize you were *in* a rut."

"Now, now, Cat, you know what I mean. Polley

has all sorts of fresh ideas for our menus." Nick gestured towards the shrimp. "Like tonight. Listen to this dish. Polley's going to prepare it for us. Prosciutto-Wrapped Shrimp with Cantaloupe *Salsa*."

"Sounds delicious," I admitted.

Nick caught the doubt in my voice. "What's up, Cat?" he asked, frowning. "Some kind of run-in with Polley?"

"No," I said. "Nothing like that. When you've unpacked, please come up to my office. I have something to show you."

"Jose can put the food away. You've got me curious."

Nick followed me up the stairs to my office above the restaurant. It's a small, airy office, shaped like a lasagna pan, just big enough for my desk and chair and a couple of upholstered client chairs. Signed celebrity photos on the wall smile down on the bookcase holding my collection of catering menus, 4-color glamour shots of flower-strewn, hope-filled wedding cakes, more glossy pictures of hors d'oeuvres: artichoke tartlets and Thai dumplings, teensy pizzas and puff pastries, mousses and cheeses, and more edibles heaped, baked or sprinkled over crusts, slices, crackers, cakes and cucumbers.

I wasn't in much of a party mood, showing Nick the envelope and its contents. Though Nick's sturdy frame usually crowds the small room, now he seemed diminished.

"Sonofabitch," he said quietly. "He can't run away from it, can he?"

Whatever "it" was.

Nick leaned over the package and sniffed with distaste.

"Should we call the police?" I asked. "It is a threat."

"No, not yet. This could make problems for Dellacasa's if word got out. First thing, we need to know if the birds are poisoned. If not, it could just be someone up north with a sick sense of humor."

We both stared at the limp little bodies in their plastic shroud.

"Are you sure, Nick?"

He shrugged. "If it's a threat, it's a long-distance threat. I'm not going to jeopardize my friends and my business until I've got a better grip on this.

"What we need is a private laboratory, some place that'll check out the birds, but discreetly. How do we do that? The Yellow Pages?"

Nick's distrust of officialdom is Sicilian and inbred. An attitude much like an echo of my own tightlipped Scottish forebears. I've heard stories of clan conclaves, surprise raids, deadly attacks, going back to the fourteenth century. Not much else to do but right wrongs, I suppose, on the moors of a Saturday night. Well, I won't say that I heard spirit bagpipes that morning. But I do understand the call of medieval value systems. I would stand by Nick.

At this time, however, the pitiful quails weren't Nick's personal challenge. Simply a matter of good business, he said.

I agreed and asked, "How about a private detective?" I told Nick about the discreet P.I. that I'd met during the police search for my murderous neighbor.

"Fine," said Nick. "You handle it. He could also call San Francisco, phone around, see if he can trace the birds. Although I doubt it. Most of the good retail poultry shops sell packaged quails. But let him try. I just don't want him talking to anyone here, in the restaurant."

"Not even Polley? Won't you tell Polley?"

"Of course. He needs to know. And, sure, he can talk to this private eye. It would be better, though, if the three of you met outside the restaurant. I'm not ready to tell Rosie about this." A rueful shake of grey-streaked black curls. "You probably won't believe it, Cat, that a woman as kind as Rosie could have such a mistrustful streak."

I balked at this. "Rosie has very good instincts. I think she should know."

He looked as betrayed as if I'd served him rancid olive oil.

"Sometimes I wonder when I stopped being the

boss. Okay, I'll tell her tonight. At home. So only the kids will hear us fight."

I smiled sympathetically. Nick was probably right. Rosie would tell him that even a bookie (her favorite expletive) could be trained to produce a silky, rich *tiramisu*, who needed this expensive, reckless choice for a substitute chef?

We agreed that I'd call the detective later, after Nick had talked to Polley. As it happened, I never did call. The day would turn into a disaster frightening enough to change all our plans.

At that time, however, I closed up the carton holding the birds, sealed it, and Nick carried the box away to a back shelf in the restaurant freezer.

The ugly smell lingered, but I ignored it and checked over my messages. Nate Greene had called this morning from San Francisco, before Dellacasa's was open. He'd left a message on our answering machine asking me to return the call.

Before I could reach for the phone, it rang.

Quick, ragged breaths. Then a harsh voice said, "Is this Dellacasa's catering department?"

"Yes, may I help you?"

"Hippolytus Arbusto. Get him to the phone, *now*."

There was a bursting, feverish emotion in the man's voice.

I heard myself chirping, like a twittering bird in

the path of a hurricane, "I'm sorry, he hasn't come in yet. May I take a message?"

Empty air, then choking, grieving words.

"A message? Sure. Tell him Mickey died last night."

"I'm—I'm sorry." Second time I'd said I was sorry. Who was Mickey? "Uh, will Mr. Arbusto know who you are? Can he call you?"

"Tell him Eddie Claire. He won't call back. He wouldn't take my calls in San Francisco either. But it's all changed now, now that Mickey's gone. Just tell that murdering bastard I'm not as forgiving as the Mick." Eddie's voice climbed into a howl. "He was my love and my life. But he didn't believe in payback, and I do."

Well, well. Though I hurt for Eddie's grief, I felt a *ping!* of excitement.

"Was that why you sent the package?" I said carefully.

"Package? What package? I've been at Mickey's bedside day and night." The anguished howl became outrage. "The only thing I'm sending him, darling, is a love letter from our lawyer. I hope it fries his hands." Eddie hung up, the sound crashing in my ear.

I was shaking slightly, caught up in the death of someone I didn't know, assaulted by the fierce mourning of his lover. Yet, if I could believe Eddie

Claire, there was more than one enemy ready to take revenge on Polley.

I reached for the phone and called Nate Greene. He was at his desk. No easy greeting when he heard my voice.

"Cat," he said, "I thought you'd want to know. Remember the AIDS patient who was one of the poison victims at Arbusto's?"

"Yes, I remember."

"Well, he died last night."

I waited for the inevitable. "And…?"

"Get this. His longtime lover is blaming your new co-worker for the death."

"Eddie Claire. He just called to talk to Polley. He got me instead."

"You're really getting deeper into this mess, aren't you?"

"I don't understand, Nate. The poisonings were *months* ago!"

"Eddie was still at the deathbed when he called his lawyer. Asked him to pressure the police to dig for more evidence against Arbusto. Also, he intends to file a wrongful death suit."

"On what basis? Wasn't his friend already dying?"

Nate sighed, as if he'd accepted the burden of Eddie Claire's grief.

"AIDS victims are living longer these days, if they get decent care. I just interviewed Eddie on the phone. He was anxious to talk to the press. That's an understatement. He yelled, then cried, then swore. But he insisted that Mickey—his friend—could have lived for years if his body hadn't been weakened by the poisoning. Says Mickey's doctor will testify."

"What does he think he'll get by going after Polley?"

"Revenge, I suppose." *Aha!* "Also, compensation for loss of affection, disability payments, etc."

A hint of amusement. "I just thought you'd want to know."

I could picture Nate's lean face, his wavy brown hair that no gel could tame, alert brown eyes behind the tortoiseshell rimmed glasses they must give out at journalism school graduations.

Right then, I should have volunteered my information. Told him about the quails, asked his opinion about the white slip of paper that said RE-VENGE. He was my friend, my source. Nate was generous and supportive.

Yet, I couldn't guarantee his secrecy. He was, after all, an investigative reporter. Suppose he decided to write about the package sent to Dellacasa's. We'd all be in the soup, not only Polley but Nick and me bobbing around like a trio of stringy stewing hens.

Dammit! The thought of dead birds was becoming so distasteful, I could seriously consider turning vegetarian. On the way home, I'd pick up a tofu stir-fry at the Chinese take-out.

But what could I say to Nate now? Nothing. Besides, he had a favor to ask of me.

"Ever hear of Agrisure?"

"No."

"Well, you undoubtedly will. It's a biotech company, heavy on medical and agricultural research and development. Everything from FatBeGone-Burger protein patties—"

"—I've tried them, not bad—"

"—to powdered infant formulas for Third World countries."

He continued, "Agrisure's headquarters are in San Francisco, but its semi-annual stockholder's meeting is down in L.A. this coming Monday and Tuesday. In a hotel near the airport."

"Should I care?"

"You bet. Your chef, Mr. Arbusto, has a personal contract as an Agrisure spokesman. It'll be interesting to see what the stockholders want to do about him."

I tilted so far back in my chair I nearly toppled over. Nate was putting me on information overload.

"Oh, they haven't actively used him since the poisonings." Nate continued. "Even yanked the TV spot he was featured in. The one they ran early Sunday mornings: *'And now, while our Washington team debates the political future of the presi-*

dent's dog, let's cut away for a brief word from our sponsor.'

"And then Arbusto comes on standing in a row of cauliflowers and fumbles through a speech about how he's a chef who's sure that Agrisure is the leader in California agriculture. Not exactly a spellbinder."

"Never seen it. Saturday's usually a working night. I sleep late on Sunday mornings."

"Well, when you can spare a Saturday night, come visit San Francisco. I know some fantastic restaurants, and you won't even have to pass around the appetizers."

"I'll think about it, Nate, I will. Meanwhile let's talk about Polley. Why did Agrisure pick him in the first place? Is he that much of a celebrity chef outside of California?"

"Yes and no. Yes, he has a good reputation for being creative. No, you need a certain charisma to be raised to celebrity status. Arbusto isn't liked.

"But this deal is more nepotism than fame, Cat. Arbusto's son works for Agrisure, in marketing. I've heard that your man agreed to do the spot as a favor. He kept vanishing like the Loch Ness monster when the boy was growing up, and he's feeling guilty.

"Probably didn't get paid much for being the spokesman, but he does have a contract. Arbusto hasn't been charged with any crime, so they must still be paying him."

I picked up my brass paperknife and made furrows on a notepad.

"At the risk of repeating myself, the poisonings happened months ago. Is it still such a big issue?"

"Agrisure is getting leaned on these days by Washington. The company has a history of problems with quality control. Last time it was their agricultural division—the one Polley speaks for. They settled some lawsuits about a health food supplement, but the FDA took its share of flak for inadequate supervision.

"The biggie right now is an improved, reputedly foolproof HIV/AIDS home detection test. Agrisure's already spent millions on development, but the FDA wants them to do more—read, expensive—testing before they'll approve it."

"So Agrisure doesn't need any more bad publicity."

"You got it!" said Nate. "I'd love to be a fly on the wall at that stockholder's meeting, but I can't break loose. I'm hoping you could get down there, hang around the lobby, listen to gossip. I hear there's a stockholder faction that wants to vote out all the rascals—including the current management and Arbusto's son. Will you do it?"

I held my paperknife like an epee and made a petite lunge at the desk lamp. The knife is a gift from La Belle Bakery. Its handle is a fleur-de-lis; I grasp it and feel like Joan of Arc spurring on her troops. Now I felt more like Joan wondering whether to stay in camp and wash her hair.

"My fridge is down to carrot sticks and two fat-free blueberry muffins. My hair needs a trim. Monday's my day off. I'd planned to do errands, but I suppose I could make the time."

"Do I detect a lack of enthusiasm? Maybe I'm wrong to ask you to get any more involved with Arbusto than you are."

I sighed. "You don't know the half of it. No, I'll do it. I owe you one. Besides, I need to know more about Polley. I'll just have to think of a reason for me to be lurking around."

"If you do get to the meeting," said Nate, "be careful about what you say. There's big money involved here. I have a hunch some desperate people are hiding under those pinstriped suits."

"I'd like to meet Polley's son. You know, see how he turned out. We're having a party at the restaurant on Monday night. Maybe he'll be there." I explained about the send-off for Mario.

"Polley's girlfriend is also going to be in L.A.," I added. "Do you think she's also a stockholder? Why else would she be coming this particular weekend? Polley's going to be busy. I'd assume he'll go to this stockholder's meeting, then he's helping Mario prepare the party food. There'll be about fifty guests."

"Maybe she just misses Polley's cooking."

"Think he's that great a chef?"

"Not to look at him. Wonder if I should throw away my Calvin Klein aftershave and take up baking."

"Oh, God, Nate, there's enough temperament around here. Stay with reporting."

A pleased laugh. "Call me when you've got some news."

Take care. Be careful.

I assured him I would, and that I'd be careful. We hung up.

So many good people suddenly worried about my safety. I thought about the confrontation with my new partner. No question that he was irritating, highhanded, a remarkably flawed human being. But a monster? I resolved not to panic.

The phone rang again. What next? I thought grimly. Probably San Francisco calling to tell me how Polley chased after his arugula supplier with a flame thrower.

SIX

"YOU HAVEN'T CALLED, so I'm calling you. I hope you're all right. It's so chilly these nights, and I know you wear those thin little dresses even when you're working very late."

Pleasure at hearing Aunt Sadie's voice mixed with guilt. I *hadn't* phoned her when I'd returned from San Francisco, though I'd meant to.

Sadie is my only living relative in what I optimistically call home. In a city where the earth can open up and falling from grace is more than a metaphor, Sadie offers as much stability as Los Angeles will allow.

"Sorry, Auntie, lots of changes at work. It's been busy."

"Well, I know I'm calling at the last minute, but I hope you can break away for a few days. Remember my little trip? Suddenly I need a roommate."

I remembered. "Oh, yes, that resort package. Wasn't Birdie going with you?"

A tch! of annoyance. "That Birdie. I keep telling her, if she were really my friend she'd be as serious about taking her vitamins as she is about feeding plant food to her violets."

"She can't go?"

"The flu," Sadie sighed. "Birdie chose *this week-end* to get the flu. And I'd hoped to start building up her stamina for our trip to China next year."

I could picture Aunt Sadie, every copper curl in place, pulling fragile Birdie up to the topmost step on the Great Wall.

Since Uncle Art died over five years ago, Sadie has been searching for a vigorous travel companion. Recently, I mentioned remarriage, but Sadie stared at me as appalled as if I'd suggested that she post the bans with Saddam Hussein. So Birdie, willing though out of shape, is the designated non-threatening companion.

"Catherine, can I talk you into coming with me? You've been working so hard, you'd certainly benefit from a spa regime for a few days. Massages, mineral baths, early morning walks in the woods! Here's what the brochure says: *'a nutritional regime custom-designed to balance all the vital organs in your body.'*"

A gentle plea. "How about it? El Encanto de California. Doesn't that sound life-restoring? We'd be back late Sunday."

I sighed. "It sounds frightfully healthy, Auntie, but I can't. I'm booked. Two parties this weekend, and Mario's farewell party on Monday." Not to mention a bit of discreet snooping.

"How about one of your gentlemen friends?"

Despite her rejection of marriage, Sadie has more eligible bachelors and widowers flocking around than any other woman I know who admits to senior status. Nothing invisible about Sadie. Sometimes when I hear about her fertile social life I feel as if I'm living on the Alaskan tundra on the longest night of winter.

"No men," she said. "I want to wear old sweats, forget makeup and work on cleansing everything-inner and outer, top to toe!"

"Sorry, wish I could."

"Well," she said, "I'll just pay the single supplement and go by myself. It's not a bad drive. Down the 405 to Escondido and then inland. I'll be there before dark."

"Call this evening and let me know you've arrived safely. If I'm not home, leave a message on my machine."

"Are you working tonight?"

"No."

A note of hope. "Anything special happening tonight?"

"Not really."

"Oh. Well, did I tell you that Gil called this week?"

"That's nice. He's always been fond of you."

"Cat, you know he was calling to see how *you* are."

"Did you tell him I'm fine, and to find himself

a new girlfriend? He's my ex-husband. You don't have to report to him."

"Now, don't be annoyed. Couples do reconcile, you know."

"Listen, my job is so exciting I can't think about marriage."

Silence, while she mulled over the excitement of serving fancy food at weddings for other women.

"Let's talk about it another day. I'd better pack and leave."

We wished each other nice weekends. I hung up, reeling from a morning that began with dead quails and ended with the Curse Of The Living Ex-Husband. I needed a breather. So I got my car and sped off to hone my killer instincts with the Fencing Master.

SEVEN

SWASHBUCKLE IS A studio for every actor who's ever yearned to play D'Artagnan, or who rather fancies himself in tights. The staff choreographs TV and movie fights. They stage exhibitions for parties.

Then there's me, the closet romantic. The girl who preferred *The Three Musketeers* to *Little Women;* who thrust and parried with Scaramouche, and Zorro, and dozed through *Rebecca of Sunnybrook Farm.* After all, how many daring role models did my generation have?

Between Joan of Arc and Astronaut Barbie there were few.

Amelia Earhardt had vanished, Nancy Drew was an impossible icon with those gleaming golden-red curls and her own convertible. I am dark-haired, hazel-eyed and sturdy, descended from some touchy Scots and a disreputable great-great-uncle who joined the French Foreign Legion. No wonder that at UCLA I went out for fencing, the loner's team sport.

Swashbuckle came into my life last year, when I hired them for a pirate-themed party for kids, complete with fencing lessons and a lot of "Avasts!" and "Yo ho ho!'s."

A visit to the studio to reconnoiter, I met the Fencing Master and became his student. A legend, winner of three Olympic Gold Medals, he is short, compact, ageless, supple as a steel blade.

I take lessons from the Fencing Master whenever I can. I focus until all my untidy emotions become a small black speck in my brain, and I am a thinking machine of incredible skill and cunning. Well, sometimes.

The studio is one big bare room with a mirrored wall. Two combatants in regulation white jackets and knickers were slashing away at each other with sabers, their shoes making light thumps on the hardwood floor.

"You are tentative today," said the Master, parrying my foil with a sharp clang of steel.

"Mmmph," I said, behind my mesh mask. "Rough morning."

He stood erect and motionless. "Hesitation could get you killed, you know. Use your mind. Anticipate, then strike."

I nodded.

"Keep your body tight and in profile. Make yourself less of a target."

Can't see his eyes behind the mesh mask. It's still unclear if the Fencing Master is profound or simply an elegant technician.

"En garde," he said, aiming his foil.

We parried, thrust and lunged. I think I scored a flesh wound, but he may have been kind. I would have bled to death, the way I'd bumbled today.

A FEW MINUTES after midnight the phone rang. I fumbled for it in the dark, instantly alert, worried that Aunt Sadie might have had trouble on the way to El Encanto.

To my relief and puzzlement, it was a man's voice, one I knew, although the words were slurred.

"Catherine? Jus' sittin' around, thought I'd say hello."

I said, "It's midnight, Polley, has something happened?"

"Well, no, thought maybe you might like company. Ah, we could discuss the catering menus. I've got a bottle of fifty-year-ol' Napoleon brandy I could bring over." A pause; I heard something gurgle into a glass.

"Ol' brandy. Bes' drink of all. What d'ya say?"

I spoke gently but firmly. "It's very late, Polley. We can talk about the menus tomorrow."

He gave up easily. "Okay." Another pause for refreshment. Then, in a whisper he said, "What I really wanted was to tell you my secret about the quails."

My heart a bit faster. "Your secret? I'd love to hear it."

"I knew I could tell you, Catherine." His voice dropped so low I had to strain to hear him.

"Goddam quails," said Polley. "You spend half a day roasting and saucing them, and then they're gone in two bites. I've always hated the little fuckers." A hiccup, and then he hung up.

SOME CATERING COMPANIES do nothing but children's cart parties. It's not our style, but this was a birthday party for the son of a longtime Dellacasa client. I'd rented a convoy of carts with red-and-white striped awnings, the machines that produce cotton candy, popcorn and frozen yogurt. I'd ordered candy-striped aprons and straw boaters for our servers.

Now, to coordinate with the chefs. They were in Mario's cubbyhole. Polley was stabbing his finger at a sheet of paper. He greeted me with all the warmth of a stainless steel sink.

"A problem?" I asked.

Mario was seated at his desk. He shrugged. Polley whirled around to face me. "Ah, Catherine. We've just been going over your menu for that children's party. I can't believe you plan to fill up those little bodies with all that obscene junk food."

I refused to be rattled. "It's a cart party, like lunch at the circus. Ten-year-old kids and their parents love it."

"Hot dogs! Hamburgers! Sugary fluff! Nitrates!

Grease! Empty calories! Is this cuisine in Los Angeles?"

My hunch was that Polley couldn't remember what he'd confessed on the phone last night. Either that, or Nick had told him about the soggy package of quails, and this ranting was misplaced anger.

I shrugged. "A day at the circus isn't exactly child abuse. I certainly want to hear your thoughts on children's parties, Polley. But for now, I'm going to lunch."

Head high, teeth clenched, I walked toward the kitchen.

THERE WAS A cardboard carton of flavored olive oils sitting on a counter. Bought that morning at the wholesale food market, I assumed. *Arrivederci,* garlic bread! Nick's Brooklyn sensibilities would never allow him to ban that garlic-cheese-and-butter restaurant staple from Dellacasa's menu, but he has seen the handwriting on the wall, and it is writ with green-gold liquid.

Ask for our *bruschetta,* spread with olive oil and garlic then grilled. Have a basket of rosemary bread studded with black olives or sun-dried tomatoes. Try our chewy sweet onion *focaccia.* No butter, please. Instead, your waiter pours a pool of extra-virgin olive oil, pure and fruity, onto your bread plate. Perch your bread on the rim of the plate and dip.

I looked over the bottles of infused oil in the carton: hot pepper oil, a branch of rosemary in another bottle, and still another oil infused with porcini mushrooms.

Ah, an intensity of mushrooms! I found a loaf of Italian bread, cut some hefty slices and twisted off the cap on the porcini oil bottle. The liquid was a soft amber, releasing a curious pungent fragrance as I poured it into a small dish.

Delicately, I dipped a chunk of bread into the gleaming oil. Whooeee! Even as I swallowed, the bitter, heavy taste of the oil made me gag. I rushed to the sink, tried to spit out the bread, gagged again, turned on the cold water faucet and splashed water into my mouth. My throat felt on fire, my lips tingled and hurt, as if I'd been chewing nettles. Hastily, to stop the awful burning, I filled a glass with water and gulped it down. Luckily, I hadn't swallowed much. I leaned against the sink, breathing hard, my thumping heart calming to an inquiring knock.

"Help," I said weakly. "I've been poisoned."

EIGHT

THE BOUQUET OF red roses and pink carnations was enormous enough for a state funeral. I appreciated it even though I was only half-dead.

In the emergency room at UCLA Medical Center they had done unspeakable things to my intestinal system, then carted me to a semi-private room. My roommate was invisible behind a grey curtain; she'd snored softly through the clatter of moving me into bed and setting up my IV. I'd been about to doze off when Nick and Rosie arrived bearing flowers and worried smiles. While Rosie fussed with the vase, Nick seated himself at my bedside. He was still in work clothes: blue chambray shirt and washable twill pants.

"In the emergency room they said you'd be okay," said Nick right off. "But you were weak. I asked them to keep you overnight, just to be safe."

I managed a smile. "Why? Do you expect a follow-up? Maybe someone with a knife in his teeth at my front door?"

"The porcini oil wasn't intended for you," said Nick. "No one knew you'd be switching from your usual tuna salad."

"Another 'to whom it may concern.' Like the quails."

"That's the way it looks," agreed Nick, sighing. "A threat, meant to be noticed, but probably not to harm anyone."

I looked at him in disbelief. "If it wasn't meant to *harm,* what am I doing here shooting up a saline solution for lunch?"

It was an intemperate remark. Rosie burst into tears.

"We were so worried about you," she said. "Nick and I followed the paramedics to the hospital, and we've been waiting outside the emergency room ever since. Everyone at the restaurant sends love. We talked to them. The police went to the restaurant, then the detectives came to see us here. Then they sent that nice Detective Wang that you know. He'll be back to talk to you soon."

Detective Paul Wang. Well, that was reassuring news. He'd protected me during the search for my neighbor, Angela. Not only was he smart, but we'd discovered we shared an affinity for Chinese food. Of course, Paul Wang is ethnic Chinese, but I see, in his devotion to pan-fried dumplings, a passion that matches my own. It had been too long since we'd shared a stuffed lychee.

Not that I had any appetite. The water I'd gulped had probably saved my mouth and throat from real damage, but they were sore.

"So you decided to call in the police."

"I had to," said Nick. "It's gone too far. How could I tell the paramedics this was an accident? I didn't believe it myself.

"Detective Wang feels," Nick added, "that you weren't meant to swallow much of what was in that bottle of porcini oil. You tried to spit it out right away because it tasted terrible."

"What was in it?"

"The police should know soon. The hospital sent the oil to their lab when you arrived in the emergency room."

I had to agree with Nick. No one would have mistaken that nauseating stuff for a lightly flavored oil. But if I hadn't been so curious in the kitchen, the diners at Dellacasa's that evening might have had a taste treat they'd never forget. I said as much. Nick moaned deeply, rather like a baritone with gas pains.

"That's what Detective Wang is figuring. Someone was trying to scare away my customers."

"Or kill them," I added. "Let's agree, it's possible, if the poisoner didn't know the oil would taste so awful."

Nick winced. "Deliberate murder? Killing innocent people in a restaurant? Why would someone want to do that?"

"It happened in San Francisco, Nick, in Polley's

restaurant. Remember? A room full of strangers, poisoned."

"Not so. It was a private party. The diners at Arbusto's all knew each other. Polley tells me the San Francisco police still think the poisoner might have had only one victim in mind, the man who died. Or, maybe, someone hates all gays enough to commit murder. Los Angeles doesn't own all the crazies in California."

There was silence, broken only by fluttering breaths that descended into deep snores, from my invisible roomie. I knew that Nick, Rosie and I had the same unspoken thought: the police had never completely cleared Polley of murdering his own guest.

Who but Polley could have been certain that only Framboise would get the lethal dose of poison? And, though this was extremely far-fetched and logistically impossible, could Polley have been angry enough to want to harm *me?* I tucked the thought away for later reflection. Right now I still felt as if a mad chef had attacked my stomach with a potato masher.

Rosie must have seen my eyes droop, because she said, hurriedly, "We shouldn't be staying this long. Catherine needs rest. Nick, tell her what we've decided."

"You'll take the weekend off, Cat. I'm bringing in Olivia on overtime to fill in at the cart party in the afternoon and the We Want Wetlands reception at night. Any instructions?"

"Tell Olivia to call me here." Mournfully, I added, "She can wear my straw boater with the ribbons to the party."

"Do you have anyone to drive you home from the hospital tomorrow? What about your aunt?"

"She's away for the weekend." Besides, I wouldn't want to alarm Sadie. She'd never trust UCLA Medical Center on digestive problems. I'd have to submit to her homemade custards and boiled chicken for at least a week.

"I'll call Marcy."

"Good, that's settled!" Nick beamed a smile at me, smoothed his trouser legs over his knees, and sat back.

"Tell her the rest," prompted Rosie.

As Thoreau so wisely said: most men lead lives of quiet desperation. I could see the truth of it in the pleading look that husband gave wife and, in return, she stared at him with the calm conviction usually reserved for martyrs and saints.

"It must be handled," she said.

A rueful nod of agreement, then Nick cleared his throat and said, "We want you to go to San Francisco, Cat. You never did interview those other two chefs. It may be a good idea to have a backup for Polley."

Surprised, I struggled to sit upright. Remembering the control on my bed, I pushed the button hard. The top part of my mattress swung up, thumping me on the shoulders.

"Now, now," said Nick, "I'm not saying I've made any decision yet about Polley. I believe some weirdo's got a grudge against the poor guy, and if ever Polley needed a friend, he needs one now.

"But, innocent people are being caught in the middle and I have to protect my staff and my customers—"

"—And Dellacasa's reputation," broke in Rosie. I was sure they'd been having similar discussions ever since Polley's arrival in Westwood; the poisoning attempt on me had created a new urgency.

"You remember very well, Nick," Rosie continued, "the one-day closing by the Health Department—just because a water pipe burst. It was enough to get Dellacasa's some bad publicity in the newspapers. Imagine what would happen if a reporter ever heard about what happened to Cat."

"You don't have to convince me, Rosie. I'm doing what has to be done." She remained standing and immoveable, a softly rounded statue in a brown silk print dress.

"Okay. Enough!" he said.

Nick turned to me. "Cat, could you leave for San Francisco on Monday? We'll tell everyone you're taking a few vacation days."

"Gosh, I'd hate to go out of town on Monday. I'd

miss Mario's farewell party." As well as the Agri-sure meeting.

"Of course. Well, then, Tuesday morning, first thing. Unless the cops catch this guy before then."

I really did need a nap. I leaned back, my eyes closing.

"We're leaving," said Rosie. "We love you. Get well, please."

They tiptoed out and I drifted into an uneasy sleep. I was in a cobblestoned town square, in some small town in Italy. There was a community well, and a dipper made of cool white marble. I leaned over the well to fill up the dipper, and saw my reflection. Polley stood behind me, holding my shoulders so I wouldn't fall into the well. (Had he held me until the paramedics arrived?) In my hair were pink, red and white blossoms. I smiled and sipped the pale liquid in the dipper. It was the finest olive oil I'd ever tasted. My question was: were the flowers in my hair for my burial or for Monday's feast day? I fell into a deeper sleep.

EVEN BLURRED, the moustache was familiar and astounding. I rubbed my eyes. Last time I'd seen Detective Paul Wang, the Charlie Chan styled hair on his upper lip had been trimmed back to LAPD regulation neatness. Now the moustache was once more luxuriant, almost hiding the lean face, contradicting the straight hair that was glossy and black as raven's wings above his high forehead. Paul was taller than most ethnic Chinese, and broad-shouldered. It had been no surprise to learn that he'd once played quarterback for UCLA; although he'd lost the bulk along with his shoulderpads, he'd kept the grace.

He still looked like a graduate student: brown tweed jacket, tan striped Oxford shirt, maroon knit tie, chinos. He was seated quietly at my bedside, observing me with a small, scrutable smile.

I dragged myself into a sitting position, aware that my skin was clammy, my hair disorderly. And yet, I was feeling better.

"Your moustache," I said. "It's grown back."

"Just so you'd recognize me," he said. "You know we Asians all look alike."

"I knew you right away. I remembered the tweed jacket with the elbow patches. But what are you doing here in Westwood? I thought you were with Wilshire Division."

"Well, in part thanks to you and your nutty neighbor, Angela, I was noticed downtown." With a touching show of casualness, he said, "Two weeks ago I got my transfer to Robbery-Homicide Division. We can be assigned cases anywhere in L.A."

"I'm so pleased for you! Congratulations!"

Paul Wang nodded in appreciation. I realized again that my hair undoubtedly looked like a wad of wet kelp, and paused to work my fingers through some tangles. Besides, I was perplexed.

"I'm delighted that it's you, but I don't understand. My bizarre little poisoning is hardly in the same league as a celebrity double murder case. How come the LAPD is sending its detective elite?"

"Elite? Aw, shucks," said Paul, grinning. Then, seriously, "Originally, the call went to West L.A. But after the detectives came to the hospital and talked to your boss—no, correction, after they talked to your boss's wife—West L.A. called and offered it to us."

Rosie must have spilled not only the beans, but the pasta, the sauce and a kettle of minestrone. I said cautiously, "What did she tell them."

"About this fellow Arbusto and the San Francisco poisonings."

"Nothing was ever proven," I said, surprised to find myself defending Polley.

"We checked with San Francisco, the case is still open. And here's Arbusto, in the vicinity of another poisoning. We have nothing—so far—to show that he was involved. On the other hand, it's more than a coincidence. We heard about the package of quails, and that you were the one who opened it."

"My name wasn't on the package. It was addressed to the catering department."

"I know. In spite of what you may have heard,

the LAPD does not always rush to judgment. No one's accusing anyone. We're just starting the investigation. I was on duty when the call came in downtown. I saw your name and thought, well, maybe I can talk her into buying me lunch at Dellacasa's again. Considering it's not Chinese, the food's pretty good. The crab ravioli tastes almost like wonton. I'll just ask her to taste it for me first."

I shuddered. "It was bitter, Paul. I couldn't have swallowed much, the oil tasted so bad."

"All we know, so far, it's not the same poison that was used in San Francisco. The police have identified that one and, since the case is open, I won't say much except that it's easy to obtain and not noticeable in strong-flavored food. Quail has a gamey taste that would mask it."

"Did Nick give you the package that's in our freezer?"

He nodded. "It's already gone to our lab. Along with the rest of the carton of olive oils. I don't expect any word for a few days. Your puzzle is a little unusual, but not an emergency. Meantime, are you up to talking about today?"

I said I was, and we went over the details: my finding the carton on the counter, choosing the bottle at random, eating the oil-soaked bread. Feeling sick instantly.

Paul volunteered that it was Jose who'd found the carton on the back doorstep just before noon. Dellacasa's kitchen helper assumed that Nick, Mario or Polley had brought it from the produce market, and had forgotten to carry it in. All three men were questioned and denied buying the oils or seeing the carton.

None of the other staff had noticed the carton on the doorstep. No one had seen any suspicious person around the back door. But, then, everyone was busy preparing for the lunch crowd.

I was sleepy again. Paul Wang rose, patted me reassuringly on the shoulder, and told me he'd want to talk to me again soon. I murmured that we could meet for lunch at Burger King if he was nervous. Then I dozed off.

NINE

It rained hard on Monday morning. One of those heavy, driving rains that made you nostalgic for drought. The rain filled reservoirs, flooded streets, and left freeway commuters splashing and sliding like salmon headed upstream.

I'd intended to arrive late at the Agrisure stockholder's meeting and slip inside unnoticed. Stop-and-start driving under punitive skies got me to the hotel near the airport even later than I'd planned. I hadn't taken the freeway. My apartment is just a zipcode east of Beverly Hills, a ten-minute sprint to Dellacasa's in Westwood, maybe twenty minutes on La Cienega and Century to LAX. Subject to change, anxiety and despair in the rainy season.

My timing wasn't all bad. There was an empty seat in the last row of the small hotel auditorium. I could see Polley in the third row on the side; he didn't notice me. Not until later, at the mid-morning coffee break. I'd hoped to avoid him completely, but I couldn't see myself crouching behind a skinny potted palm.

My story, admittedly, was as thin as a soup kitchen sandwich, but he might accept it. My aunt Sadie, I'd tell him, was out of town (true); she owned some Agrisure stock (I'd never asked, could be true); she'd asked me to attend and report back to her (a lie).

I did see part of the morning's session. The trim, silver-haired man on the podium sported a ruddy tan that made me think of yacht races and open seas. According to the program left on each seat, this was William L. Metcalf, CEO of Agrisure. Other executives, less buoyant, sat in front. From the photos I picked out Ben C. Foley, President, and Basil P. Doyle, Controller.

There was a lone woman in the group, Laura Ferris-Flood, the Vice-President of Marketing. Homer Arbusto's boss. She was much younger than her male colleagues, maybe late twenties. Thin face, intense eyes, thick black curls tumbling to her shoulders.

The CEO was introducing a film that would, he said, sum up the diversity and excitement of Agrisure today.

As I slouched down in my seat the room darkened for the three-screen presentation: intensely colored stills, live action, shots of glossy corporate reports, all pulsing in quick, almost dizzying cuts to an uptempo music track that sounded like an MTV sound engineer on speed. Dynamic company, yes, yes, yes. Eeh, eeh, eeh. Ooh, ooh, ooh. Unh, unh, unh, unh. Agrisure, with its high profile research and development on an HIV AIDS test, was sure to be a hot stock to the baby boomers and dot-com crowd. I thought I recognized a snippet of Elton John, a trace of the Stones, a dash of heavy metal. But the music and the visuals whizzed by so fast, the message blurred in my mind. Possibly that was the idea. When the lights went on, doors opened and the stockholders, all jazzed and noisy, headed for the coffee and pastries arranged on refreshment tables in the corridor.

A long side table held annual reports, the current prospectus, four-color brochures showing Agrisure products. Trays of souvenir keyrings were tagged with plastic Wild-Oat Weiners, the Agrisure entry into the growing meatless deli business. Other trays were heaped with sample boxes of TeaTime For Tonic teabags, the top-selling product in Agrisure's health supplement line.

Pushed way to the back of the table, almost hidden behind a pyramid of TeaTime For Tonic boxes, was an untidy stack of orange flyers. I hardly needed my best powers of deduction to guess that the flyers had been hastily moved back sometime during the break.

"STOCKHOLDERS! YOU HAVE A CHOICE!" headlined the flyer.

Copy went on to urge stockholders to vote for an alternate slate of officers, to be nominated from the floor this afternoon. The broadside ended, "It's legal. It's urgent. It will protect Agrisure's reputation—and your profits!"

I was so busy collecting these materials for Nate, I became careless. When I looked up, there was Polley standing with a younger man at the far end of the corridor. Polley's hand clutched a copy of the orange flyer; his other hand tapped the paper as he spoke to his companion. They both seemed worried. As I stared, Polley looked up and saw me. Surprise, then a frown.

Oh, hell! I tried out a genial smile and a wave. Polley hesitated, then walked towards me, slowly edging his way through the chattering crowd. The younger man, in his late twenties I guessed, followed and now I could see the family resemblance. Same hawkish nose and black hair. But the clarity of the green eyes was blurred by thick, black-rimmed glasses, his grey-suited frame was slender and his shoulders stooped. As he came closer, I noticed a small tremor in his hands. If this was Polley's son, did daddy always make him so nervous, or was it a crisis brought on by the orange flyer?

Polley this morning, in contrast, looked like a model corporate spokesman, almost handsome in his navy double-breasted pin-striped suit and starched white shirt; perhaps the red paisley tie was a tad too bright, yet it bespoke his creative nature and was understandable.

He questioned me cautiously. "Catherine? I didn't expect to see you here. Did Nick send you?"

"Oh, no. My being here has nothing to do with Dellacasa's."

I told my little story about my aunt, the stockholder. The tense lines in Polley's face faded, although I think he didn't quite believe me.

Confidently, though, he said, "Well, what did you think of this morning's film? Did you see it?"

"Um, very lively. It certainly makes Agrisure look like a progressive company."

"It was my boy's idea," said Polley, turning to his son. "Let me introduce you. Cat, this is Homer Arbusto. Homer, meet Cat Deean, she manages the catering for Nick and Rosie."

Homer ducked his head shyly as I said my how-dya-do.

"This smart fellow is in marketing at Agrisure. Just a few years on the job, and he's brought some very creative ideas to the table. You have a bright future there, son," said Polley with a heartiness that was, just possibly, less fatherly pride than an apology for the years of neglect.

Homer's face turned almost as red as his father's tie, but Polley didn't seem to notice.

"Are you staying for the afternoon session?" Polley asked me, looking worried again. "There's an election, you know. Do you have your aunt's proxy?"

I concentrated on looking vague. "No, I don't. I think, I'm pretty sure, she sent it in, oh, a long time ago."

"That's all right, then. Will you be staying for the luncheon?"

"No, I can't." That was truthful enough; I wasn't on the guest list. "I'm taking a few vacation days, and I need to go home and pack." I wasn't sure if Nick had told anyone at the restaurant that I was going to San Francisco.

"Of course! It completely slipped my mind. I should have remembered. How are you, are you feeling better? You know, sometimes those imported olive oils can be tricky. They can spoil, if they're not shipped at the right temperature. The importer has to be very careful about his supplier and the shipping company."

I stared at Polley. Talk about denial! He smiled broadly, as if we had cleared up the matter of my slight indigestion, and could dismiss it. I started to say something heated and nasty, then shut my mouth. Nothing to gain by tangling with Polley.

"But I will see you tonight," I said, dredging up a smile that was equally cheerful and false. "At Mario's party. Homer, very nice to meet you. I hope we can talk tonight. I'd love to hear about how that film got made."

Homer sent me a pleased look that made me ashamed of myself.

"Well, if you can't stay—" said Polley, looking puzzled.

No wonder. It must have unnerved him to see me pop up like Hamlet's father's ghost. To what purpose? Did I lurk among the ramparts groaning about revenge? Did I point a shaky finger at him? No, I babbled on about my aunt sending me for information she could easily have gathered by phoning her broker. If I were Polley, I wouldn't be puzzled, I'd be alarmed.

The stockholders were beginning to head back into the auditorium for the rest of the morning session. I left Polley and Homer in the corridor, heads bent in conversation. Wondering, as I walked to the hotel parking structure, if Polley, with his gift for creating enemies, was really helping Homer's marketing career. More likely, Agrisure's CEO would dump Polley if the stockholders protested their spokesman's involvement with mass poisonings.

My footsteps echoed on the concrete ramp. There was the sound of squeaky wheels behind me and, startled, I turned. A young woman was pushing along a sleepy toddler in his stroller. We smiled at each other, glad for the company on that deserted parking level. Take a deep breath, Cat. Push aside the troubles with Polley. If rain doesn't make your hair frizzy, paranoia will. Get to that appointment with Mr. Joseph. It's been a long time since you've been to a party where you didn't have to work for your supper.

TEN

To BEGIN, a small plate heaped with caponata, some crisp-fried artichoke hearts, a slab of carrot-zucchini-mushroom pate. A regretful glance at the curried shrimps, the rounds of brioche stuffed with leeks. Better to save myself for the five varieties of pasta to follow. Usually, I view gorgeous food with professional detachment, but I was hungry after a weekend of canned vegetable soup and dry toast, and feeling vulnerable as well.

Nick and Mario, in chef's whites, greeted me at the door. "Welcome home. You're pale. Eat something."

"The chestnut puree is special for you."

I'd been hugged by Rosie, looking lighthearted and pretty in a green silk brocade dress, her black hair swept back and curled. Polley, I could see, was presiding in the kitchen. My hello could wait. The trip to San Francisco tomorrow bothered me. It seemed underhanded, as if matters should have been resolved with Polley first. Of course, there was no reason for me to protect Mr. Macho Man. And yet—

The police hadn't dug up any proof that Polley was a psychopath, poisoning his perceived enemies with cunning and guile. On the other hand—

Laughter wafted from the bar, presided over by Nick's nephew, Joe. ("Please, Nick, don't call me Giovanni, we're not in Brooklyn anymore.") Joe, at 21, is slender with thick-lashed dark eyes and perfectly shaped lips. Many girls in Brooklyn wept when he left. He welcomed me with a hearty kiss on the cheek, and poured a glass of white wine. I took the glass and my plate and made my way through the clusters of guests to a quiet corner table in the small bar. A first grateful sip of wine, and then a husky female voice interrupted.

"You must be drinking the Pinot Grigio. Nice, isn't it? I mean, pleasing bouquet, I should say."

I turned towards her. She looked like a woman who ran five miles every morning for fun. Good tan, a cap of short and sleek blond hair over a round, almost babyish face, blue eyes edged by sun-etched fine lines. Her dress was black, bare-armed, brief, slinky and expensive. If it wasn't a Donna Karan, it was a good knock-off and I looked at it with mild dismay. I'd gone semi-punk to the party: my totally extravagant red leather bomber jacket, with slim black jeans, black tank top, low black boots. *This is some tough broad, nothing gets her down,* was my statement, I suppose. On the other hand, this woman was too sunny for the sexy black dress. We were both in costume.

"May I join you?" she asked, strong white teeth showing in a hesitant smile. She was holding a salt-edged, bathtub-sized margarita that sloshed as she set it on the table. Not her first drink of the evening.

"Sure," I said. "I'm Catherine Deean, Cat to my friends. I work here."

"I guessed that. Nick and Mario have been waiting for you to show up. I heard about your, um, accident. Terrible, just awful."

She looked pained, like a baby about to bawl. For a stranger, she was taking my, um, accident, pretty hard. Of course, a couple of Joe's margaritas could bring out the blues in Pollyana.

I must have stared, because she drew herself up and said,

"Here I am, taking off—zip—like a roadrunner, and you don't even know me. I'm Lila. Well, Lila Sue Fulcher, to be formal."

Lila. I'd heard the name. This must be Polley's girlfriend.

"I'm Polley's friend," said Lila. "I drove down from San Francisco this morning."

"Nice to meet you, Lila. That's a long way to come for a party."

A rueful laugh. "I really came down for the Agrisure stockholder's meeting, and then I almost missed it. Left San Francisco before dawn, right in the middle of a downpour, still thought I'd be at the hotel before lunch, but the rain was too heavy. I got to the meeting just in time to vote my shares."

"How did the election go? I understand there was a second slate."

"Nah, they never really got organized. Started too late. Billy Metcalf can sail off to Australia on his 64-foot sloop and not worry. The old guard is still in."

"Then who's minding the store? Will Polley's son still have a job?"

"That's right. Polley told me you were at the meeting this morning." She looked at me with open curiosity. "Your aunt has some stock, he said?"

I nodded, but didn't volunteer.

"Well," she shrugged, "Don't worry about Homer. Polley is just discovering what it feels like to be a father. But the old management got a vote of confidence this afternoon, and that includes the marketing department."

Would it also include Polley as company spokesman? I wanted to ask Lila without pushing too hard.

"If Mr. Metcalf is away for long periods, who runs the company?"

Lila ran a finger around the rim of the margarita glass. I recognized the shade of polish, Wantonly Pink, on her blunt cut nails. She peered down into the icy green drink and said, "It's all right, really. Tell your aunt to relax. Agrisure has a full quota of professional managers. Very bright and bottom line. New products roll off the assembly line every year. But they keep tight control of the money for research and development, so there's always a profit for us stockholders. When it comes to making money, I can't complain about Agrisure."

Very clearheaded. I looked at Lila with fresh interest, and she caught my glance. She beamed, crossed her long, slightly muscular legs, tugged down the black skirt to a semblance of modesty.

"I know," said Lila. "You're thinking, how come this country girl sounds like the whiz of Wall Street? I'm not, really, but I've been following Agrisure ever since I met Polley."

"Have you known him long?" My interest was real: like it or not, I was involved with Polley's fate.

Dinner was being served at the long buffet tables at one side of the restaurant. Gradually, the other guests moved out of the bar, and Lila and I were enveloped in silence.

"Ever since I moved to San Francisco," sighed Lila. "He changed my life, you know. I mean, I had *planned* to change my life, but Polley made it happen."

"I don't know much about Polley," I admitted, an open invitation for her to say more.

"Well, I don't want to keep you away from dinner with my life story—" She leaned toward me hopefully.

"After those appetizers, dinner can wait. Please, go on."

"Thanks. You're easy to talk to. Polley's busy, Homer hasn't shown up yet, and I don't know anyone else here."

She'd been drinking away at her margarita and now she drained it. "We need refills," she said.

I obliged by finishing off my glass of wine. Lila Sue stood, walked with almost steady steps back to the bar, offered Joe her empty glass and pointed to mine. She waited, smiling dreamily, one elbow on the bar, one black silk pump on the rail. Presently, she returned, bearing the two drinks.

"There, that's better. I can tell you're a good listener, and it *has* been a long day, so let me tell you how little ol' Lila Sue broke into the San Francisco in crowd." She raised her fresh margarita in a toast, and took a genteel sip. I drank companionably from my glass of the pale Pinot Grigio.

"I'll begin with my little home town. It gets so hot in summer, everybody who can, leaves. The tourists, for sure; then the restaurants, except for Mexican Annie's; even the local dentist. Need a filling during the summer, you have to drive into San Diego.

"After my husband Charlie died," said Lila, "in a freak accident—he got caught in a gully during a flash flood—I had my son Dan to raise alone. Once he was grown and gone, there was only me and Henry, the dog."

I looked more closely. Some of the faint lines

feathering out around Lila's eyes and mouth could be more than dryness. She was a few years older than I'd thought.

"Henry was a loving, intelligent Golden Lab, but he died of old age. Then there was only me, talking to the sagebrush, actually looking forward to the Chamber of Commerce pancake breakfast and the Rotary barbecue.

"I had plenty of money from the insurance settlement, so I took what the travel agency called the Grand Tour—England, France, Germany and Italy. Then I came to San Francisco. That's where Charlie and I spent our honeymoon. I rented an apartment up high enough to see the fog roll over the bay, fog was such a relief after the desert. Then I looked up some famous restaurants I'd read about from our subscription to *Bon Appetit*. After Europe, I wanted more gourmet stuff. You ever go to San Francisco?"

"As often as I can."

"I mean, *alone*," said Lila. "You ever sit alone, taking up a whole table in a popular restaurant when people are waiting, or you look around and everyone else is laughing and eating and having relationships?" She plunged into her margarita.

I nodded sympathetically. "What did you do?"

"I joined this singles club. After all, that's what I was again, right? Single." Lila's tight black skirt had crept up, showing even more thigh. She stood, gave it a vicious tug, sat and crossed her legs.

"'The Singles Supper Club,'" the newspaper ad said. "The idea was, you'd have adventures in dining, and meet other sophisticated people.

"Well, most of the singles were sophisticated, I guess, but I was too old and dressed too dumb for most of them. But we did go to these really elegant places, so I stuck with the club. Once a week, every Tuesday night.

"Then, about the third month, we met at Arbusto's. The group was younger than usual that night, and they paired off. So it felt like I was back talking to the sagebrush again.

"Then Polley came out of the kitchen, saw me sitting off by myself, and sat down with me. One thing led to another and, there I was, hanging out at Arbusto's almost every night. I'd stay until the last diner left, then Polley would close up, and we'd go off somewhere for a light bite.

"Pretty soon I was learning about food and wines from one of the best chefs in San Francisco. So Polley and I were together for over a year until he had this trouble in the restaurant. I could have helped him out with money, you know, to keep Arbusto's going, but he's too stubborn to take help, even from me. Then your boss offered him this job, and now he's in Los Angeles."

"Do you miss him?"

Lila's margarita glass was empty, but she pushed it away. A little tired, a little sad, coming down from a tequila high.

"Do I miss him? I miss the excitement of the restaurant at night, all those smart-looking people praising him and the dishes he creates—he really cooks like a god, you know. It was like being at a party every night.

"We still talk on the phone, and he's accused me of finding other men as soon as he left, but he's wrong. Polley sulks and then explodes. I don't miss his moods. But I'm not interested in other men, not right now. He's given me a lot, in his own way.

"Even investing. I knew Polley was a spokes-man for Agrisure, and he got me turned on about investing. I've done all right so far, and it's fun to use my brain instead of going back home and try-ing to make gardens grow in the desert. I'm going to hang around the big city for a while, with or without Polley."

She raised her big empty glass, salt still dotting the rim. "To more adventures in dining," she said wistfully.

I realized that I wasn't seeing much of Mario's farewell party. How I'd miss him! I picked up my drink and stood. The feeling of loss was making me hungry.

"Come on, Lila, let's see what the god's been cooking up."

ELEVEN

The intruder found a parking place on the third level, across the aisle and a few spaces down from the red Geo. At mid-afternoon, the lunchtime traffic had slowed to an occasional dawdler. The last car was a silver Mercedes. It was easy to hear it careening around corners, tires squealing, proclaiming power even before the driver, hunched over the wheel, red-faced, middle-aged, wellgroomed, raced by.

The three martini lunch lives, thought the intruder with a bemused shake of the head, not even bothering to slouch down as the car passed. There is, after all, nothing more anonymous than the exit side of a parking garage. The driver's eyes are on the arrow, the preordained path; the car twists downward, following the curving ramps, gravity pulling towards the freedom of the streets.

Who would even notice an ordinary person sitting quietly in a parked car? Just me and my shadow, hummed the intruder, slightly offkey but with feeling, we're walking down the avenue. Coming a few steps closer to settling old scores.

A glance up and down the parking ramp. No

*traffic, no noise in either direction. Time to walk.
The intruder reached into the glove compartment,
pulled out a well-worn ice pick, left the car and
strolled casually across the aisle to the shiny red
Geo.*

WHAT STARTED OUT as a happy Bon Voyage party
would end in disaster. Who knew? We thought it
was enough to protect the food.

"Don't worry," Rosie had told me, "Nobody is
going to poison anybody tonight."

Nick had checked out every delivery, sniffing
like a curly-haired bloodhound at everything but
the canned tomato paste. Mario fearlessly sampled
the dressings, the sauces, each finished dish before
it left the kitchen. Polley hovered over the stove,
green eyes intense, squinting through the steam, as
if his future could be read in the simmering sauces.

But what precautions would Dellacasa's take tomorrow? And the day after? Nick couldn't run a
restaurant on fear. I began to feel better about San
Francisco.

Besides, the guests in the main dining room
were twirling their way through mounds of pasta.
I could see trays with spaghetti, linguini, and spin-
ach-green tagliatelle; the tube-like penne as well,
and my favorite, seme di melone, a slippery little
pasta the size of rice grains. And the sauces! Tomatoes and fennel, clams and cream, mozzarella

and prosciutto and—oh, why chatter on? The night was scented with garlic and Parmesan. I was determined to get my share.

Lila in tow, I greeted Nick's cousins, Mario's proud mother and sister, a few favored customers, and what seemed like a reunion of Mario's entire graduating class from the Professional Culinary Program at L.A. City Tech.

The guest of honor and Polley were seated on a large red banquette, deep in discourse about wild asparagus. When we approached their table, Mario moved over to make room for us. Polley did not appear delighted to see us together, but he nodded to me before quickly appraising Lila head to toe, her basic blondness in her basic black dress. He must have approved because he said, almost tenderly, "Looking good, kid."

"It's the dress, Polley. Remember? You helped me pick it out."

"I remember." He looked at me, arching thick black eyebrows in a questioning stare.

"You two girls have been having a cozy little talk, eh? I could see you in the bar."

Girls? Ech! Lila said, "Well, Cat and I were just getting acquainted, Polley. You told me to go around and mingle. Well, I'm the mingler and she's the minglee. Right, Cat?"

I nodded. "The minglee, yes indeed."

Polley looked disgusted. Mario stood; I could tell he was sensing tension and wanted to move on.

"My friend Wayne Yoshitomi just came in," said Mario. "I want to lead him to a drink and some of Polley's hot hors d'oeuvres. Wayne's become a sushi bar chef, and I think he's forgotten what cooked food tastes like." He eased away gracefully.

"Please lighten up on the booze, Lila," said Polley in what was an attempt at a pleasant tone.

"Sure, Polley, it's just that I was feeling a little lonely. I'm better now."

"Where's Homer? I asked him to look after you." Polley's eyes scanned the room.

"No sign of him yet," said Lila. "I've been looking."

Polley shrugged. "That bastard, old Basil P. Doyle, is probably keeping him late. Doyle is always thinking of extra things for him to fetch and carry. Busywork, that's what controllers want, I suppose, but it really burns me."

"Homer was supposed to take down and pack away all the Agrisure exhibits," said Lila. "I heard his boss in the marketing department—what's her name?—"

"Ferris-Flood, you know, the hyphenated bitch."

"Still giving you trouble?" Lila was sympathetic. "Anyway, I heard her asking Homer to take charge."

"Take charge?" Polley snorted. "Like asking the

janitor to *take charge* of the mops and pails. Homer deserves a promotion, not a slap."

"Aw, Polley. Homer's just starting out. They gave him their film to produce. That's a big step forward."

"You didn't see it, did you, Lila? It was good. Of course, Agrisure hired an outside film production company. But Homer worked with them. He told me he interviewed every division head in Agrisure to get the information. Then researched all the company files for the best pictures. Big responsibility for a young guy. His bosses wouldn't have picked Homer for the job if they didn't trust him to do it right."

"Sure, Polley. But maybe they're doing this packing up stuff just to keep him humble. Companies do that, you know. Saves them giving a lot of raises."

"That's true," said Polley, shaking his head at the perfidy of big business. He settled himself against the banquette, lifting a hand to massage the back of his neck, as if his head needed support against the accumulated weight of the day.

"You're a smart woman, Lila. Sometimes."

She shrugged, folded tanned hands in her lap and looked at him. Watchful, waiting—for what? Another Olympian nod?

This unrestrained display of affection was getting to me. I decided to hit the pasta bar. They didn't seem to notice when I stood, murmured something about hunger pangs and wandered off. I had just lifted a warm white china plate from the stack when the restaurant's front door opened. To my surprise, Detective Paul Wang entered, bringing in a gust of chilly night air. How nice, Nick's invited him to the party.

"Paul," I called, walking to meet him at the door, "so glad you could come. You're just in time for dinner."

He seemed tired, not in a party mood at all. But his smile was genuine. "Cat, glad you're out of the hospital. You're looking terrific. How do you feel?"

I touched my transformed hair. Mr. Joseph, bless his talented shears, had salvaged this creature from the Black Lagoon.

"Shook up, but glad I didn't die. Just between us, I'm having my own quiet celebration tonight. Why don't you join me? There's champagne and wine. Or anything else you'd like to drink."

The smile disappeared. "Sorry, Cat, but I'm on duty." A hesitation. "Look, I have to see Mr. Arbusto. Is he around?"

"Why, yes, he's at a table near the back of the dining room." I nodded my head in that direction. "Is there anything—"

Somberly. "No, I should talk to him first. Wait, you *can* help. I'd like to find a quiet room and take him there. Is there somewhere we could go?" he asked. He looked around at the clusters of party guests then turned to me.

The color of his eyes seemed lighter than I remembered, an amber so intense and hard that all thoughts of asking questions left my mind.

I said, "There's a small dining room in back that we use for private parties. Ever since that package of quails arrived, Nick's kept the room locked up. See that door next to the kitchen? Open it and go down a short corridor, you'll see the dining room door on the left. I'll get the key and meet you there."

Our keys were on hooks inside a kitchen cabinet. I hurried, fumbled through the key tags, and was unlocking the dining room door when Paul arrived, followed by a grim-faced Polley; a half-step behind was Lila, gripping her lover's hand.

Paul motioned to me to wait outside. He closed the door but it didn't quite shut. I stood in the corridor, irresolute, knowing I should retreat to the party, but drawn to the open door like an over-the-hill Nancy Drew. Eavesdropping wasn't worthy of me but, what the hell, standing there, ear close to the door, I decided that I'd packed away the word *genteel* along with my late mother's lace collar.

Paul's voice came through, but pitched too low for me to understand what he said. Then a wordless cry of despair that I knew arose from Polley. And a horrified: "Not Homer! Oh, no!" from Lila.

I'd heard enough for now. Shaken, I tiptoed away, back to the party. I found an empty table facing the door to the corridor, sat down and waited. In less than five minutes the door opened, the detective followed by two people whose lives had just changed forever. There was violence involved; I didn't need the details to be sure that Homer was dead, his end in some way connected to the deaths and near-deaths that had sent Polley fleeing from San Francisco, to Dellacasa's uneasy embrace.

Paul saw me and I stood as he came over; the other two waited as if fixed to the floor.

"It's Homer," I blurted. "Something's happened to Homer."

"A car accident—only it wasn't an accident."

"What do you mean?"

"Someone tampered with the brakes on his rental car. Punched holes in the brake fluid lines. Effective but not very subtle. Whoever it was just wanted this guy dead, and didn't care if we knew it was murder."

"Where—where did it happen?"

"Arbusto got as far as Sepulveda and Wilshire. According to eyewitnesses, he tried to make a turn, lost control and wrapped himself and his little red Geo around a power pole. He was dead when the paramedics arrived."

"How's Polley?"

"Holding up. He and his ladyfriend—"

"—Lila, she knew Homer—"

Paul nodded. "—they're coming with me to the morgue to make a formal identification. It happened a couple of hours ago. He must have been on his way here."

"Yes, he was coming to the party."

"The detectives at the crash scene traced him through the car rental agency, which gave them the name of his hotel. He was registered there as part of the Agrisure group. The desk clerk managed to find one of the executives who was staying over until tomorrow. He confirmed that Homer was Polley Arbusto's son."

He smiled ruefully. "That's becoming a well known name around here. The first squad car on the scene was the same pair of cops that responded when you were poisoned. They remembered an Arbusto who was a chef at Dellacasa's and alerted the detectives, who contacted me. Mr. Arbusto certainly draws attention, wherever he lands."

My fingers felt like dead things packed in ice. "Paul, what are you saying? Polley's son was just murdered!"

Paul placed a steadying hand on my shoulder. "Calm down, I'm just thinking out loud. I'm not saying anything right now. Really. But this isn't a package of butchered poultry. The sender wanted a stronger message. Don't you think so?"

"What do you mean? Are you blaming Polley in some way?"

He was either still thinking out loud, or evasive. He said, "The car was parked all day in the hotel's parking structure. I wonder how many people there knew what the victim was driving."

"I don't know. It's a five-level garage. When I was there this morning, I didn't notice any reserved spaces."

Paul looked at me sharply. "You were at the Agrisure meeting? Why?"

Now *that* was a familiar question. At least I didn't have to repeat the lie I'd told Polley and Homer this morning. "I was picking up some stockholder literature—for a reporter friend of mine."

"Interesting. I want to hear more about it, but not now. What time will you be at Dellacasa's tomorrow?"

"I hadn't planned to be at work. I'm supposed to leave for San Francisco in the morning. My flight's at ten a.m."

"Better change it to an afternoon flight. I want to see everyone who works at Dellacasa's right here, in the restaurant, around ten in the morning. Will you tell Nick?"

"Yes. But why? I was the only one from Dellacasa's who was at the hotel."

"I don't know yet where this case is leading," Paul replied.

"But it's likely that the more I know about Mr. Arbusto, senior, including his movements yesterday, the sooner I'll find answers.

"Right now, first things first, I need to take him to the morgue."

Polley and Lila hadn't moved. They'd drawn a circle of sorrow around themselves, standing quietly, unnoticed, walled away from the room's cheer.

Paul looked at them with dispassionate policeman's eyes. He had, he'd once told me, worked on a case where a father had hacked his young son to death, cutting the body into stew-size pieces for easier disposal. Paul would not be sentimental about biological fatherhood.

I found myself once again feeling protective about Polley.

Not that I'd become one of his kitchen groupies, not yet. Why, it was only this evening, tasting his tri-color pate, that I'd begun to understand why he had a following. That first taste was, well, as if Cupid wielded a fork instead of an arrow. It would have to do for now; the rest of my appetite had fled.

And my concern for this difficult man wasn't misplaced affection for the underdog. Sure, I helped find homes for stray puppies and donated to the Wildlife Waystation to feed endangered bobcats and bears. Even so, Polley was hardly a help-less pup.

Nor was I a masochist shriveling inside my militant leather jacket as Polley postured like Stallone Of The Simmering Stockpots. Truth is, I sometimes don't understand myself and must trust to my instincts, fallible as they may be.

So when Paul beckoned and Polley and Lila moved like sleepwalkers past me to the front door, I didn't attempt to touch them in sympathy. Closing the door behind them, shutting out the moon-less night, I said my own stumbling prayer.

I didn't know if Polley finally had loved Homer, or what kind of peace the son had made with his father. Although I'd mourned the deaths ten years apart of my parents, although I'd grieved for illusions that ended along with my marriage, I could only guess at the raging loss that must come after violent death. I didn't know how much Polley was capable of love but, just in case, I prayed that he'd be comforted.

Nick was standing at the kitchen door with his cousin, Frankie the baker. They were drinking ruby red wine and laughing. I went over and gave Nick the news.

TWELVE

EIGHT-THIRTY ON A cool but sunny Southern California morning. At hotels around town, the tourists clump like metal filings at the doors of their tour buses, cameras ready for the peak moments of their Los Angeles visit.

A block from where the librarian from Duluth waits, a jackhammer goes rat-a-tat-tat, and she shivers and wonders whether the riots ever explode onto Wilshire Boulevard. A sixteen wheeler rumbles over deep potholes on Hope Street downtown, and the Hong Kong businessman braces himself for glass towers that will crash down as the sidewalks split open, swallowing him up and leaving his six children fatherless.

Soon the tour buses will load and leave, windows sealed against dust, heat and crimes against the innocent, carrying the visitors around town, from the old pueblo ambience of Olvera Street, west to Brentwood and the photo-op of the century: O.J.'s neighborhood. ("Sorry, folks, this is as close as our bus is allowed to get.")

At some point, the buses will stop, belch, and unload at the stalls and shops of the Farmer's Market.

There the locals will be overwhelmed by tourists in urgent need of waffles and enchiladas, stuffed dates and strawberries, Dodgers caps, suntan lotion, and Hollywood t-shirts, not to mention short lines at the rest rooms. I avoid the Farmer's Market during the July and August crush. But at eight-thirty on a serene March morning, before the shops open, when the loudest sounds at the outdoor tables are senior citizens and out-of-work actors rustling the pages of the *Times* over their coffee cups, the Market is my hangout.

I'd agreed to meet Aunt Sadie and her new friend at a table near one of the coffee stalls. Sadie had called yesterday evening; the message was on my answering machine when I'd returned, distraught and tearful, from Dellacasa's.

"Where are you, Catherine? I had a fantastic, inspirational weekend, and there's someone I want you to meet. Please call no matter what time you get home tonight!"

Dutifully, I'd called. She'd sounded so happy, I couldn't bring her down by telling her that I'd been poisoned on Friday, in the hospital till Saturday, and that our chef's son had been murdered on Monday. With great restraint I said that I'd had a busy weekend and was leaving for San Francisco on business at one p.m. Tuesday.

"Well, then," said Sadie, "Can you join us for breakfast? Ricardo is only here for one day. He has to get back to Rosarita, and he's been looking forward to meeting you."

Ricardo? From Rosarita? That's a beach resort over the border in Mexico.

"I have to be at Dellacasa's in the morning, at ten. How about a cup of coffee early, at the Farmer's Market?"

With the fervor of a recent convert Sadie said, "I don't drink coffee anymore. Neither does Ricardo. But there's a juice bar, so we'll find something."

No more coffee? Sadie has Southern roots, and her coffee is famous for being strong, rich, fortified with chicory. I had to assume this new phase was some temporary aberration. Or could it be love? I was used to Sadie's flights of enthusiasm, but this time her feelings seemed more intense, certainly more than those of your average 68-year old widow. I should be supportive.

Which was why I sat, tired and depressed, with a double-size cafe latte and a fresh rye bagel, waiting for Sadie and Ricardo.

I had packed my suitcase before last night's party, and it was stowed in my car trunk. After meeting with Paul Wang and the staff at Dellacasa's, I'd go directly to the airport.

My clothes were as droopy as my spirits. I hadn't bothered to dress with any thought, either for meeting Detective Wang, greeting Ricardo, or for my arrival in San Francisco. This morning, I'd begun with the usual routine of make-up base and mascara, stared in the mirror at my emerging Lancome glow and said, ah, the hell with it. I'd thrown on clean but shapeless grey sweats, Reeboks and dark glasses, locked up my apartment and left. This is me today, world, take it or leave it.

By contrast, Aunt Sadie appeared trim and radiant in her cerulean blue jogging suit, copper hair a-gleam, as she threaded her way through the tables towards me. Behind her, and about the same height, was a perfectly pink man in a navy sweatsuit.

He had the high pink color of a man who'd stayed in the sun too long, though I soon realized this was his natural skin tone. His scalp was shiny pink and nearly bare, save for a frizz of close-cropped white hair that started over his ears and continued in a low band around the back of his head. Ricardo's cheeks (yes, this must be Ricardo) had a robust blush; even his fingernails were shell pink. His build was sturdy, not muscular but solid and broad-chested for a rather short man. I guessed him to be about seventy years old.

I rose and gave Sadie a real hug, which I needed more than she did. She looked surprised and pleased, and I realized with pain that too many times I was stingy with my hugs.

"Catherine, this is my new friend, Ricardo Winesap. Ricardo, meet my darling niece, Catherine."

I smiled, Ricardo beamed, we said our how-do-you-do's, and sat. Like the fine hostess she is, Sadie remained standing, ready to offer hospitality.

"Cat, do you want a refill yet? No? Well, Ricardo and I are having Green Cocktails, so I'll go to the juice bar while you two get acquainted."

"Green?" I was dubious.

"Spinach, parsley, celery leaves and pineapple juice, dear. Probably not organic here, but still a wonderful way to get your daily carotene and anti-oxidants." This was Aunt Sadie, who'd won prizes for her seven-layer coconut cake? Amazing.

Ricardo had risen to offer his wallet, which Sadie waved away.

With springy steps, she left us.

"Remarkable woman, your aunt," said Ricardo fondly.

I nodded, trying not to show my curiosity. Wine-sap from Rosarita Beach, eh? And where was the accent?

"You met at the spa, Aunt Sadie told me. Do you go often?"

"Every couple of months or so. Or if I'm stressed out." He patted his stomach gingerly. "I was on the verge of an ulcer. My doctor told me I needed changes in my lifestyle. Slow down, eat healthier, that kind of thing. I go to El Encanto to relax."

"Sadie's brochure talked about 'balancing the vital organs in your body.' How does that work for you?"

Ricardo leaned forward and said, "Confidentially, your aunt really got into this yin and yang stuff. After we met that first evening at dinner, I went to the lectures with her, just because I like her, you see, but I'm not convinced. A few soybeans go a long way with me. On the other hand, if eating like a Japanese monk makes her happy, sure, why not?"

Other people's strong, ugly passions had been tearing apart my life. Here's to kind hearts, I thought, deciding I liked Ricardo very much.

Sadie reappeared, a clear plastic glass of green liquid in each hand. "Adelle Davis said we should have an intensely green leafy vegetable daily."

I nodded respectfully at the name of the pioneering nutritionist. "Hello Adelle Davis, goodbye Julia Child?"

"I'm thinking about it. At El Encanto, they told us it's okay to relapse every now and then."

"Auntie, they make it sound as if eating is a disease!"

"Catherine," she said impatiently, "I've been at some of the parties that Dellacasa's catered. I realize now that your guests become walking time bombs of cholesterol and fat."

I groaned. First a confrontation with Polley, now my aunt. Would chocolate mousse tarts die off like tiny brown dinosaurs?

"No one eats like that every day, Aunt Sadie. If

we did, we'd have to have carts rolling down the streets to carry away the corpses, the way they did in the plague days. I'll grant you, even Dellacasa's is cooking lighter these days. But an indulgence every now and then doesn't hurt."

I'd raised my voice. Next table over, the actor who'd just been written out of his soap opera, dying of a tarantula bite, caught my eye and winked. Be kind: I offered him a prim smile.

"Whatever works, Aunt Sadie. Meantime, what are you and Ricardo up to today?"

"We're going to find a health food store and buy miso—"

"—fermented soybean paste," volunteered Ricardo, clear blue eyes twinkling.

"Yes, I'm going to cook a miso soup for Ricardo so he'll know how to prepare it when he returns to San Diego."

"I thought Ricardo was from Rosarita Beach."

"Both," said Ricardo, answering my questions before I could think of a tactful way to phrase them. "I was born in San Diego to an American father, but my mother was from Rosarita, and my cousins still run our family's ranch down there. It's not huge or fancy, but it's near some spectacular beaches. I hope Sadie and you will visit someday soon."

"I'd like that," I replied, meaning it. "So, you're a rancher?"

"Catherine," protested my aunt, "You're quizzing Ricardo as if you were my father."

Perhaps I was; trust didn't come easily to me these days.

"It's all right, Sadie," said Ricardo. "I can tell your niece cares about you.

"My son grows avocados in Oceanside, and I'm a partner in his ranch. Mainly, I'm a food broker with an office in San Diego, Catherine. I deal in the usual national brands, but I also represent some smaller California companies. Like the agricultural co-ops that package their own product, raisins and artichokes, that sort of thing. Some health food lines, too, which is how I got to know El Encanto."

"Then you're not a novice at this spa regime."

"Yes and no. I deal in the foods, I don't necessarily buy into the philosophy. They have this theory about balance: you eat some foods one week, other foods the next. Sounds a little extreme to me."

"Now, Ricardo," said Sadie, "that's because you haven't accepted the idea that everything in nature is in balance." She raised her arms upward and moved her graceful hands in slow, widening circles.

"We are all collections of atoms," opined Sadie in what I can only define as a mystical voice. "We spin around in a cosmic balance that holds us together. When our souls or our bodies go *out* of balance, we may sicken and even die."

She lowered her hands, picked up her Green Cocktail, looked at both of us and said, "This weekend has changed my life. I'm so glad I've learned in time to pass on this wisdom to you." She smiled her warm Sadie smile and sipped at the green drink.

"A little balance goes a long way," said Ricardo carefully.

"Oh, my," said Sadie, laughing. "I'm not going to start wearing a homespun robe and playing the tambourine at the airport. Don't worry, you two. Just give what I've said a little thought. Catherine, when you have time, I'll explain the program in detail."

The sun was higher, warming my face. The Farmer's Market had come to life. Smells of frying eggs and freshly made fudge drifted our way.

I looked at my watch. "I have to leave."

"Let me remind you, dear, that Easter is just two Sundays away. You said it was all right with you, so I've invited Gil for Easter dinner. Gil," she explained to Ricardo, "is Catherine's ex-husband.

"Ricardo," Sadie explained to me, "is invited, of course, but he's spending the holiday with his son in Oceanside."

"A family tradition," said Ricardo. "My little grandson would miss me."

"Someday," I told my aunt, "Gil will break loose and find some traditions that don't include us."

"Gil is coming along very well. He misses you, you know."

This was not a proper discussion in front of Ricardo. But I did have an inspiring thought.

"Remember how Gil loves your baked ham with the brown sugar and mustard glaze? And the scalloped sweet potatoes?"

Sadie nodded.

"How about trying out the new regime on him. Something festive, like—oh, say, mung bean loaf and kale?"

Ricardo repressed a smile.

"You're joking," said Sadie, unperturbed. "But I'm glad you're thinking in that direction. I already have. We will have a healthful Easter dinner, for once."

I returned my untouched bagel to its paper bag and dropped the bag into my purse. I would find butter and jam at Dellacasa's, eat the bagel and self-destruct.

We said our goodbyes and I left, relieved that Sadie's solitary vacation had brought her both revelations and romance. She'd almost made me forget the feeling of dread that had given me a restless night and lasted into the morning.

Not quite. Just my luck, I thought, I'd order a Green Cocktail and there'd be a leaf worm waving up at me from the bottom of the glass.

THIRTEEN

THE OCTAGON-SHAPED floor tiles had been scrubbed to bleached whiteness; copper saute pans and cast iron skillets shone on overhead racks above the tidied counters and butcher block worktables. It was as if the kitchen fairy had risen early, waved a magic scouring pad and whisked away all traces of last night's party fare, spills and sorrows.

More likely it was Jose and Damien who'd been cleaning since dawn; they now sat in the dining room with mugs of coffee and slabs of leftover sausage pizza. Rosie had stayed home with a headache that began at midnight. Mario, bartender Joe, hostess Winona, our waiters and waitresses were scattered at other tables. I missed the usual morning activity. Nick had decided to stay shut for lunch today; the "CLOSED: Open For Dinner" sign was hung in the front window.

I was relentlessly determined to be depressed. Alone in the kitchen, I'd set myself up with a cup of fresh coffee and my buttered bagel. Just before 10 a.m. a distressed Nick appeared.

"More bad news for Polley," he said. "Agrisure didn't even wait a day, those sons of bitches. They must have been burning up the phone lines from L.A. to San Francisco. Their controller, a guy named Doyle—I guess he's their hatchetman—called Polley at his apartment early this morning.

"He offered the company's condolences to a grieving father—and then fired Polley as Agrisure's spokesman. Too many unexplained deaths around Polley, and the company must avoid scandal. Doyle was sure he'd understand."

"That's disgusting," I said.

"Yeah," Nick sighed, "business is business. Anyway, Lila was at the apartment. She asked if you'd call her."

"Any idea why?"

His answer was cut short as talk in the dining room stopped. The silence invaded the kitchen and we went to investigate.

Paul Wang had arrived with his new downtown partner, a veteran homicide detective. Swanson was a study in monotones: silver hair combed carefully back over an emerging bald spot; grey worsted suit, its open jacket only partially hiding a waistline thickened, most likely, by long stakeouts fueled with stops at the doughnut stand. We were introduced. Swanson appraised Nick and me with steady grey eyes, more the color of steel than silver; there was none of the hidden softness of silver.

Polley had not shown up; that was expected. He

was arranging to fly his son's body home to San Francisco after the autopsy.

"When?" Nick asked.

"No firm date yet," said Swanson. "It might be two or three days."

Added Paul with grim pride, "The coroner's office performs 18,000 autopsies a year. They have bodies waiting in line."

Although I was the only one among us who had met Homer, there were uneasy sighs around the room. Sighs, I suppose, for those bodies lined up waiting to check out of L.A. County's air-conditioned, personal attention, no mints on the pillows, no pillows hotel. Because they had died violently. Or mysteriously. Perished because of vengeance. Or greed. Or, who happened to be standing on the wrong corner when death drove by with a gun and an itchy finger.

Outside our front door, under the beamish Westwood sun, the streets were clean and wide and graced with green early spring shrubbery. Past the wine displays in our front window, I could see a couple wearing UCLA t-shirts and jeans, slouching towards the nearest espresso bar. Dellacasa's suddenly felt stifling.

Thankfully, our meeting with the police was brief, even anticlimactic. What time, they asked, did Polley arrive at Dellacasa's yesterday?

"Exactly three o'clock," Nick answered, "so he

could help Mario prepare the party food. Just like we planned." Nods of confirmation around the room.

Was Polley upset? Acting strange, or different?

Not noticeably, the kitchen staff agreed. They'd already learned that he was quick-tempered. They expected it.

Had Homer Arbusto ever been to the restaurant?

Mario spoke up. "No, Polley told me his son would be interested in looking around an old-fashioned Italian restaurant."

Old-fashioned? Nick frowned.

The questioning ended soon after. Paul asked me to stay; the rest of the staff scattered for a long break. Nick retreated to the kitchen to keep his hands busy with dinner preparations.

When the dining room was empty I asked the two detectives, "Could you really build a case that Polley killed his son?"

They had seated themselves at my table. Swanson seemed bemused by my empty coffee cup. I offered them both coffee and rolls.

Swanson was grateful. "I haven't had breakfast. Black, please, with sugar." Paul declined. As I returned with coffee and fresh, crusty rolls, Swanson fumbled in a jacket pocket and took out a package of Tums.

"Just in case," he said apologetically. "I shouldn't be drinking too much coffee."

Slim, fit Paul Wang sat impassively. "So I've heard."

Swanson was cheerful. "It's okay, partner. If your stomach isn't full of holes by the time you're fifty, I'll treat you to a month's worth of chili dogs. With peppers."

Paul smiled as if the very idea was incredible, shrugged, and turned to me.

"We don't have any answers, Cat. This is the routine detail work, checking out times and alibis. Not just for Arbusto. I'm looking at everyone in that Agrisure bunch.

"Could be someone in Agrisure's management had a reason to get rid of Homer. Meanwhile, what were you doing at the stockholder's meeting?"

Swanson took notes, between sips, as I told them about Nate's request and my impressions: A possible flare-up among the stockholders in the morning that had, I'd heard later, been put out by the time the day was over.

I asked my own question. "Any more news about Homer's car?"

Paul shook his head. "Just what we thought, a sharp instrument jabbed into the three brake fluid lines. Probably an ice pick. A few seconds work if the killer knew what he was doing. Homer picked up the car rental at the airport the night before. The mileage records indicate he didn't drive it until he left for Dellacasa's the next evening. He was too busy at the meeting.

"So, the tampering could have been done anytime between, say, eight o'clock Sunday night until just before seven o'clock on Monday when he crashed. His red Geo would have been easy to spot. All our killer needed was a few minutes alone in the garage."

Swanson had decided that if I was accepted by his partner, I was okay with him, too. He reached into his jacket pocket for a pack of Camels, took out a squashed cigarette, looked longingly and replaced it. His thumb stroked the pack as if it were a lover's skin.

"What narrows it down," said Swanson with a raspy cough, "unless this was a completely random act, which we doubt, the killer knew in advance what car Homer was driving. Since most of the Agrisure people went back to San Francisco on Monday evening, we're still checking. *Who* reserved the car for him in San Francisco, *who* saw him drive it away from the rental agency, or could have seen him arrive at the hotel. We don't know any of that yet."

"But why suspect Polley?"

"We don't know much," said Paul, "about Arbusto's relationship with his son. The San Francisco police talked to the mother. She says he wasn't much of a father until recently.

"And, he hasn't been cleared yet for the murder at his restaurant. Or for the attack on you down here."

"Isn't it possible someone has a grudge against him?"

"Sure. That's why he's still a free man."

Not much more to say. The detectives left.

Nick and I had agreed last night that I'd return from San Francisco on Thursday or Friday. Nick would fly up for the funeral, whenever that would be. Since Mario was leaving for France tonight, Frankie the baker, who was semi-retired, would fill in as needed.

I felt a gentle stirring of blood in my veins. Like Joan of Arc, I'd accepted my mission. I didn't hear her "voices," *Grace a Dieu,* but I'd go north to help bring order out of the chaos that was threatening Dellacasa's existence. This wasn't as dramatic as saving France, but our friendly Italian restaurant in Westwood was as dear to me as home and country. I'd raise my sword and—

Hell, I'd nearly forgotten to call Lila. Looking at my watch, I dialed Polley's apartment. Lila answered. She talked, I listened, she wheedled, I reluctantly agreed.

Was I doomed to be tangled up in Polley's troubles? But as I brooded on my way to the airport, it suddenly became clear that Lila had, without knowing, presented me with an opportunity. How big it was I couldn't yet tell.

Somewhere in size between France—and, well, a soggy eclair.

FOURTEEN

ONE INTERVIEW and two miserable tasks: that was my new agenda for San Francisco.

I was down to one candidate for standby catering chef. Our other choice, Chef Max, hadn't waited after I'd cancelled our meeting during the Fancy Food Show. He'd easily found another berth, he assured me when I'd called from L.A.; it was on a luxury cruise ship. He'd be leaving next week, cooking for a 16-day voyage through the Panama Canal. Fitness A-Float, he said in a rich Austrian accent, was the theme.

"Will you be serving soybeans, mung beans and lots of greens?" I asked with genuine interest.

"Nein," said Max, chuckling into the telephone, "after a couple of hours of aerobics on deck at sea, my guests want their handfuls of vitamins and green salads, of course."

"Of course."

"Followed by lobster with drawn butter and filet mignon."

"It figures."

"After all, it is a luxury cruise."

I sighed. "And we are hopeless bundles of contradictions."

"The eternal struggle," said Max with gusto. "Purity or passion. The ascetic and the voluptuous. We should taste both, Miss Catherine, or life is too bland. I've given this much thought. In my life, in my cuisine."

"I'm sorry we've never met, Max." My regret was real. Kitchens are too busy for philosophers; in our haste we put the sauce before Descartes.

"Come take a cruise with us," said Max. "Only costs you $2,000 to get away from L.A. and eat my Tarte Tatin whenever you want it."

He knew we'd hired Polley and though he sounded a trifle smug I forgave him. I wished him Bon Voyage and told him to call Dellacasa's if he ever felt like jumping ship.

So I was left with just one chef to interview, on Wednesday morning. Before I did my nasty errands.

Lila had said, on the phone, "I'm embarrassed to ask you, Cat. I know you and Polley aren't too friendly—"

And the Civil War was a minor skirmish.

"—but since you're going to San Francisco anyway, it would only take a few hours of your time. And it would be so absolutely *nice* of you."

I gnawed at the edge of my left thumbnail. "What would be so nice, Lila?"

"Well, Polley's ex-wife called him. Anna had given Homer an engraved black marble clock when he started to work at Agrisure. Homer kept it on his desk and now his mother wants it back. She's too broken up to get it, and the other personal things in his office, and Cassie won't even talk to her father—"

"Cassie?" That's right, Polley talked about his *children.*

"Cassie, well, Cassandra. She hasn't talked to Polley since the divorce and, besides, she's pretty broken up, too."

"So," I said slowly, "you want me to go to Agrisure and get Homer's things and—?"

"Bring them over to Anna, you know, Homer's mother. You've seen the Agrisure people. You're smart, you'll know what to say. It would be touchy for Polley to go. He may have to sue them over his contract.

"It's a mess. I mean, Anna barely talks to Polley, either. I can't imagine how they'll behave towards each other at the funeral."

"What about you?"

"Oh, I'm going to stay with Polley until the autopsy is over. Maybe I'll drive him back to San Francisco. But Anna, and especially Cassie, don't particularly think much of me. I don't know why. I didn't meet Polley until after the separation."

Lila hesitated. "Maybe they don't think I'm elegant enough to be out in public with a famous chef."

Maybe Polley was lucky to have such unquestioning loyalty.

I said, "Lila, don't worry about what they think. Sometimes divorce makes both sides act as if they have to—"

I had begun to say, put poison in the other one's oatmeal but, to my credit, I stopped myself in time.

"—be enemies," I finished lamely.

"Then you will?" said Lila, though I hadn't said yes.

"Well, okay, I suppose I should pay my respects to Homer's family anyway. I only met him briefly, but I liked him."

"Oh, you are a good person!" said Lila with fervor.

How others must see me! Chin up, shiny-eyed and noble, like Lassie. And that's when, panting with self-adoration, I allowed myself to be pulled deeper into the murders.

OF COURSE, I'd come to San Francisco partly to check on the quails sent to us by someone who'd vowed "REVENGE." Although the LAPD now had the package, I didn't imagine they'd be setting up a quail-tracking task force anytime soon.

I wanted to talk to two people whose friends had died: Blaine Shepherd, according to newspaper accounts, had been the murdered Perry Framboise's business partner. And I'd heard Eddie Claire's anguished cries after he'd lost his lover.

Nate Greene had agreed to help. He called soon after I checked into the Brittany, my small, familiar hotel on Geary Street.

"Cat? Welcome. Can you be ready in an hour? Shepherd will be at his video store in the Castro. He's expecting us. And Eddie Claire, well, he'll also be in the neighborhood. I'll tell you about it later. Be in front of the hotel at four o'clock, because I can stop but there's usually no place to park. I don't take my car out of the garage for just anyone, so feel flattered."

Nate was as staunch a skeptic as any good reporter, but I could hear the excitement as he spoke. Polley Arbusto was an enigma, but he was also a helluva story. I had a feeling that Nate would stay close to me while I zigged and zagged around the city trying to make connections with Polley's foes, family, and past employer.

No problem; I'd have access to sources all around San Francisco. Nate had already opened doors, which helped. While I didn't expect any of these folks to greet me with an assault rifle, hey, I also wasn't visiting to say they'd just won the five point two million dollar California lottery.

Time to get out of my sweats, take a quick shower, and dig around in my suitcase for moisturizing makeup, blusher, mascara, black slacks, turtleneck and walking shoes. It had been threatening rain when I arrived, so I donned my dashing khaki trenchcoat, ignored the elevator and ran down four flights of stairs with a step that was surprisingly light.

Traffic was already fender-to-fender on Geary Street, and a sharp, cold wind had gusted in from the ocean. The Brittany's blue canvas canopy gave some shelter and I amused myself watching the pedestrians.

There was a steady, easy pace to the way they walked: the homeless man wearing dreadlocks and dirt-caked Army fatigues; a tourist couple, both in white shorts and thin purple windbreakers; a sleek woman in a black fitted coat and black sheer stockings. They walked as if the clouding-up sky and the forceful wind were part of San Francisco's charm, along with the bay and the hills. This city fitted comfortably into its skin.

L.A. was once that easy.

There were stories to tell my grandchildren. One day, I'd gather those cute rascals around my arthritic knees and say, I can remember when L.A. was so young and giddy, why, we had buildings shaped like derbies.

And a working stiff could drive down to Santa Monica on a Sunday afternoon and watch the polo matches.

And when we looked over our shoulders, it was because we weren't so rude as to stare directly at Miss Lombard and Mr. Gable. And your grandma went to maybe three or four parties a week where everyone was friendly and smiled while she helped them to champagne and punch and canapes that looked like tiny cream puffs.

'Course, little darlings, grandma may have got some of the years a bit mixed up, but it's all true.

That's what I'll tell them, and about how I waited with the clean wind dancing around my feet, feeling that somehow San Francisco would set me in the right direction.

So I watched for Nate and waited for rain, and thought about finding answers to questions I hadn't yet imagined.

FIFTEEN

WE'D TURNED OFF Market and parked on Castro Street, taking the only space in sight. It was directly across from a gilded dowager of a movie house, with an Art Deco marquee that announced: GAY AND LESBIAN FILM FESTIVAL TONIGHT AT 7.

"What luck," said Nate. "Another hour and we'd have to park in the next county."

Approaching dusk and rain were making the sky darken rapidly, but there were flashes of color along the street from the flags and banners of the Castro. I'd noticed them in other districts of San Francisco as well: vivid stripes of red, orange, yellow, green, royal and purple that waved above a homosexual-owned business or dwelling. In the Castro, the colors were everywhere, proclaiming unity and gay pride. But AIDS had decimated the neighborhood, and the flags put me in mind of a battlefield where young men rallied around bright banners, only to find that victories and death were handed out unequally.

On the surface, the Castro had the pleasing mixture of shops and people that livened many San

Francisco neighborhoods. Chinese mothers in somber tweed coats hurried with their shopping, wheeling round-faced toddlers strapped in strollers. Young couples window-shopped and stopped for cheeses and bagels, books and antiques.

The men walked in twos and threes on Castro Street, gathering at this hour at the cafes and bars. Nate and I left his car, heading for Blaine Shepherd's video store near the end of the block. I dawdled in front of an airy-looking cafe with wide front windows, ferns and pale blond furniture. Two doors down, the smell of beer wafted to the sidewalk from a dark bar crammed with hard bodies armored in leather jeans, jackets and studded wristbands; circled with thick brass buckled belts; festooned with strange hardware. Nate pulled me along.

Perry's Video Place had advertising posters in its windows: a gay cowboy on a stallion, yippee-ing for an upcoming rodeo; The Milk Institute's spring catalog; the latest CD of a Madonna concert; videocassettes of Hollywood blockbusters; a video manual about sex that was gay, safe and erotic.

A buzzer sounded as we entered, and a tall, lean man in his early forties came toward us from the back of the store. Black leather cap at a rakish angle over a well-shaped head, trim pepper-and-salt goatee, a small gold hoop in his right ear, slim black leather jeans. A tucked-in t-shirt read, "All That Glitters Isn't Gold Lame." A cautious smile.

"That's Blaine," said Nate.

"I guessed."

"Hi, Nate, glad to see you. This must be your Los Angeles friend. Catherine, is it? I hear you've inherited trouble."

"Just call me Cat. And, thanks for agreeing to talk to me."

The store was neat, brightly lit, with wide aisles. At the rear was a small counter with an espresso machine and white china, a couple of white ice cream tables with black ladderback chairs. Blaine led us to a table and chattered amiably as he measured out a densely black grind, turned spigots, and poured steaming coffee into demitasse cups.

"Easy entertaining," he said. "I'm in the store so many hours, this little space is my second living room. The espresso machine was Perry's idea. I'd have been using that instant cherish-the-times-you-got-laid stuff, if not for Perry."

Turning to Nate, he continued, "You knew him. For such a big man in every way, he really cared about the details." Blaine became quiet, shook his head then said simply, "I still miss him."

I accepted a coffee cup and ventured, "I'm sorry if my visit upsets you, and I wish I could be more precise about what I'm looking for. Maybe some insights into the relationship between Mr. Framboise and Polley Arbusto. Do you know Polley?"

Blaine reflectively scratched his goatee and said, "I'd rather not but, yes, I know him. The man wants to be America's most honored chef, and God help anyone who gets in his way."

Nate laughed. "Perry liked him, you know that, Blaine. I'd see them talking together at a fundraiser or some other event, and it was always friendly."

"No, Perry *admired* him, that's different. He had great respect for Arbusto's talents as a chef. Liked to talk recipes and wines with him, that sort of thing. But Polley's too ambitious. I suspect that he's capable of great harm if he's threatened."

The buzzer sounded and two handsome young men in bulky turtlenecks, jeans and boots came in.

"Excuse me for a few minutes." Blaine rose and walked to the front of the store to meet his customers.

"Are you learning anything?" asked Nate in a low voice.

I whispered, "Only that Blaine could have been upset enough to want to frame Polley."

"I know Blaine. He's not the vengeful kind. He's a good businessman, thinks clearly. He kept Perry calm and rational during this raging debate about stopping AIDS by closing the gay bathhouses."

"Maybe, but his good friend was murdered by someone who may be targeting gays. And he's told you what he thinks of Polley—doesn't sound very calm to me."

"He's coming back."

Blaine apologized. "Usually I have a clerk here helping me. But he wanted time off and, with the film festival down the street, it'll be a quiet evening.

"Perry left me his share of the store, if you wondered, and it's profitable. No worries about slack times. Now, where were we?"

"Let me tell you about what's happening at Dellacasa's, our restaurant, since Polley arrived."

I told Blaine everything: the package of poisoned quails with a threat, an attempt on me, the murder of Homer Arbusto. Even some of the details I had withheld from Nate until now.

They stared at me: Nate looking more upset than I'd expected, Perry Framboise's partner intent on my words but blank-faced.

"Well," said Blaine, "it's certainly never dull when Arbusto's around. Oh, speaking of quails, I have something for you."

He walked to the front of the store, reached under the counter to retrieve a rectangular package and returned with it.

"There's a syndicated cooking show, *Northern California Chefs,* that Arbusto's appeared on several times. I told you that Perry was a fan of his. He always taped Arbusto's cooking demonstrations.

This video should fascinate you. Your new chef prepares the quail recipe that he used at the—to be melodramatic—fatal dinner."

Aha! A clue? With so little else that was tangible to carry me forward, this was exciting.

"Of course, I'd already taped a copy to give to the detectives. I don't know if it's helped them. If nothing else, they'll have a tasty recipe for their next department barbecue."

"Were you at the dinner?"

"No. I was here, minding the store. Not that Perry really spent much time here, I'd always run the business."

He waved a hand towards the tidy rows of shelves. "This was too small an arena for Perry Framboise. He needed to be in the center of things. He liked power and drama. He had presence, you know. The sheer height and size of him, three hundred pounds he weighed, and a voice like rolling thunder." Absentmindedly, Blaine balanced the empty demitasse cup on the palm of his hand.

"There was so much to love although he and I were never lovers. After his longtime companion died of AIDS, I think Perry was so relieved that he wasn't infected, he gave up on romance and sex. Poured all his energy into gay rights."

"Then he must have been very angry at Polley over the scene in the restaurant," I suggested.

"Betrayed," said Blaine. "I know he felt betrayed.

After all, they shared interests, at least that's what Perry thought. He assumed that those happy chats about food and wine made a bond between them. But suddenly here's his buddy, his mentor, acting like his unforgiving Basque father."

I didn't know much about civic conflicts in San Francisco, but I could believe it was possible— just possible—that Polley was getting a bum rap.

I asked, "Was there any other business that Mr. Framboise picketed? All this street theater must have made him more than one enemy."

Blaine nodded calmly. "Oh, there were several, over the years. And you're right, Perry put on a good show. But San Franciscans are extremely tolerant, and most people enjoyed the theatrics. I can't think of any other business owner holding a serious grudge."

"Whatever happened to the two fellows who started it all at Arbusto's?" asked Nate. "I never saw them marching during the protests."

Perry's good friend looked pained. "Truth is, Ron and Bobo were—and are—a couple of twits. They're always outrageous, playing Superqueer, the gay crusader and his sidekick, Barboy. They just adored picking the most conservative restaurant owner in San Francisco and making a scene at his place.

"Perry decided to protest because he'd heard that Arbusto roughed them up when he threw them out.

But he didn't ask the dreadful duo to march, simply because they'd give idiocy a bad name."

"What you're telling us," I said, "is that both sides were acting stupid."

"Exactly," said Blaine. And because of some slobbering kisses, one very fine man had to die and dozens of others suffered.

"You must have thought about it," said Nate. "Any ideas you want to share about Perry's killer? Even though I can see Arbusto becoming so angry he'd want to strike back, this seems to go beyond anger into hatred. After all, twenty-four other people were poisoned as well. Can you think of anyone who hated Perry so much that it didn't matter who else was hurt?"

Blaine's hands gripped the edges of the table, he leaned towards us and, for a second, I thought I saw fear in his eyes.

"I've thought about it till my brain shuts off. Why don't you look at it the other way? It's possible the killer hated all gays. Very possible. Most of the guests, not all, but most of them were gay or lesbian. It could even be a hate *group,* who knows? But so far, no one's claimed responsibility. Not even any rumors.

"And if it was someone in the gay community who had a grudge against Perry, would he have poisoned all the others? Would he?"

While we mulled it over, Blaine stood, went

to the cupboard under the espresso machine and brought out a package of cookies.

"I'm being a poor host," he said. "Here, have some of these. Fat-free fig newtons. I adore them. It's enough of a problem being queer without getting fat."

We all helped ourselves to nutritionally correct Newtons and chewed.

Said Nate, "This was a small, fairly private dinner party to settle a dispute. Yet the killer had to know about the party in advance, in order to tamper with the quails. And if he did want to target Perry, that means he also knew the guest list. Which is why the police are still fond of Arbusto as a suspect."

Blaine nodded his agreement. "I'm convinced that Perry didn't have any other real enemies, certainly not among the gays. As far as I know, no one besides Arbusto in the straight community. Even at City Hall. And his family, they were Basque farmers, had decided he was dead a long time ago."

Blaine stopped abruptly and cleared his throat before he continued.

"I don't know. Unless it was an anti-gay act—or Polley Arbusto, who's probably anti-everyone—what other straight person could have hated this upstanding man enough to push him into a heart attack?"

"Heart attack?" I said. "Mr. Framboise was poisoned."

"Perry had a weak heart, he was on medication. Most of his friends knew it. The convulsions from the poison triggered a heart attack, that's what it said in the autopsy report. One of the detectives read me the results."

In the silence, Nate removed his tortoiseshell rimmed glasses, squinted at them, pulled a handkerchief from his pocket and began to polish the lenses. A gesture I remembered from the hours we'd spent together at UCLA studying for tests. Nate gaining time while trying to create logical solutions from unruly facts.

There was a lot to chew on besides the Newtons.

For starters, if Perry Framboise died of a heart attack, were the poisoned quails a sick joke that went too far? Or did the killer really intend to kill *all* his victims—gay and straight?

Was Polley capable of such a terrible act of revenge against Framboise—even at the risk of destroying his own career?

Or could it be that Polley was the intended victim—his reputation demolished, his restaurant closed? Set up by a killer who hated him enough to plan a mass murder?

A killer so passionate about his hatred, he could not let Polley start his life over in Los Angeles without following him.

To devise such mischief as the contaminated oil that sent me to the hospital.

To carry through the murder of Polley's only son. (Assuming *temporarily* that this was a personal vendetta and not a corporate plot at Agrisure to ensure Homer's silence.)

Sitting in the quiet enclave at the back of the video store, we sipped our espressos and considered motives that were as dark as the coffee.

The buzzer had *breeped* again at the front door. Blaine uncrossed his long, leather clad legs and stood, looking down at us like a bright-eyed raven.

"Does it really matter what killed him that evening—the poison or his heart?" he asked. "After all, dead is dead."

SIXTEEN

"It isn't a *wake* for Mickey MacHugh, I'm told, it's a celebration of life." Nate peered through the windshield at the first spatters of rain.

"Whatever," I said glumly. "Next time you come to Los Angeles, we can visit Forest Lawn."

Nate looked at me in mock surprise. "What happened to that 'It's my mission to save Dellacasa's' stuff?"

"It's there. I'm just feeling a little bad that I'm dealing in other people's misery."

"You're too sensitive. You'd make a lousy reporter."

"I'm tougher than you think. I did cry when I learned how many fat grams there are in Kung Pao Chicken. But not since."

"That's reassuring. But, listen, these folks are looking for justice. Or resolution. They're glad to talk if they think you can help."

"If. If. It's a struggle to stay objective. I've been feeling so sorry for Polley after his son's death."

Nate angled the white Honda to the curb. "Here we are. Let's see how Eddie Claire's dealing with *his* sorrow. This is the house that Eddie owned with Mickey MacHugh."

Light rain was falling and Nate had raised the car's windows. The glass was partly fogged with our breaths but, looking out, I could see a two-story wood frame Victorian. It was one of the more colorful restorations on a harmonious, tree-lined street: light grey paint, arched entranceway and second-floor balcony outlined in turquoise, the lacy fretwork a pale peach. A short flight of grey stairs led up to a small landing protected from rain by the balcony's overhang; the front door was open.

I raised the collar of my trenchcoat and we hurried up the stairs. Voices and laughter met us on the landing. Nate knocked on the front door and after a polite pause we entered.

We were in a narrow hallway: pale pine floors, grey wallpaper strewn with small pastel posies. The voices were coming from a room down the hall. As we listened, a tall, slender wood nymph popped out. She inhabited a moss green velvet slip dress over a creamy lace tee; long black hair framed milk-white skin and wide-set green eyes. Her cheekbones were the high, serious kind that a camera loves; even an incompetent leprechaun could easily get her on a cover of *Vogue*. She wasn't much older than seventeen.

"Oh, here you are," said the nymph. "I thought I heard you knock."

"Eddie's expecting us, sorry we're a little late. I'm Nate Greene, with the *Post-Ledger,* and this is Catherine Deean. Cat."

"I know who you are," the nymph told me with a friendly smile. "The poor unfortunate from L.A. I hear Eddie screamed at you. Don't take it too seriously. He's usually very sweet, but he's been under a terrible strain."

"I understand. But thanks for telling me. Are you family?"

"Sorry, forgot my manners! I'm Phoebe, Mickey's sister." Nate had given me some background on Mickey and his lover, Eddie. He hadn't mentioned any relatives.

"It was good of you to come," said Phoebe. "Don't feel that you have to tiptoe around me and Eddie and Mother. Naturally, we're feeling sad. But we're trying hard to be thankful for Mickey's life."

The clear young voice wavered, then Phoebe continued, "Let's not stand in the hallway. Come in and meet Mother and Eddie. There's lots of food, our friends brought all sorts of nibbles and casseroles and desserts. Everyone's been so kind. Please help yourselves."

The sitting room we entered did suggest more of a party than a wake. Its ceiling was a bobbing mass of balloons. They floated above us like puffs of rainbows, their streamer ties twirling lazily over museum-white walls, polished pine floors, a long grey leather sofa, a simple, eclectic mix of furnishings.

Guests nearly filled the small room: mostly, the men and women were young, attractive, dressed for their day at the brokerage office or ad agency. It was an ingathering. No one turned to wonder who the strangers were. I didn't mind; we were here as observers. I paused to admire the balloons in their airy dance.

Perhaps I was getting into the spirit of what Phoebe, Eddie and Mother had planned as a tribute: sorrow lifted, and a release from cruel memories of how Mickey's life had ended. "That's my mother on the sofa. We came in from Santa Rosa this morning and we'll stay here a few days." She sighed.

"We have to face sorting through Mickey's things. We've told Eddie to decide about his clothes, but there are photos and some mementos we'll want to take home."

I was almost shocked to see a tear roll silently down Phoebe's perfect cheek. She wiped it away, smiled wanly and said, "After all, he was my big brother."

A thin man with sparse blond hair was leaning over the leather sofa: Eddie Claire, most likely. As we approached, I heard him say, "You're worrying about nothing, Peg. I'm under control. Let me handle them."

He straightened up and I saw that his face beneath the lank hair was flushed, from emotion or illness I couldn't tell.

He was dressed for winter: white tee under a heavy tan corduroy shirt tucked into 501's, thick brown socks, polished brown loafers. Although the room was heated, he looked as if he was perpetually chilled.

Phoebe frowned. "Eddie," she said loudly. "Here are Nate Greene and his friend, Cat Deean."

"Hello, Nate. What's new on the street?" The men shook hands.

"Not much, Eddie. If there was, you'd hear from me. Meet Cat, I've been taking her around the Castro."

"Well, you won't find a murderer here," Eddie told me.

He eyed me as if I was about to pull out a dagger and yell *Death to gays!* I offered my best calm, reflective nod, the one I use with clients who are questioning their catering invoices.

The woman on the sofa sat taller and said, "Eddie! You promised!"

"Mrs. MacHugh? Thank you for letting me intrude. Is this a bad time?"

"Call me Peg. All of Mickey's and Eddie's friends do. And, no, it's not a bad time. We've been through that and now we're getting better."

Peg was dark-haired like her daughter, but

smaller, rounder, her body more seductive. Fine lines were beginning to appear at the corners of the violet eyes, otherwise she could have passed for early thirties, around my age. Even younger. Her simple lilac silk dress intensified the color of her eyes. She hadn't the height for high-fashion modeling, but she was beautiful. She might cast a long shadow for her daughter; a son would be proud.

Mickey's mother smiled up at Nate and said, "Eddie tells me you met my son at the hospital a few times. So you know what happened. Why don't you find yourself some refreshments while I visit with Cat?"

"Sure," said Nate. "Phoebe can introduce me around." The reporter's instinct never dies.

Phoebe took his arm; she was about his height. Easy for her dew-fresh nymph's eyes to look into his eyes. Um, Nate, remember: she's hardly more than a child. They went in the direction of a small dining room. Eddie planted himself behind the sofa.

Peg patted the leather seat beside her and said, "What a shame you never met Mickey. I have his scrapbook, here on the coffee table. Would you like to see it?"

"I would."

"At first," she said, "I wondered if I could ever look at his picture again. I was grieving but I was also terribly angry at him for leaving me. Angry that he was selfish enough to catch a disease that would take him away from me."

She looked up at Eddie, who still stood motionless, only the spots of high color in his cheeks revealing any emotion.

"Sorry, Eddie, but you know that was the hurt in me talking."

Peg looked at me and said, "Eddie knows that I always accepted Mickey's life. How could I turn away my child? Just look at my wonderful son."

She opened the gold-embossed scrapbook and I saw the happy infant and later the awkward child. Family pictures, friends. Pages turned, then there was a snapshot of a tall young man in khakis and a windbreaker, standing in what appeared to be a clearing in a park. He was smiling into the sun, black hair tousled, chin held high, green impudent eyes. An Irish sprite like his sister, but Mickey was older, wiser and ready to take on the demons that assuredly hid in the woods.

"A fighter, that was the Mick," said Eddie, over my shoulder.

"I snapped that in Golden Gate Park, just after we learned he had AIDS. He said it wouldn't get him down, that he'd go on forever. God didn't want him, he said, and the devil was too busy keeping an eye on the politicians."

There were more pages in the scrapbook but Peg

snapped it shut. "That was two years ago. He lived two more years."

"It was that bastard, Arbusto." Eddie's voice was harsh. "If it hadn't been for the poisoning, Mickey might have gone on, *almost* forever."

I turned and looked up at him. "How do you know it was Polley Arbusto? Why are you so sure?"

"Why are you defending him. Are you in love with him?"

I shook my head, stifling a laugh. "Even Polley agrees that he's not very lovable. No, I care about my friends and I hate being a victim. Nate told you about what's been happening in L.A. Nick, my boss, is protecting Polley but it can't go on. Suppose there was another incident at the restaurant. What I'm asking is, do you have any proof that Polley Arbusto poisoned his own guests?"

"Jimson weed," said Eddie. "The juice is deadly."

"What are you saying? Was that the poison?"

"Yeah, I pestered the detectives on the case until they told me. No rat poison for Mr. Arbusto. He's always been the big guru for *natural* ingredients."

"Where would he get it?"

"I've been reading up. It grows wild. In the foothills, in pasture land, even in that vacant lot in your neighborhood."

"I sound like a broken record, but why Polley?"

Eddie came around to the front of the sofa and sat down, cross-legged, on the floor in front of me.

He demanded, "How much do you know about A
busto's background?"

"Just that he has a fine reputation as a chef an
that he's been an awful husband and father."

"Arbusto's been around San Francisco for de
cades. Don't know where he came from originall
but he popped up in Haight Ashbury in the late six
ties. A psychedelic love child. It was a time whe
you could buy pot as easily as chocolate milk. Bu
Arbusto was into full-color visions. Some LSI
here, a few fancy mushrooms there.

"He'd hooked up with an old Indian shaman wh
taught him about jimson weed. D'you know it
nickname? The mad apple. The Indians called
mani. They dried and ground the roots to make
potion for religious ceremonies. It made them se
spirits and have strange dreams. But the shaman
were expert, they controlled the weed very care
fully.

"I haven't heard that Arbusto experimented o
anyone but himself, but he did learn a lot from
that shaman. He knew how much weed would tak
you into the spirit world—and he knew how muc
would kill you."

Hard rain was hitting the windows now, an
the sound blended with the rush of Eddie's words

"Maybe he never intended to kill Perry Fram
boise. It was just a practical joke, you know, th
way there's always some smartass who spikes th

punch at the senior prom. Suppose Polley Arbusto wanted his guests to see fabulous visions, like the quails on their plates taking flight. Only, the old shaman died years ago, and Arbusto got the dosage wrong."

"It would be a pretty sick joke," I said.

"Arbusto is hardly a mental health poster boy."

"But you're saying that the hippie turned into a successful restaurateur. How did that happen?"

Eddie shrugged. "He got older."

"That's too simple. What happened to him in between?"

"Oh, sometime in the early seventies, he got tired of living in a commune in the Haight. Found a job in the kitchen of a big hotel, discovered he had a flair for cooking, worked hard and eventually got his own restaurant."

"Would he give it all up for a practical joke? Or, let's say, to pay Perry back for challenging him?"

"As The Shadow might have said, who knows what evil lurks in the heart of an ex-wacko cook?"

"Eddie, you're so sure of your facts. How come you know so much about Polley Arbusto?"

Peg had been sitting quietly next to me. Now she and Eddie exchanged glances.

"It's for the lawsuit," Peg said. "Eddie's been researching Mr. Arbusto's past for the lawsuit."

"Mickey's immune system had been weakened by AIDS," said Eddie, "but he was by no means terminal. The poison was such a shock to his body—he was already going into convulsions on his way to the hospital—that he never recovered."

"And you're blaming Polley? Your case is circumstantial."

"Our lawyer thinks we have a chance. Look, Arbusto had liability insurance. But Mickey didn't die on the way to the hospital. It took a few months. So the insurance company won't pay off.

"If we can't prove wrongful death, although I haven't finished my research, then we're going for negligence. Loss of income. Whatever we can throw at them. We're naming both Arbusto and Cal First Insurance."

Peg's eyes closed, holding back the tears. Eddie looked at her tenderly.

"By the way, the lawsuit is in Peg's name. The Mick had a great career going, art director in a top ad agency, but he hadn't hit his big earning years yet. This house is wonderful, but it's been a bottomless money pit."

He rubbed his jaw, as if he'd shaved too close. "Animals are lucky. They may know when they're facing death, but they don't burden themselves with worrying about who'll take care of the family. Higher intelligence isn't always a blessing.

"You may have guessed, I'm HIV-positive. I'm not ready to pack it in yet, but I'm thinking ahead. Who'll take care of Peg, and Phoebe? I've got a steady job teaching night school, English as a Second Language, very big in California, but that doesn't bring in much money. The lawsuit is important. You're not planning to throw any wrenches in it, are you, Cat?"

"Lord, no! I'm just trying to understand what's happened."

I wasn't sure that Eddie would trust anyone outside of Mick's family, but he was less edgy.

"You seem to be decent," he said. "Go back to your boss and tell him not to take chances. Get rid of Arbusto before he destroys all of you."

Eddie slowly got up from the floor, supporting himself on one thin arm. I had a dark feeling about him: he was more ill than he'd admit, to me or to Peg.

"I should talk to some friends," he said. "Take care." He moved to join a group that opened up and enveloped him.

Peg faced me but her eyes were following Eddie.

"He's given me such strength," she said. "I'd have been lost without him these last months. My daughter is so young. She's in her last year of high school. She'll go off to New York and leave me right after graduation. Phoebe wants to be a model and I'm told she'll do very well. Quite beautiful, isn't she?"

"She's exquisite."

"Well, we were never that close until Mickey got

sick, so there's no reason for her to stay here for me now. Mickey was my pride and joy. Of course, I was disappointed that I'd never have grandchildren, but I came to accept that.

"Eddie's hiding the truth from me. He doesn't want me to know that he has full-blown AIDS but I see the signs. He's become family, I'll look after him. But he's slipping away from me, too."

She looked perplexed. "This isn't the way it's supposed to work out when you have children, is it?"

SEVENTEEN

PUT YOUR BUTTER into a large casserole, heat until the butter foams. Add the quails and saute them for about twenty-five minutes until they're a golden color.

Saute...twenty-five minutes...golden color. I was watching Polley on the TV screen and scribbling the recipe on one of Nate's lined reporter's pads.

Heat some oil in a frying pan, add the chopped onion and crushed garlic, and cook until the onion is transparent.

Put the red wine vinegar and the dry white wine in a saucepan. Add the chopped parsley, rosemary, sage and crushed juniper berries, season with salt and pepper...

Polley, in his white chef's jacket, deftly heaped the herbs into a copper saucepan. I watched as intently as if I might catch him adding a vial full of dark, sinister liquid to the pan. Nate put a glass of brandy into my free hand and I sipped without taking my eyes from the screen.

...and simmer for ten minutes. Combine the wine and herbs, onion and garlic. Pour the mixture over the quails. Marinate in the refrigerator about eight

hours. Drain the marinade and arrange the quails on a cold serving platter. Garnish with watercress.

With a smile as triumphant as if he'd invented fire, Polley displayed the platter of eight golden quails dotted with greenery. I took another sip of brandy, and wrote "Marinated Quails Arbusto" at the top of the notepad page as the kitchen scene dissolved into an Agrisure commercial.

This was Polley at a different location, still clad in a white chef's jacket. He was seated at a picnic table next to a fancy wicker basket. He pulled back the red checkered napkin that covered the top of the basket, lifted out and set on the table a platter of what appeared to be hamburger patties, another plate of no-nonsense whole grain buns, a bowl of salad greens, condiments and a bottle filled with blue tablets. He pointed to the display and said, "At Agrisure, we're on the side of nature. No fat, no cholesterol, just gourmet great taste in our FatBe-GoneBurger protein patties. And, if you're not sure you're getting all the veggies a good diet demands, consider our NutriMore nature supplements...."

I never did consider NutriMore. At that point Nate came up, leaned over the sofa and kissed me on the nape of my neck.

"There," he said. "I've waited for fourteen years to do that."

The kiss didn't surprise me: after slogging around in the rain and gloom all evening, we both needed more warmth than a bottle of brandy could supply.

Nate sat down on the sofa, neutral space between us, the moment *fraught* with possibilities. I like the world fraught: it is a classy way to say that we were both breathing a little faster than one would expect from watching a video about cold poultry.

An hour earlier, we'd dashed in the rain to Nate's apartment building on Russian Hill, leaving his car parked in a space down the street. Neither of us had much of an appetite. Phoebe had plied Nate with enchilada casserole; Peg had apologized for Eddie's abruptness by personally serving me with chocolate truffle cake. It made sense to stop at Nate's apartment ("If it weren't for the rain, you could stand on tiptoes on my balcony and see the bay"). We'd view the cooking show video, have a drink, and then decide about dinner.

His kiss was not on our agenda, but we'd already done our duty; now there was all the time in the world.

At some point, we moved to the bedroom and made love. It was not an elegiac act to blur the pain we'd felt in the Castro. This was happy, sweaty sex between two people who ought to have been lovers a long time ago. If there is such a thing as fate, it must sometimes get tired of detours.

Later, the rain stopped and we walked around puddles to the Italian restaurant on the corner.

The owner greeted us with glad cries and led us through the half-empty room to a table with a hurricane lamp that cast a soft glow. It was a setting for easy talk, but contentment and a certain shyness had set in, and we didn't say much.

Just some silly things that don't need repeating.

We ate baked artichokes, and spaghetti in a seafood-rich tomato sauce, and drank a smooth red Petite Sirah that shimmered in the glass. The owner insisted on treating us to brandies. Nate chose an Italian one, which is rawer than the French kind, and its kick is fast and strong. I worried about falling asleep at the table, which could seem like rejection, so we left soon after.

I didn't stay at Nate's apartment that night. There was, I explained, my early morning appointment; I'd need fresh clothes.

To myself I admitted that I'd gotten out of the habit of intimacy and looked forward to my own bed at the hotel.

Nate didn't fall to his knees and paw my hem, which was a slight disappointment.

"That's okay," he said. "I've got to cover a breakfast meeting at the Fairmont at seven-thirty tomorrow morning. At least I'll get a cup of coffee. I don't have any. No chance to stop at the market tonight."

"I'd never fall for a guy who couldn't serve me a cup of coffee the next morning."

"I'll pick up two pounds of premium blend to-morrow. Who knows? There might be a storm. Could last for days," he said cheerfully.

The streets were slick and iridescent on the short ride to the Brittany. Nate stopped in the 5-minute parking zone at the entrance and we used up most of the time in a goodnight kiss that tasted like clams, wine and heat. He told me he didn't mind Byron but he was a dirty limericks man himself. I left him at the curb and wondered if I should have stayed over after all.

Fatigue won. I was in bed in minutes, spent with emotion, sex, wine and brandy. Dreamless sleep came so quickly I didn't even have time to wonder what kind of person would scavenge through empty lots in a search for deadly jimson weed.

EIGHTEEN

THE RED LIGHT on my room telephone was winking at me. *Getyourmessages,* it said, *Getthehellupandgetyourmessages.* I hadn't thought to check the desk last night. But it was only six-thirty a.m. according to the clock on the nightstand. So why was the phone ringing? Not only winking but ringing. I pulled the covers over my head and practiced being a single cell amoeba.

Too early for my wake-up call. Suddenly, I opened my eyes. It must be Nate, megastar reporter and lover, calling to say I was on his mind, needing the sound of my voice even more than he wanted an early cup of coffee at the Fairmont.

I reached for the phone. "Good morning," I said tenderly.

"Cat? Is that you? You sound different. Did I wake you?"

It was Nick Dellacasa.

"Oh, hi, Nick. No, I'm awake. How are you?"

"Fine, fine. I phoned twice yesterday. Did you get my messages?"

"Not yet. I was just about to call down to the

desk. Had dinner with a friend. Italian restaurant. Good, but Dellacasa's is better."

"What did you order?"

"Baked artichokes. Spaghetti con Vongole."

"San Francisco has the knack with seafood. If Polley was in better shape, I'd ask him for recipes."

"What's happening with him?"

"He hasn't been at the restaurant at all, but Lila phoned in. They expect Homer's body to be released anytime now. It'll be sent home by plane, and Lila will drive Polley back to San Francisco. Today or tomorrow, I suppose."

Nick sounded dispirited.

"Any problems that can't wait?"

"Well, that's why I called. I'm hoping you'll be able to wrap up your interviews by tonight. Forget about checking out suppliers for the quails. We'll leave it to the police. It's their job, not yours. I need you first thing tomorrow morning, here in L.A."

I swung my legs over the side of the bed and sat up. Unfair!

"Why the sudden rush?"

Nick sounded surprised. "Well, things pile up and, as I said, Polley's not around. Understandable," Nick hastened to tell me, "but we can't run a catering business with both my manager and my chef away. Frankie and the staff will do a good job on the Citizens Against Potholes luncheon today, but *you* set that menu months ago. Now there's a problem with the Dillenbeck wedding."

"That's three months away!"

"Not anymore. The bride is pregnant, and the family wants the wedding moved up to next month. Mrs. Dillenbeck called me yesterday afternoon. They left their round-the-world cruise when Debbie gave them the news. Now they want to meet with us at eight tomorrow morning, change the arrangements, then catch a plane to Borneo to pick up their cruise again."

There was a pause while I envisioned the buttons on Debbie's wedding gown popping open. We all have our fantasies.

"I need you, Cat."

"Okay, Nick, I'll wind up everything this afternoon and take a plane back to L.A. tonight."

"How were your meetings yesterday?"

I told Nick about Blaine, and Eddie, and about Polley's experiences in the sixties with psychedelic drugs.

"Did you ever hear that Polley was tripping back then?"

"Oh, the year we worked together, we'd go out for drinks afterwards and he'd laugh and tell me about the Haight and his adventures. The stories were so wild, sometimes I thought he made them up. Rosie and I got married so young, you see. Besides, in Brooklyn if you wanted an out-of-body experience, you drank an egg cream."

"Did you envy him?"

"No regrets, ever. It wasn't my kind of life. I always liked being married. But I still can't believe that Polley would ever harm anyone. He says the drugs expanded his mind."

"Only his mind? I heard they called him the mattress surfer."

"Sometimes, Catherine, I think you're too puritanical."

I leered at the phone. "Not so! Anyway, I'm talking to Bianca DeSavio this morning. If she can peel a banana and she's available, I'll see if she'll come to L.A. and work for us until things settle down."

"Let's hope. Maybe you could finish up, take an earlier plane, and stop in at the restaurant this afternoon."

How nice to be needed. I reminded Nick that I'd promised to pick up Homer's clock at Agrisure and take it over to Mrs. Arbusto.

"That's right! You do it, Cat, and give her my condolences. Tell her Rosie and I will be at the funeral. So then I'll see you first thing tomorrow morning."

He hung up and I thought of calling Nate, but realized he'd be leaving his apartment about now. I'd call him later at his office and break the news. Duty before romance. I padded over to the window and opened the drapes. It was a foggy San Francisco morning, rather like the mists around Ingrid Bergman in the last scene of "Casablanca." Ingrid, baby, isn't life the pits?

Sighing, I called down to the desk.

"Hello, Catherine Deean here. I didn't pick up my messages last night."

"Yes, Ms. Deean. The bellman slipped them under your door a few minutes ago."

So he did. There were three slips of paper on the carpet.

I picked them up. Two were the calls from Nick. The third said, at ten p.m. a Mister Quail had called. He'd be in touch later.

I rushed to the phone and called the desk again.

"Do you know who took the messages last night? There was one at ten o'clock."

"That would be George, our night clerk. He'll be back on duty at nine p.m. You could call him then."

"Thanks, maybe I will," I said, knowing that I wouldn't.

It appeared that I'd ruffled the elusive Mr. Quail. Something had happened in San Francisco to alert him. And it had become personal.

This was no bloody package directed to-whom-it-may-concern in Dellacasa's catering department. This message had my name on it.

Worrisome, but also progress.

But what had I discovered? As I showered and

dressed, there was a teasing memory of something out of place, as if I'd seen a Twinkie riding by on our pastry cart. I'd think about it later, after today's priorities. A temporary catering chef to replace the equally temporary Mr. Arbusto. Then an errand of what? Kindness? Curiosity? Crass snooping? After that, well, planes left for L.A. every hour, on into the night. There'd be time to linger awhile at Nate's apartment on Russian Hill before the last flight.

CAFE ARGENTINA SAT in the middle of a grim mini-mall, its graceful script sign dwarfed by a giant LAUNDROMAT announcement on one side, HOT QUICKIE PIZZA 24-HRS flashing in neon on the other. If the top three criteria for choosing real estate are location, location, location, this place was at the bottom of the list: loser, meltdown, flop. At nine-thirty in the morning I hadn't expected throngs of customers, but Cafe Argentina had an aura of failure that seeped out past the perky green and white striped awning, the calligraphy menu in a display box outside the door.

Bianca DeSavio sat waiting for me, chin propped on one hand, at one of the twelve tables crowded into the small room. As I entered she stood and smoothed her fresh white apron, a tall woman, about forty I guessed. Bright red lipstick, pretty smile, curly dark hair pulled back with combs, a formidable bust, slender waist and ankles. Even

through the long-sleeved, severe black dress I coul
see that her thin arms were muscular, as if mos
of her waking hours were spent slinging aroun
brimming stock pots and hot, sputtering skillets.

"So. You are Catherine. I have coffee made
please sit down, darling." (Actually, she said *dah
link,* in a liquid Latin accent.)

We exchanged pleasantries as she poured coffee
I was grateful, and hungry. I'd bypassed breakfast
since Bianca had promised me a sampling of he
specialties.

"You didn't eat breakfast, no? I can tell. So be
fore we talk business, I want you to eat. You wil
feel better, you will know what I can accomplish
I cook Argentinian. I cook Italian. And French
And Californian. And, believe me, Polley Arbust
thinks he is *le dernier cri,* but I have more clas
sic training than he, and I'm a sweeter person be
sides." She looked boldly for my reaction from
under thickly mascaraed black lashes. I burst int
laughter.

She seemed pleased and turned towards th
kitchen, calling over her shoulder, "I'll be bacl
right away, darling."

Left to wait, I looked around the spotless littl
restaurant. Travel posters on the walls, of Bueno
Aires, and the Andes mountains; other posters o
Rome and the ruins at Agrigento.

Near the kitchen were twin display cases tha

should have been filled with cheeses, desserts and eye-catching delicacies for take-out. The cases were empty. And where was Mr. DeSavio? In our first phone conversation, before the Fancy Food Show, Bianca had mentioned a husband who was also a chef. Had he left her alone, trapped between the Laundromat and round-the-clock pizza?

Bianca returned with a tray that held three appetizer-size dishes. On one plate was a trio of puffy, golden envelopes of baked pastry.

"Empanadas," said Bianca, pointing. "Filled with picadillo, you know." I nodded and filled my mouth with the sweet spicy chopped mixture of beef, onions, raisins and green olives. The pastry was of extraordinary lightness.

"Cumin?" I guessed about the spice.

Bianca nodded. "Very good."

I moved on to the next plate. Spears of lobster tail in a lacy tempura batter, accompanied by a cup of tart apricot dipping sauce: magnificent.

Bianca placed her third sample before me: a crystal bowl of chocolate banana bread pudding. It was warm and it sang on my tongue. I dipped in again, trying to identify the bite that underlay the chocolate's sweetness. Bianca chuckled.

"It's there but it's subtle. Chili powder. A pinch."

"Chili!"

"One of the things I do with chocolate," said Bianca.

This talent wasting in a moribund cafe? Shocking.

"I'm convinced. When can you start?"

With a proud nod, Bianca accepted my offer.

"Anytime, darling. As you'll have guessed," she glanced around the restaurant, "we are not terribly busy."

We? Where was her husband?

"My Carlos is in Buenos Aires," she answered my unspoken question, "raising money from his family. We need to reopen in a better location.

"Here, they are not our customers. The people, they go to the pizza palace while their clothes are washing in the laundromat, they get tomato sauce on their sweatshirts, then back to the laundromat to do more wash. Back and forth." She shook her head.

We had talked salary earlier, so that was settled. She'd be staying with an aunt in Los Angeles and keeping her San Francisco apartment. No problem there.

"The question is, Bianca, how long can you stay?"

"The question is, Cat, for how long will you need me?"

Would Polley come back? Did Nick want him back? I had to be fair to Bianca. I sighed.

"I don't know, Bianca. Things are so unsettled with Polley."

"It's all right, darling," she answered, firmly reattaching a tortoiseshell comb in her thick curly hair. "No one ever got carried out on a stretcher from my cooking. That should make Mr. Nick weep for joy, don't you think?"

NINETEEN

WHEN THE TAXI dropped me off, the sun was shining over the Agrisure headquarters: three stories of used red brick, a front of floor-to-ceiling windows, their black glass dazzling in sunlight like light on a becalmed sea. Light that bounces and shimmers, and hides the monster resting underneath.

The building was about a block from the waterfront and had once been a warehouse. Coffee, spices, silks from Siam and porcelains from China had given way to marketing plans and pie charts, chemical formulas and dubious liquids sealed in test tubes and held in locked rooms.

It would be impossible to tell, from the look of the stark, glass-fronted lobby, just what kind of business went on upstairs. My footsteps made sound bites on the marble floor. The reception desk was teak and sleek; other than a telephone, there were no papers or signs of useful activity to mar its surface. The receptionist, sleek and blonde, had nails so long, pearly pink and flawless, I wondered how she managed the pushbuttons on the phone. As I offered my name, I wondered what she did all day, whether her nail polish chipped from punching pushbuttons. It was possible, with this biotech lily of the field, never called upon to spin or weave, that repairs to her polish could occupy much of her day. One puzzle solved.

Her smile was as impersonal as the teak desktop; no discourtesy intended; hers was simply the corporate way.

Earlier in the day I'd phoned, spoken to someone named Grace in the marketing department, and explained my errand.

"Oh, I'm so glad you called," Grace had said in a tearful voice. "Poor Homer, we're just devastated here. I tried to contact his mother and sister, to ask whether anyone would pick up his things. And about the funeral, you know. But all I get is an answering machine. Maybe they're too broken up to talk."

"Have you met them?"

"No, not really. Just talked to Mrs. Arbusto or Cassandra on the phone every now and then. You know, to take a message for Homer." A pause. I could hear a coolness creep into Grace's voice. "Of course, we all know Mr. Arbusto."

"Yes, well," I said awkwardly, "I'm sure they'll all appreciate your help. May I stop by this afternoon?"

"Of course. I was very fond of Homer. He was a dear, sweet young man. I'll put his things in a carton, all ready for you."

"His mother particularly asked about an engraved clock."

"It's right on Homer's desk. I'll make sure it's well packed."

A few hours later and I was at Agrisure, doing my good deed.

Fascinated, I watched the receptionist delicately tap out an extension number on the phone. I could learn from this woman.

"Grace? There's a Ms. Deean to see you?"

I was approved, given a visitor's pass, and pointed towards the elevator. Marketing was on the second floor.

Its reception area was smaller, functional, bleak. The single armchair for visitors was covered in a tweedy, hard-finish synthetic that could send you sliding to the floor. No magazines, ashtray, or hospitable dish of hard candies beckoned on the fake walnut side table. Five framed Agrisure ads on the wall were what passed for decor. The blank outline of a rectangle hinted that a sixth frame had been removed. An ad with Polley's picture?

The standard beige metal desk held a calendar, a computer, an in-and-out basket empty except for a single sheet of green paper. I peeked: a memo to remind employees to lock their desks when leaving at night. Security, it said, was everyone's duty.

I felt as if unseen eyes were on me, tracking my movements, watching to see whether I'd tiptoe out, down the corridor to the fire exit, open the door and bring in the Fat Man and Joel Cairo.

Information was certainly buttoned up in Marketing. Not a scrap of paper lying around to reveal Agrisure's secrets. A door half-paneled in opaque frosted glass undoubtedly led to the inner offices. As I wondered whether to try the handle, the door opened.

A tall, slender woman, fiftyish emerged. Her hair was the brash red of a young fox, if the fox had spent Saturday night with plastic gloves and a dye bottle. Nice brown slightly watery eyes, heavy on the charcoal eyeshadow, even heavier on the black mascara.

Miss Deean? I'm Grace Upland, the department secretary. Sorry to keep you waiting. We're in between receptionists." She waved vaguely at the empty posture chair.

"You must be busy. I'll try not to take up too much of your time."

She was clutching a wet blue Kleenex, as if she'd been blotting up tears. I sensed a private grief that went beyond the unexpected loss of a co-worker. She stepped back through the door and beckoned me to follow. Grace said, "I have Homer's things all packed and on his desk. Let's go into his office. It isn't a big carton. And I've already cleared it with Security."

We passed a row of modular beige-walled cubbyholes; possibly a dozen employees were hard at work. Fingers flew silently over computer keyboards; a sallow young man, shirtsleeves rolled up, bent over a drawing board and frowned. The quiet was more than concentration. Was the Marketing department fearful today because of Homer's murder? Or did peddling soy protein burgers to a meat-eating nation demand this kind of intensity?

Grace was no fool; she'd seen my side glances. Leading me into the last cubbyhole before a big corner office she smiled wearily and said, "Everyone worked late last night. We're going into test markets next month with a couple of new products."

I'd only planned to carry off Homer's few possessions. But my nerve endings had begun to tingle when I walked into the Agrisure headquarters. Standing now in the dead man's office, I felt as if I'd downed a double latte with an espresso chaser.

It wasn't just the precaution of the inevitable hidden security cameras. Agrisure, after all, had to protect itself from industrial espionage. But I had an undefined feeling of menace that might be traced to the act of violence in L.A.: silence assured by an icepick plunged into a lightweight compact's brakes.

What did I really know about Homer's job, whether he could have stumbled across information that made him a danger?

So I asked earnestly, "Anything coming on the market that would interest me? I can't remember if I mentioned that I'm a caterer. Always like to know about new products."

Grace seemed amused. "Everything we do here is very hush-hush, you know. I'm surprised Penny let you upstairs without the guard. He must have been on his break."

"I look wholesome. It's a blessing and a curse."

"Well, we are so security-conscious, if you went to the ladies restroom, I'd have to be with you, stand outside the booth and make sure you weren't stuffing secrets into your pantyhose."

"Like a nuclear plant."

"Not that different. Some of Agrisure's research could revolutionize the entire practice of medicine."

It dawned on me that Grace was being unusually chatty with a stranger, a voice on the phone who'd asked to enter and take away the contents of a desk.

I glanced around, at the bare walls, at the small cardboard carton on the clean desktop. No trace of Homer would remain once the carton was gone. I felt unutterably sad.

We were both focused on the carton, as if Homer had been neatly folded, slipped into an envelope and packed away out of sight. Perhaps Grace had chattered on from a need to connect with another human who'd touched his brief life.

"About Homer." I cleared my throat. "I only met him once, just for a short time at the stockholder's meeting. But I liked him, and what happened is just terrible."

"I'm taking it very personally," Grace admitted. "My only son lives in Anchorage, my daughters are in Fresno, and I suppose I enjoyed mothering Homer. He seemed to like it. I'd invite him to my apartment for dinner and every now and then he'd take me to a concert or a movie."

She paused, hid a sob, busied her hands fussing with the floppy tie on her white blouse. The blouse, under a severely cut grey suit, had a '70s dress-for-success look. My mother owned a few floppy tied blouses. She dressed in them most mornings, along with her tailored navy or brown suits, hoping for success. It was after dad died, she was raising me alone, proudly setting forth to what she called "the business world."

If Grace was that stuck in the '70s, her interest in Homer had to be maternal. I couldn't see them as an older woman-younger man pair.

"He wasn't that close to Mrs. Arbusto," said Grace. "From what Homer told me, she wasn't a bad mother, just very excitable. She made him nervous."

Homer's hands had trembled while he talked with Polley at the stockholder's meeting. Poor guy was at the end of the line when parents were being handed out.

Click, click. High heels made sharp sounds on the vinyl floor in the corridor.

"Grace, *Grace?* Oh, there you are!"

The VP of Marketing stood in the doorway. I'd noticed Laura Ferris-Flood at the stockholder's meeting, but she was tinier and tougher than I remembered. The glossy black curls were the only soft thing about her, framing steely grey eyes and carefully outlined lips in the hottest shade of the year, Puma Blood.

So young to have climbed to a vice-presidency. Her bio in the stockholder's program had mentioned an MBA from Stanford. Most likely it was contacts there, plus her own drive, that put her on the fast track at Agrisure. There was an aggressiveness to the linebacker shoulder pads in her pale crepe suit, its waist cinched with a wide matching belt for which a calf had died young. I admit, she raised my hackles. I disliked her on sight.

"Grace, where are the revised roll-out plans? I wanted fifteen copies printed out, collated and on my desk by three."

"You'll have them, Laura. Everyone worked past midnight last night."

Ferris-Flood peered into the older woman's face. "If the late nights are getting to you, Grace, just let me know. Maybe you can't take the pace anymore."

"I'm used to hard work," said Grace quietly. "I've never complained."

Abruptly, Ferris-Flood turned her attention to me.

"Who's this?"

"Catherine Deean," I said, ignoring the rudeness. "I came to pick up Homer's things."

Her glance went to a four-drawer file cabinet standing against the rear wall.

"What are you giving her?" asked Homer's boss. "Have you cleared out his files, as I asked you to?"

"Yes, the files are cleared out and locked up," said Grace in the same dead-quiet voice. If she reacted at all to the imperious Ferris-Flood, she hid it very well. "Homer's personal things are in that box."

Ferris-Flood stepped over to the carton, poked around at Kleenex, a fresh shirt and tie in a laundry wrap, an electric shaver, some framed pictures, an oblong box.

"What's in the smaller box?"

"It's a clock. The clock Homer's mother gave him."

The VP walked to the cubbyhole's door, turned and darted a smile at me. It was as phony as the beef in a tofu burger.

"Please give my personal condolences to Homer's family. We are all very sad at his passing."

I nodded, struck dumb. She disappeared down

the corridor, the click of her heels sounding warnings to her staff.

"Well," I said, "she certainly expects her department to jump. I'll bet she wasn't too good for Homer's nerves."

"She wasn't too bad with him. Laura likes her people young, ambitious and scared," said Grace with a rueful smile.

"Homer worked very hard for her, especially on his last project, the Agrisure film. He put in hundreds of hours, sometimes all night, researching the company and its products. She was pleased, because the film made her look good."

"You're more generous than I'd be," I said bluntly.

Grace shrugged. "I've worked for Agrisure for thirty years. I've seen 'em come and go."

I picked up the carton. "You have deadlines. I'll leave now."

"I'll walk you to the front entrance," said Grace. "It's faster than calling the guard to accompany you."

She waited until we were in the elevator to say, "Have you seen Homer's clock? Black marble with gold numerals, quite handsome, you know."

"No, I haven't."

"Then I strongly suggest that you look at it before you leave it with Homer's mother."

"Oh?"

"Yes," said Grace, lifting a red-fox eyebrow at me. "Definitely worth a peek."

"Then I shall," I said.

Grace walked me to the front entrance, opened the black glass door, smiled and said, "So nice to meet one of Homer's friends. Do have a nice day."

TWENTY

A TAXI CRUISED BY; I hailed it and gave Mrs. Arbusto's address. When Agrisure was out of sight, I attacked the carton as eagerly as if it hid my Dick Tracy decoder ring.

Grace had sealed the small box inside. Under the tape was a polished black cube, gold numerals, gold plaque engraved, "Wishing You Success, Son." It was cushioned by wads of tissue paper. My probing fingers touched an envelope tucked away under the tissue.

A plain white envelope, with a yellow Post-it note tacked on. The note, written in ink in a precise hand, said: *"Found this today in the back of Homer's desk drawer. Good luck."*

Inside were four sheets of paper. The top sheet was a memo from Laura Ferris-Flood to Homer Arbusto, sent about two months ago. It said:

"Do you have a death wish in this company? Never, I repeat, never, show or mention anything about Bio-Valerio in the film—or anywhere else. See me at once with your file."

Underneath were other memos, dated four years earlier. Too much information to study now. I replaced the papers, tucked the envelope into my purse, closed up the carton and leaned back. What d'ya know? Grace, the good soldier, has defected.

The taxi had taken me to the Sunset district. It was close enough to the beach to see seagulls wheeling overhead and smell the brine in the wind that careened through the open spaces between narrow houses. The Arbusto house was a faded blue, more weatherbeaten than most on the street, its low picket fence enclosing a sandy front yard with a few shrubs losing their will to survive.

Homer, I'd heard, had taken his own apartment in the city when he went to work for Agrisure. Polley had left his wife and kids long before that. No one, it appeared, cared about keeping up the family manse. Could be Mrs. Arbusto was depressed, short of money, or a combination of both.

I asked the taxi to wait, mounted the steps to the porch and pushed hard at a bell that had been pitted by the salt air.

A brief wait, and then a female voice on the other side of the door.

"If you're the press again, go away! My mother's lawyer says not to talk to you!"

"It's Catherine Deean, Miss Arbusto." Surely this was the dead man's sister. "I have Homer's clock for you."

The door whipped open and a pale-faced, sturdy figure in a black dress separated itself from the gloom inside. She was a few years older than Homer, and she looked too much like Polley, complete to the hawk-like nose, to be conventionally pretty.

"Oops, sorry. The reporters have been such damn pests," she said indignantly. "It's bad enough that Homer was murdered, but they're trying to tie it into my father's troubles. They won't leave my mom alone."

"Well, this is short notice to show up on your doorstep, but I'm going back to Los Angeles tonight. Please tell your mother that Nick and Rosie send their deepest sympathy, and that they'll be at the funeral."

"You're so nice to help us. Come in, come in. I'm Cassie. Here, let me take that carton. My mother is a little emotional today, but she'll want to thank you."

I glanced back at the taxi waiting at the curb, meter ticking. "Just for a minute."

Cassandra beckoned into the dark interior, led me down a hallway to a small parlor. Its blinds were drawn, but I could see a couple of chintz covered sofas, a few rattan chairs, the casual comforts of living near the beach. A large framed photo of Homer in a black cap and gown had the place of honor on the mantel of the brick fireplace. Behind it was a smaller studio photograph of Cassandra in a white dress, holding a diploma.

Anna Arbusto was tense and watchful, sitting erect on the sofa, a white, lace-edged handkerchief the only relief from her head-to-toe mourning garments. Like a solitary black rock in a sea of tears. The olive skin was splotchy with grief, the grey-streaked dark hair unkempt.

"Thank you for coming," she said with a good try at politeness. "Please stay and visit. Would you like coffee?"

Cassandra stood behind me and said, "Mom, Catherine's taxi is waiting." I murmured my inadequate regrets.

Mrs. Arbusto beckoned to me, as if to draw me nearer, as if my leaving was unthinkable. "Wait, before you go. Did you meet that Laura Ferris-Flood?"

Surprised, I said, "Yes, but only for a few minutes."

"I believe she murdered my son." Not crying now. Pinch-faced. Emphatic.

"Mom!" exclaimed Cassandra, "You don't have any proof. Don't say such things."

"Homer found out something about her. Maybe she was covering up for her boss, that awful old man, Doyle. Maybe they killed him together."

"Mom!" Cassandra was shocked.

"Don't be so wimpy," said her mother. "You and Homer always let everyone walk all over you. But I'm strong, and I want revenge."

Mother and daughter glared at each other out of red-rimmed eyes. I broke in.

"Mrs. Arbusto, have you told the police about your suspicions?"

"Of course. They said they'd look into it. But I don't know. After all, it happened in Los Angeles. It has to be a celebrity murder to get any attention there."

She looked up at me, pleading. "Will you tell the police in Los Angeles? Promise me. I don't know you, Catherine, but you must help me avenge my son. Polley won't do a thing, he never cared about Homer. Will you help a grieving mother? Will you?"

"I'll do what I can," I said, wondering how I'd blundered into adopting Polley's family.

"Thank you! Oh, thank you many, many times!"

Cassandra said, "Catherine has to leave now. She has a plane to catch." She took my arm firmly, and we backed out of the parlor.

"Don't pay too much attention to my mom," said Cassandra. "She has absolutely no proof at all. She's heard that Laura is the boss from hell, so she's built this up in her mind. She has to take her anger out on someone, or she'll go crazy."

We said goodbye and I got into the taxi. A seagull was gliding down toward the ocean, keeping a sharp eye out for tonight's seashore dinner.

I wished I could be that focused: circle, swoop

and pluck out answers. There were still too many questions. Certainly, it was a bad year for mothers who grieved over sons who died too young. Last night, Mick, a victim of AIDS, his death possibly hastened by poisoning; mourned by Peg. Today, Homer, killed along with his mother's hopes, in a car crash. Both connected somehow, for reasons still hidden, to Polley. And were these deaths linked to the alarming acts against me, my agreeable career among the cakes and canapes, and my dear friends at Dellacasa's?

Of late, I'd been both hunted and hunter. Well, Cat, I told myself, sure as fog will creep in tonight over San Francisco Bay, being the hunter is better.

TWENTY-ONE

BACK AT MY HOTEL, I called Nate from the lobby.

"Guess what? I've got to be in L.A. at eight a.m. tomorrow. One of our brides-to-be is pregnant, and we have to move up the nuptials."

"Bummer," said my lover. "But listen, there's at least one flight to L.A. that leaves around six a.m. We can share one more night of wild, uncontrollable passion and then I'll put you on the plane in the morning."

I thought of Ingrid saying goodbye to Bogie, tasteful tears glistening in her eyes, mists swirling around them. My duty call to save the Dillenbecks from social disgrace was not the stuff of heroism. On the other hand, planes also flew back to San Francisco almost every hour. Today's frequent flyers have taken much of the romance out of airport farewells.

"Sure," I said. "Works for me. I came back to the Brittany to get my suitcase. Do you want to pick me up here?"

Sounds of dismay. "Sorry, Cat, I just can't do it right now. I'm covering the governor's speech this evening. It's at a fund-raising banquet, but he may announce whether he's running for re-election. I can't break loose till about ten o'clock."

"Chicken and peas and speeches. I'll have to think up something special for dessert."

He said hoarsely, "With whipped cream?"

I laughed. "Something sweet. I've got about five hours to kill. So there's time to have dinner, maybe see a movie and then, around ten, I'll take a taxi to your apartment."

With mutual vows of more-or-less eternal devotion, we hung up.

My last meal had been Bianca DeSavio's lobster tails tempura and espresso early this morning. I was ready for the hotel coffee shop, and its time warp menu. Tuna on whole wheat, inoffensive vegetable soup, and sympathy for the guests who'd supposed everyone dined exquisitely in San Francisco.

The best thing about The Brittany cafe was its dark wood booths, the seats padded in brown leather, its amber glass shaded lamps giving enough light for me to read the pages in the envelope Grace Upland had smuggled to me.

Under Laura Ferris-Flood's warning memo to Homer were the pages dated four years earlier. Well before Homer went to work at Agrisure. They were a set of internal memos on this same product, Bio-Valerio. A health food supplement from their agricultural division. I knew the name but not much else about it.

At first glance, nothing sinister. References to a person, place or thing called "Bundesgesundesheit-sant." For short I'll call it Bundes. The first memo, Ferris-Flood to her marketing staff, stated curtly that Bundes had rejected sales of Bio-Valerio. There would be a staff meeting that afternoon to discuss any possible changes in strategy.

Memo two, a week later, cautioned her staff not to discuss the Bundes decision with other departments at Agrisure or their ad agency. There would be a full-staff review the next morning of the revised plans.

The last memo, dated the following month, said that the revised Bio-Valerio marketing plan for the U.S. and Europe had been approved by the Agrisure executive committee and was ready to be implemented.

"Congratulations to Marketing," wrote Laura Ferris-Flood. "We can all be proud of our quick work on a difficult project."

My veggie soup and sandwich arrived and I put down the papers. Sipping the lukewarm broth, I puzzled over the significance of the memos. Homer, I guessed, had stumbled across them as he researched files to find material for his stockholder's film.

But why these memos? None of them said,

"CLASSIFIED," or "TOP SECRET" or "SHRED THIS AFTER READING." What was there about Bio-Valerio that made it dangerous reading for Homer? Possibly supplied the motive for his death.

I should have told the waitress to toast the whole wheat. I could see my thumbprints in the limp bread. Bio-Valerio. It was a product I knew about, but had never tried. Vaguely I remembered that it was supposed to make you feel energetic and sleep well. Haven't heard about it the last couple of years.

Maybe I should hang out more in health food stores. Even Aunt Sadie, the coconut cake maven, has fallen for green, growing things.

But why not go to the source? Grace Upland might be willing to talk to me about Bio-Valerio. It was just before five-thirty; with luck she'd be working late, hiding a simmering anger under her corporate grey suit.

I threw cash on the table to pay for dinner, and hurried to the lobby phone. The number I had was a direct line to the marketing department; my call was picked up on the fifth ring.

"Hello. Marketing." A woman, sounding annoyed.

"Um, is this Grace?"

"No. The department closes at five-thirty. She left exactly on time." There was a scowl in the voice.

"Ms. Ferris-Flood?"

"Yes. I'm at Grace's desk."

I had this flash: Joan of Arc on horseback leading her troops into battle. Fate had delivered Laura Ferris-Flood to me. If I retreated now, I'd be good for nothing but mucking out the stables.

"Who is this?"

"We met this morning. Catherine Deean. I came by to pick up Homer's things."

"Well, did you forget his Kleenex?"

I took a deep breath and raised my banner.

"Actually, Ms. Ferris-Flood, I came across something that may concern you. After I left Agrisure, I went to see Homer's mother."

"So?" Impatiently.

Crossing my fingers, I said, "Mrs. Arbusto had found some papers that Homer hid in his room. She didn't know what to do with them, so she asked me for help."

"What papers? Why should they concern me?"

"They were memos you wrote. About Bio-Valerio. I want to ask you some questions about them."

Dead silence. Then in a tightly controlled voice she said, "Listen, lady. Blackmail is a serious business. If you think you can threaten me, that's a major mistake."

Blackmail? Hey, I've shook something loose here, but what?

"Who mentioned blackmail?" I protested. "Now I really think you have something to hide."

"There's nothing to hide. The Bio-Valerio cases were settled years ago. Everyone's happy."

Joan of Arc raised her banner and stabbed the air.

"Let me offer one word, Laura. Bundesgesundesheitsant."

I stumbled over the pronunciation. It sounded so melodramatic even to my ears, I nearly laughed. But Ferris-Flood's reaction almost knocked me off my horse.

She gasped. "What about that? What do you want?"

Well, I wasn't quite sure what I wanted, but it was impossible to stop now.

"Homer's death could be connected to some others. I want to find out how."

"Agrisure is *not* to blame!"

"Then don't be afraid to answer my questions. Let's meet for a drink," I suggested. "I have time this evening. You can name the place."

She said angrily, "A drink? Just girl talk?"

"Why not?"

"I don't know what kind of scheme you've got, Ms. Deean, is it? But I'll meet you. Just remember, I'm the youngest top executive in the history of Agrisure. I didn't get there through sensitivity training. I'm a tough bargainer."

Patiently, I repeated, "Where do you want to meet?"

"Where no one I know will see us. There's a small noodle shop in Chinatown. I used to eat there in my student days. It's on Sacramento, near the corner of Stockton. You can't miss it."

"What time?"

"I have a report to finish first. Eight o'clock."

Ferris-Flood didn't waste words. The phone slammed in my ear.

I checked my watch. Not quite six p.m. Okay, what should Cat Deean, blackmailer-in-training, do for the next two hours?

I'd noticed a health food store just down the street from my hotel. It would help to know more about Bio-Valerio. Then, a stroll through China-town to stretch my legs and focus on the questions I wanted to ask Homer's boss.

In my other life, I've kept my cool when the groom's spaniel knocked over the wedding cake. When my client insisted on a garden party during the rainy season, and the tent leaked. When half my waiters dropped with flu.

But my heart raced a little at the thought of this meeting. Suppose she called the police and they wired her. Remember to say *nothing* that could sound like blackmail.

Or, what if Mrs. Arbusto was right and Ferris-Flood had killed Homer? A small possibility but it had to be considered.

I saw her as a woman who'd crashed through

the glass ceiling with a hatchet. She'd be ruthless to anyone who'd found out her secrets, got in her way. And she had been at the stockholder's meeting with Homer. Staying at the same hotel.

"Homer, remember that distributor's list I asked you to keep for me? Is it still in your car? No, you stay at the meeting and get ready to show your film. Just give me the keys, tell me what kind of car you're driving and where you're parked. I'll take care of the rest."

Could be. But if she'd murdered her assistant, was there also a connection to the poisonings at Polley's restaurant? To AIDS victims and Agrisure's hefty investment in AIDS research? Who knew what I'd find tonight, metaphorically speaking, at the bottom of a bowl of noodle soup?

I shivered as I left the hotel lobby. It was dusk and fog had rolled in, touching my face with clammy fingers. My raincoat was packed, so I turned up the collar of my jacket. It was a fine navy gabardine, better for taking meetings in Century City than for night games in San Francisco.

Well, Nate would be waiting for me later on at the apartment on Russian Hill. I glowed at the thought, and walked down the street to the bright lights of the Sane Mind & Body Store.

TWENTY-TWO

THE CLERK BEHIND the counter had "college student" written all over her, and wore a UC BERKELEY sweatshirt to prove it.

She was about eighteen, fit-looking, springy auburn curls, milkmaid complexion, a slick of gloss instead of lipstick.

"Hi, I'm Chris. Can I help you?"

"I'm looking for a health food supplement called Bio-Valerio."

A thoughtful frown. "Gosh, I don't remember seeing it. What's it for?"

"It's supposed to make you feel healthier."

The frown cleared. "Oh, like melatonin. We have lots of that, in tablets, powder or liquid. It really pumps you up. Especially at exam time." She held up a package of tablets.

"Is it safe?"

"Sure, look what it says on the package. '"Approved Food Supplement."'"

"Who approved it?"

She squinted down at the fine print. "Doesn't say."

"No, I really want Bio-Valerio. It's a product that's been around a long time."

"Well, my dad stepped out to have dinner. He should be back soon. If you can wait, he might know."

"Could you look it up? Bio-Valerio is manufactured locally by Agrisure."

She was a bright, helpful young woman. "I can check Agrisure's order forms, see if it's listed."

"Thanks, that would help."

She walked with a bouncy step to the back of the store. Meanwhile, I browsed along the tidy aisles, checking out the shelves. Vitamins. Natural Health and Beauty Aids. Meditation Books and Tapes. An entire section devoted to health food supplements, herbs and antioxidants: for improving digestion, energy, muscle tone, sexual prowess and stamina; formulas for promoting sounder sleep, healing shredded nerves, lifting you out of your body for a virtual romp in a field of wildflowers.

Aunt Sadie might like the satin sleep mask packed with fragrant, soothing herbs. Or, how about a package of fancy healthful tea? At least for now, she'd sworn off coffee.

There were several brands of something called Valerian Root tea. I chose a box of teabags and brought it to the counter. Chris had returned.

"Sorry," she said, "Bio-Valerio isn't on the Agrisure list. Could be they've taken it off the market."

"There was a problem with it," I told her. "A few years ago. I thought maybe it was selling again."

"I just remembered," said Chris. "I've only been helping my mom and dad in the store this year, but long ago they talked at home about something awful that happened. It could have been about Bio-Valerio. They were worried that the scare would hurt business."

"Do you remember anything more about it?"

"No. Just that some people got sick from a bad batch of the stuff. I didn't pay too much attention."

I held up the box of Valerian Root teabags. "This sounds something like it," I said. "What's it for?"

Chris's clear hazel eyes sparkled with enthusiasm. "You'll love it," she assured me. "My mom drinks it at bedtime to help her relax. Like a sleeping pill, only natural. It's been around for, oh, centuries."

I looked at the name on the box. The teabags were made by a company called "Heavenly Earthy Teas." I said, "I never heard of this brand."

"Don't worry. My folks have been doing business with them for years and years. See? On the box? They've been making herb teas since 1922. Or, you can get this as loose tea, even liquid drops. That's more concentrated."

"If your mom's been drinking it all this time, I suppose it's safe. I'm cautious about brand names I don't know."

"There are lots of small, reliable companies my folks do business with. Agrisure is unusual. Most of the big guys want to be in drugstores and supermarkets."

I filed this comment in the growing Agrisure file tucked away in my little grey cells.

"Then a healthy woman in her sixties can drink this brand of Valerian Root tea without any scary side effects?"

"Absolutely!"

"I'll take two boxes. One for my aunt, another for me. There are times these days I could use a cup of magic tea."

"You'll both love it," said Chris. "Look what it says right here on the box. 'Gives you a great feeling of contentment.'"

"Can't turn that down," I said cheerfully, taking my purchase. "Thanks, Chris. I should pay more attention to my health. Sometimes I get too busy and I forget."

"The future of health is in natural therapies," Chris affirmed. I could just imagine her, reddish curls bobbing, leading a 10K walk to send fast food junkies into rehab. "My mom and dad believe it and I do, too. I'm studying food chemistry at Berkeley, but they're a little conservative for me. I have my own ideas, you know." She sniffed with the awesome disdain of youth.

I sincerely wished her luck and left with my two

boxes of teabags. I didn't know whether Valerian Root was any relation to Bio-Valerio, but I was looking forward to contentment in a cup. Although Nick and I had discussed it once, I'd have to remind him that the New Age had arrived in beverage service; it really was time to be listing Herbal Fantasy on the menu along with the cappuccino. For a former pepperoni pizza virtuoso from Brooklyn, this would be disturbing news.

A cab came along and I took it to Chinatown.

TWENTY-THREE

THE EVENING WAS too damp for strolling. Fog made a lurid blur of the signs on restaurants and curio shops; a light but steady drizzle seeped its chill into my bones. It was dinner hour and the more sensible tourists were at table, finishing their tropical Monsoon Mary rum drinks, negotiating over Family Dinner A, B or C. Sad-eyed shopkeepers studied their newspapers, spreading the pages of Chinese characters over glass showcases of jade necklaces and ivory earrings, patiently waiting for customers who'd looked around the emptied streets, patted their wallets and hailed taxis back to the hotels.

After meandering along for a while, I'd worked up an appetite again. As Ferris-Flood had promised, it was easy to find the noodle shop at Sacramento and Stockton. A tiny place, with a half-dozen vinyl topped tables, tubular steel chairs, neon panels that hung from the ceiling and lit the room like daylight; on each table, a plastic rose in a porcelain bud vase was the only attempt at decor.

The customers seemed happy enough, both Chinese and Anglos, slurping away at bowls of noodles and other floating things. Trouble was the large plate glass window that fronted the shop: if I could see in clearly, so could anyone who was watching me.

I didn't want to spend the hour until eight p.m. placidly demonstrating my skill with chopsticks to a woman who might want to see me dead.

There was a bakery and cafe hole-in-the-wall across the street. The window table was empty; it would give me an excellent view of the noodle shop entrance. As I entered I saw, oh, joy! in the bakery case was my favorite version of char sui bao: fluffy buns with a brown glaze and barbecued pork inside. I could take out a couple of orders, nicely arranged in a pink box tied with a string bow. A late night snack for Nate and me.

Did the thought of sex make me so hungry? Or was I looking for a reward after a long, tense day? In the future, I may write a monograph on the relationship between Chinese food, sex and danger. For now, I'll take a bowl of hot and sour soup and a plate of pan-fried dumplings, please. I was *ravenous*.

An hour later, I'd collected my take-out buns, paid my bill and returned to the window table to watch for Laura Ferris-Flood.

She arrived a few minutes late, her black BMW cruising to the curb a few feet from the noodle shop. The tumbling black curls emerged from the car. She was still wearing the cinch-waisted crepe suit, its pale lavender color washed to greyness by the fog-shrouded street lamps. At this distance, away from the force of her presence, her body under the outsize shoulder pads was thinner than I remembered, almost fragile.

She was walking towards the noodle shop entrance. Then she turned abruptly, looking towards a noise or a person beyond my line of vision. She yelled in surprise, although I couldn't hear her. I saw her head jerk backwards. She raised her arms, crossing them over her face as if warding off horror. In the next second she crumpled and lay sprawled on the ground.

I ran across the deserted street, the sound of my footsteps pounding like frantic heartbeats. At the corner a dark car, lights off, screeched into motion, made a U-turn and sped away.

She had fallen facedown. I could see a large, irregular patch of blood, like a sticky red flower, blossoming out of the black curls. It dripped and a small pool of blood was already thickening on the pavement.

I grabbed her shoulder and turned her over. There was a small, smudged hole in her forehead where the bullet had entered. It had emerged from the back of her head and bloodied her curls. That was obvious, even to an amateur like me.

She was alive. In the stunned face, her eyes glared at me and her lips moved. I bent my head to listen, her shallow breath fluttering in my ear like the passage of tiny wings.

"I would have paid," said Laura Ferris-Flood with her dying breath, then she was gone.

Her eyes were still open and surprised. I had to get away from her stare. I stood and discovered that I was trembling.

The door to the noodle shop flung open and a young Chinese couple rushed up to me. The girl looked down at the body, awkward in death, and softly said, "Oh, poor lady."

"We saw her fall," said the young man. "Was it an accident? What happened?"

He bent to look at the wound in her forehead. Startled, he said, "Hell, she's been shot. Right here in front of us."

"You didn't see or hear anything?" I asked.

"No. I was looking through the window. I thought she'd tripped."

We won't be helpful witnesses, I realized. Whoever did this had taken dead aim from a distance, through fog and night, and then coolly vanished.

More people were emerging from the noodle shop, led by a middle-aged man in a white apron.

He knelt down and peered at Laura's face. "I think I know her. Our customer. This is very bad." I didn't know if he meant for Ferris-Flood, for business, Chinatown or the whole human race. It wasn't the time to ask.

"Please call the police," I said.

"Yes, yes." He dashed off. My view through the window showed him gesturing to a waitress, a slender young woman in jeans and a t-shirt. Soon she came out carrying a white tablecloth and spoke to us.

"Mr. Chang says to cover up the lady. It shows respect."

I seemed to be in charge, so I nodded, and the waitress gently placed the cloth over Ferris-Flood's body.

We stood in a semicircle around the dead woman; me, the waitress and the manager, and the dozen or so patrons who'd joined us, ignoring the drizzle, frozen in place like porcelain figurines in a haunted curio shop.

Nothing to do now but wait for the police. There was a tug on my arm; it was the waiter come running from the cafe across the street.

Little more than a kid, long limp black hair, acned skin, a son or a cousin of the owner. He couldn't keep his eyes from the cloth-covered figure, even as he held up two small packages.

"You forgot your things."

He'd brought me the pink box of barbecued buns along with the bag of Valerian Root tea. Wow! Souvenirs of my fun evening in San Francisco. I thanked him and asked if he'd noticed anyone hanging around the noodle shop. He hadn't, which wasn't surprising.

After all, only two hours had passed since I'd arranged the meeting with Ferris-Flood. Not enough time to plan a killing in advance. The most likely scenario was that she'd been followed. Had she told someone at Agrisure that she was meeting a potential blackmailer? Did this person, or persons, feel so threatened that murder became the only way to assure her silence? If so, the stakes must be very high.

And did the killer usually pack a gun, just in case? I knew people who kept a gun for protection; Nick, who often carried large amounts of cash from the restaurant receipts, was one of them. His small Beretta was registered. If this crime was done on impulse, perhaps the gun that shot Laura Ferris-Flood was registered and traceable.

I was very conscious that I'd pressured her, insisting on this meeting that led to her death. The thought was sickening. Drizzle was trickling under my coat collar but, so help me, I was rooted to the sidewalk. At last, to my relief, police sirens shrilled and lights from two squad cars flashed in my face.

"I'M BEING QUESTIONED over at the Hall of Justice," I told Nate. "In one of the interview rooms on the fourth floor. Can't tell how long this will take. Inspector Hanlon is plying me with coffee, but I'm

Homicide's best witness, and they're not ready to let me go."

I'd gotten the newsroom at the *Post-Ledger* to call Nate away from his banquet and phone me.

"Are you all right?" he asked anxiously. "You're not hurt, are you?"

So nice to be in trouble in a strange town, and have someone to fuss over me.

"I'm okay. Cold, shaky, upset. But okay."

"Good. I'll be there as soon as this dinner for the die-hard party hacks is over. The governor is still playing coy and the duckling and peas tasted like chicken and peas. And you don't know it yet, but I'm very good at back rubs for attractive young women who can't seem to stay away from homicides."

Shaky and upset, but getting warmer. I said so.

"Tell Hanlon that you're my friend," said Nate, "and to treat you right."

A pause, then he blurted, "God, Cat, this is getting too dangerous. Wrap it up and then forget about Polley Arbusto, Agrisure and this shifty bunch of characters."

It wasn't that easy. I was in too deep. But I simply said, "Sure, Nate. As soon as I can."

The detective had taken a break while I made my phone call. I shifted around on the battered wooden chair, trying to find a comfortable place. The wooden table in the interview room was scarred with generations of gang graffiti carved into the top. My fingers traced words and names. The suspects who jabbed the letters into the wood, were they still alive? Their angry messages could live on for all ages in this stuffy, sweat-scented room.

Thoughts about Nate didn't help my mood. Even the best of men, I decided glumly, offer you a back rub and clean sheets and then they want to tell you how to run your life.

I'd been poisoned recently, threatened, and had just witnessed a murder. Tomorrow morning I could get on a plane. I'd have my meeting with the Dillenbecks in the early morning quiet of the closed dining room at Dellacasa's. My most harrowing moment would come when I gave the father-of-the-bride the cost estimate of the menu chosen by his wife and daughter. Caviar from the former Soviet Union is, and always will be, costly even when it's stretched in an aspic.

Afterwards, I'd meet with Nick and we'd go over this week's schedule. Then a call to Bianco De-Savio to find out when she'd be ready to start. I'd slip back into my normal routine: the job, the gym, a chat with Aunt Sadie, who'd be planning Easter dinner.

Not so easy. Polley was still under a cloud, Homer was dead and his mother had accused his boss of murder. Which might have made sense, except that now Ferris-Flood was dead, too. And the

San Francisco Homicide Unit was not quite satisfied with my answers.

Inspector Hanlon returned. He was a red-headed bear of a man, tall and husky but not fat. Looking at his ruddy, weather-beaten face, I figured he'd risen through the district ranks, from street cop to Homicide. The paper cup of coffee almost disappeared in his large, freckled hand. From the pocket of his dark grey suit he exhumed little packets of sugar and ersatz creamer.

"For you," he said genially. "Better coffee than you'd get in an L.A. precinct. I know, I've visited there."

No reason to challenge him. I accepted the paper cup with thanks. My watch said 9:25. Let's get this over with, Hanlon. Nate would be coming for me soon. Trouble was, Hanlon suspected that I wasn't telling the truth, the whole truth and nothing but. He was right.

I'd left out the part about Grace Upland passing me the Agrisure memos. To begin with, I still didn't know why they were important, whether they'd been a reason to kill, not only Ferris-Flood but Homer Arbusto.

The memos were in my purse. If I showed them, I'd have to implicate Grace. When Agrisure heard about it, most likely they'd fire her for disloyalty to the corporation. A lousy payment for her help, to be avoided if possible.

"Tell me again," said Hanlon, "why did the victim agree to meet you? You hardly knew each other."

"I called her after I met Homer's mother. Mrs. Arbusto definitely felt that Ms. Ferris-Flood had murdered her son."

"Why?"

"You'll have to ask her. She actively disliked the woman, but that's not proof of murder."

"So you acted on behalf of the family, and called the victim."

I wished he'd stop reminding me that Ferris-Flood was *the victim*. Hanlon was making this an in-your-face kind of interview.

"Yes, I called her. I said that Mrs. Arbusto was suspicious of her. She agreed to meet me. I think she wanted to find out what the Arbustos knew."

"So she rushed to Chinatown for this secret meeting."

"Something like that."

Better to keep quiet about Laura's last words to me: *"I would have paid."*

I'd told the police about the dark car that sped away. Hanlon asked me to describe it again for the tape recorder on the table.

He said, looking at me speculatively, "I called L.A., like you said. That detective friend of yours, Paul Wang, says you're okay."

"Thanks."

"He filled me in on Homer Arbusto's car crash. Laura Ferris-Flood was one of the Agrisure people who were interviewed; he's faxing me that transcript."

I sighed in relief. "So now you have the background on, well, two murders. I have to believe that they're connected."

"Wang also told me that you'd been poisoned, maybe by someone trying to make trouble for Polley Arbusto."

"That, too. Do you know Polley?"

Hanlon raised blue eyes to heaven. "By now, everyone in this unit knows Polley Arbusto. The poisoned meals in his restaurant kept us hopping for months. And the case is still open."

I nodded in sympathy, but he wasn't through with me.

"Why do I have the feeling that you haven't told me everything? At this point, I'm going get the transcript of this interview typed so you can sign it. It's okay, you can take your flight back to L.A. tomorrow morning. Where will you be tonight, if I need to reach you?"

I said, "Nate Greene is picking me up here. I'll stay at his place. I can give you his number."

"Greene, huh?" said Hanlon, looking surprised. "For an out-of-towner, Ms Deean, you have some interesting contacts. Well, he's better than most reporters. At least fifty percent of the time he gets the facts straight."

We smiled warily at each other. I hung out until the transcript was ready and signed it. By that time, Nate had arrived, out-of-breath and concerned. Hanlon had gone off to talk to the medical examiner, so I was free to leave.

My suitcase was still in the luggage room at the Brittany, so we stopped there. Nate parked at the curb, and I went in to the lobby. Even though I'd checked out that morning, I asked at the desk for messages.

"Yes, Miss Deean," said George, the elderly night clerk, looking dapper and efficient in a starched white shirt and royal blue bowtie. "You have one message. Mister Quail called about nine p.m. He was sorry he'd missed you again but he'd be in touch."

Wearily, I said, "Did you happen to take the message?"

"I did, indeed."

"Did he say anything else?"

"No, it's hard to understand him. I think he has a cold."

Shoulders slumped, feeling terribly fatigued, I retrieved my suitcase and shuffled out to the car.

"Mr. Quail called again," I told Nate.

We looked at each other and shrugged. I didn't

even want to think about this bird and his cat-and-mouse games.

When we got to the apartment, Nate thanked me and heated the char sui bao, we had our snack, and he ran me a warm bath. He'd promised a back rub, but I fell asleep before he could get his hands on me.

Around three a.m. we woke up and made love, slowly and with great tenderness. I'd tried shutting out everything beyond the boundaries of this bed. Until Nate propped his head on one elbow, kissed me, lifted an eyebrow and said, "Do you ever have sex without being involved in a murder? I mean, I don't want our relationship to get kinky."

I pulled his head down and told him there was such a thing as being too fastidious.

Before dawn, we got up and dressed. Nate drove me to the airport and I caught my flight home.

TWENTY-FOUR

FOR THE DILLENBECK MEETING, Nick had prepared fresh orange juice, croissants, thick toasted slices of fig bread, sweet butter, ricotta and jam. The espresso machine, with its curlicues of chrome and brass, hissed a welcome. It was wonderful to be home.

I'd made good time from LAX, and we had half an hour for catching up before the clients arrived. Nick poured me an espresso.

I was hungry again, but the platter of breads was heaped so artfully, I raided the kitchen for a few chunks of leftover rosemary bread and yellow cheese.

It helped to fortify myself before telling my boss about the most recent murder. Nick is the kind of stouthearted man you'd trust to ford a raging river or halt a rampaging gorilla, when fording or halting would seem necessary. But now his face paled, and he set down his demitasse cup with such force, it overturned. We grabbed paper napkins and blotted up the coffee.

"Sorry, Cat," said Nick grimly, "but I'm worried. This is terrible. Shocking. I was trying to help an

old friend, and ended up putting you into danger
I should never have sent you to San Francisco."

"I'm okay, Nick. The killer wasn't after me."

Don't blab to him about the taunting message
from Mr. Quail, just an hour after the murder.

"Some of these big corporations," he said, "make
the mafia look like St. Ignatius choirboys. From
now on, Cat, you leave this mess alone. Leave i
to the police."

Emphatically, he added, "You're out of it. And
that's an order!"

It was ungenerous, but I had the grudging
thought that if he hadn't rashly hired Polley, Nick's
biggest anguish now would be the rise in the price
of imported Parmesan.

As I said, ungenerous. Because Nick has a good
soul and would certainly have come to *my* rescue
if, say, the trout mousse at our Save-the-Retired-
Greyhounds brunch had poisoned a roomful of
patrons.

On the other hand, who was Nick to *order* me
to stop? *Order?* I glared at him. Right now, I'd had
enough of Polley and the disasters that followed
him around. However, we might as well repeal the
Nineteenth Amendment, if I'd allow anyone to tell
me when to gather up my skirts and hide.

"Where is Polley?" I snapped. "Still in town?"

Nick looked at me in surprise, but he said mildly,
"No. Homer's body was released earlier than we

expected, so Lila drove Polley back to San Francisco yesterday."

I calmed down. "When are you going?"

"The funeral is Friday, but I told Polley that I'd drive his car to San Francisco for him. Rosie and I will leave early tomorrow. After the Dillenbecks, I'll tell you how this weekend is shaping up. A reception, two brunches and a wedding. What a bad time to be short staffed!"

I needed a full night's sleep but, after that, it would feel good to be working hard. I should phone Paul Wang, first thing this morning, thank him for smoothing the way for me with San Francisco's finest.

I'd call Nate tonight, hoping that wasn't too pushy in what was really (in the dreary morning light) only a two-night stand. We'd touched briefly on the frustrations of a long-distance relationship, assumed we'd be meeting again, but left it open-ended. I'd still been wary after my divorce, no serious attachments in the last year. I couldn't assume that Nate had been a recluse, or celibate, before I came to town waving my banner of Truth and Justice for besieged restaurateurs.

Dellacasa's front door opened. A white baseball cap appeared, followed by mother-of-the-bride Clarisse Dillenbeck, showing off great legs and a good tan in a brief white t-shirt, shorts and sandals; behind her, husband Bruce, two weeks of cruise ship buffets partly covered by a brilliant salmon colored polo and print bermudas. After them came a radiant Debbie and her fiance, the fecund Benjy, both in matching Levi's and cool House of Blues black tees.

"We're here!" chirped Clarisse across the room. "And we're getting ready to party!"

"Come in, it's a pleasure to see you," said Nick, always the genial host. Nothing faked; he genuinely enjoys his guests.

I hoped my eyes weren't too bleary; that my complexion had lost its police station pallor; that I could feel genuinely pleased for Debbie and Benjy.

After all, why not? Too much death and grief lately; a beautiful wedding with festive food and drink would reaffirm the fullness of life. My smile, as I greeted the reunited family, sparkled like imported champagne at a really decent price per case.

Nothing urgent on my desk. Or sinister in my mail. We'd wished Clarisse and Bruce bon voyage for the final month of their cruise; I'd promised to keep in touch with Debbie as the wedding date drew nearer.

The tears came on me suddenly. Nick visited my office and found me crying big fat sobs, mascara leaking down my cheeks.

"Delayed shock," he pronounced gravely, and I knew he was right. "Go home and get some sleep. Then come back later, but only if you feel like it."

"I'll be all right," I sobbed. Like it was a quarter to three in the morning, the saloon was empty, the eternal bartender had set me up with another martini, dawn would never come and, boy, did I have the blues.

"You'll bounce back," Nick assured me. "Discovering bodies isn't what you do best. Just leave it to the police."

I grabbed another Kleenex and sniffled. "I'll go home soon. Just one phone call to make first."

"Can I leave you?" asked Nick, peering into my face.

I attempted a laugh. Shaky, but still a laugh.

"Sure, I'm feeling better already. After all, Mr. Dillenbeck didn't even whimper when he signed the revised estimate."

"Good. Then I'll go. It's time to get started on lunch."

Nick backed out of my office and I reached for the phone. I knew Robbery-Homicide's number by heart. It was a little after ten a.m. and Paul Wang was at his desk.

"You're back in town. San Francisco didn't lock you up."

"Thanks to you, Paul. Otherwise, I don't know if Inspector Hanlon would have let me leave this morning."

"It's okay. I told them we'd caught up with the freeway bandit and it wasn't you. Cat, we need to get together. I talked you out of there—after all, you're a material witness to a murder—but I've got my own questions to ask."

"That's why I'm calling. Maybe we can sort out what I know. Homer Arbusto's murder has to be connected to Ferris-Flood's."

With luck, I could talk to Grace Upland before meeting Paul. Otherwise, the memos would have to be my own puzzle for a while. I told him I'd be back at Dellacasa's late in the afternoon.

"By the way," I said, "I found out that they call themselves Inspectors in San Francisco, not Detectives."

"That's because those guys sit around and read British mysteries. I think they think they have classier criminals.

"But we have our celebrity crimes. In the past, as you know, even I have had my fifteen minutes of fame."

Said with the perverse pride that Angelenos develop from making deals on their cell phones while driving one-handed along the edge of a bottomless chasm.

TWENTY-FIVE

THREE HOURS OF dreamless sleep before the clock-radio woke me with news of an office building holdup near Century City. The two robbers wore Shakespeare and Jane Austen masks. I yawned, idly fantasizing that the perps were just desperate writers trying to get an agent. Or Bill and Jane demanding their back royalties.

Sleep had chased away the blues. It was mid-afternoon. Grace Upland should still be in her office. I found the Agrisure marketing number, reached for the phone and pushed buttons. First ring and she answered, sounding crisp but harried.

"Marketing. This is Grace."

"Hi. It's Cat Deean."

A gasp. "Miss Deean! Where are you? I heard the police were holding you."

"I'm back in Los Angeles. And you heard wrong. I'm a witness not a suspect."

"Oh, that's a relief. I thought, maybe—you know—"

"Know *what*?" This conversation was taking an odd turn.

"Well, after all, Mrs. Arbusto sent you to our

office." Grace was hesitant, almost embarrassed. I gathered that she was asking me, with great delicacy, whether the Arbusto family had sent me to off Laura Ferris-Flood.

Me, Cat Deean, The Noodle Shop Killer.

To be fair, Grace had only met me once, as a representative of the Arbustos. What had she told the police?

"Have you talked to Inspector Hanlon?"

"Yes, yes. The police were here this morning, asking all sorts of questions, going through Laura's desk and files. They've put tape across her office door. They asked about you, and I said that we'd met briefly when you came to pick up Homer's things." She cleared her throat.

"Inspector Hanlon wanted to know if you were upset."

"And?"

"I said no, you were calm and friendly."

"Thanks. That can only help. Listen, Grace, I'm sorry about your loss."

"My loss?" She sounded puzzled. "Oh, you mean Laura."

"It must be difficult for you, having to carry on. Is it business as usual today?"

"Well, it's been crazy. The police. And the media. And the Agrisure executives. The detectives notified Mr. Doyle and Mr. Metcalf, you know, our controller and our CEO, last night at their homes."

She hesitated, then whispered, "I shouldn't be telling you this, but they had me come in early this morning, to help them look through Laura's office before the police arrived."

Her voice dropped even lower. "Mr. Doyle took away at least six of her files."

She'd made me her ally by passing along Homer's memos. Now she was anxious to share more of her employer's secrets. I'd been right about Grace Upland. Harassed by Ferris-Flood and distressed by Homer's murder, she'd decided that loyalty to her company was as obsolete as the ditto machine. I hoped she wasn't being careless.

"Are these phones all right?" I asked. "You have such security over there. Don't you worry that there could be a bug on the line?"

"No. This line doesn't go through the switchboard. And I'd have heard if it was tapped. I know everything that's ever gone on in this department."

She sighed, as if with relief. "Besides, after thirty years with Agrisure, I can retire anytime with my full pension. They can't touch that. So, Miss Deean, how can I help you?"

"The name's Cat. And you can help in a couple of ways. First, the memos. I haven't told the police about them. I was afraid you'd get into trouble."

"Not to worry. But to cover me, if the question

comes up, I'll just tell the brass that the envelope was with Homer's things and that I never opened it."

"That's good. Because I want to show them to a detective here in L.A. The one who's investigating Homer's death."

"Fine. What else? I'm trying to run the department until Mr. Metcalf decides on a replacement for Laura. I'm really a marketing assistant, you know." The bitterness came through the phone like a splash of arsenic.

"Laura demoted me back to secretary when she came in. She wanted someone younger, with a degree. Nobody was ever hired, and I was too close to getting my pension to quit."

Hmmn. Did Grace have anything to gain by killing Ferris-Flood? Doubtful, but possible. As she talked I imagined her, secure in her retirement, raising roses and volunteering at the pet shelter. Of course, revenge is a powerful motivator. Did she hate her awful boss that much? Add Grace Upland to the list of suspects.

"I won't keep you long. But you'd be the best person to ask about Bio-Valerio. Why was it taken off the market? And why, do you think, did Homer save those particular memos?"

She hesitated as if, even now, the subject of Bio-Valerio was too hot to discuss with an outsider.

Finally, she said, "There were problems with a

few batches of Bio-Valerio. The formula had been changed and a quality control step eliminated. A lot of customers got sick, and some died. It was a terrible accident. Agrisure spent millions settling the cases, most of them out of court."

I persisted. "But the memos, what about the memos?"

She dropped her voice again. Nervously, she said, "I have some suspicions, but I don't think it's smart to talk about this from the office. Too many people around."

"Call me at home," I said promptly. "Let me give you my phone number."

I did, and she said, "Not tonight. I'm taking off tomorrow afternoon to attend Homer's funeral. So I'll work late tonight."

"Tomorrow, then," I said. "After ten. I'm catering a reception during the evening."

I wanted to ask Grace for *her* phone number, but held back, not yet sure that I had her complete confidence.

Instead, I asked, "Will anyone else from Agrisure be at the services?"

"Most of marketing. Maybe Mr. Doyle. Mr. Metcalf has a meeting over at our lab in Oakland."

"Well, look around during the funeral. Since you know the department so well, you might hear a remark, or notice something out of the ordinary. We can talk about it tomorrow night."

"Of course. Anything to help. Honestly, Cat, I can't imagine that Homer was killed for what he knew about Agrisure. He was hardly more than an ambitious kid."

I said my thanks for the information and, just to cover all the bases, added, "By the way, Grace, be careful. Your department is shrinking fast."

No reaction but an uneasy laugh, so I left her to run Agrisure's bereft marketing department. It was time for me to return to Dellacasa's.

By the merciless light of the afternoon sun, I could see that my apartment desperately needed dusting. Low priority. I showered, put on jeans and a cotton sweater, and noted that I also urgently needed a trip to the laundromat. And the supermarket. A few murders can really screw up the housekeeping. I tried to compose my shopping list, but Grace's words intruded between the whole grain bread and the fat-reduced cheddar.

Ambitious. Maybe that was the key. What if the kid had learned too much as he researched his film? Suppose he tried to blackmail Ferris-Flood. If not for himself, to help his father. For sure, Laura had blackmail on her mind when she agreed to meet me. So she stopped Homer from exposing some dirty secret by tampering with his car brakes in Los Angeles.

And Grace Upland killed her in retribution?

Almost believable, if it weren't for the two phone

messages from Mr. Quail. Which led me back to the earlier mystery: Perry Framboise dead and 24 other guests poisoned in Polley's fancy restaurant.

I carefully applied mascara and blanked out my mind. Time to go to work. The immediate question was: even though I'd taken a stand, would Frankie the baker forget and once again pour a godawful amount of sugar into his double double fudge brownies?

TWENTY-SIX

"KILLER BROWNIES," said Paul Wang, nabbing a second one.

We'd taken a back table during the post-lunch, pre-dinner lull in Dellacasa's dining room.

"Not too sweet?" I asked.

"Just like the ones my mom bought at Mr. Chen's bakery."

"Brownies? Whatever happened to winter melon buns and little custard tarts?"

He busied himself with a paper napkin, wiping chocolate off his fingers. "Such stereotypes," he chided. "It was layer cakes and jelly rolls. I was born in Santa Monica."

"I knew that," I protested. "You told me once at lunch, when we were exchanging growing up in L.A. stories."

"Sorry. It's my cop mentality. Don't trust anyone."

Really saying he didn't trust *me*. I didn't look at him, busying myself by making wet rings on the table with my bottle of San Pellegrino water.

"I thought we had a kind of friendship going,"

I said, trying not to sound coy. "Did I miss something?"

Paul laughed, not a jolly laugh.

"Cat, let me lay it out for you. There's a stockholder's meeting in L.A., put on by a company in which you do not own stock. You show up at the hotel, and a company executive gets his brakes slashed."

"Coincidence. I was there doing a favor for a friend."

"Then you fly to San Francisco and say a few words to another executive, someone you've only known for a few minutes. But you talk her into a nighttime meeting. And she ends up murdered."

"I suppose from your viewpoint it does look suspicious."

"Yeah, it does."

"Well," I sighed, "I'm not holding back. Let me tell you everything I know, from the beginning. It all started when Nick hired Polley Arbusto, who was slicing up sausages at the Fancy Food Show the first time I met him." And so on.

Paul, of course, knew about the poisonings at Polley's restaurant, but I brought out the newspaper clippings to show him.

He had nothing new to tell me about the package of dead quails that had followed Polley to L.A. No fingerprints; mailed from a busy post office in downtown San Francisco. The plastic bag of quails available from any number of retail and wholesale markets.

I told him about the phone call from Eddie Claire vowing revenge after his lover, Mick, died.

I listed my reasons for being at the Agrisure stockholder's meeting. Gave him my review of Homer's film. And talked about Polley being the corporate spokesman, and their nervousness that an AIDS activist had died at his restaurant. Just when Agrisure was about to market a heavily-researched AIDS home detection kit.

Then the trip to San Francisco. To interview a replacement for Polley, just in case. And to meet Eddie Claire and Mick's family, as well as another person who had reason to hate Polley: Blaine Shepherd, whose partner had died during dinner at Arbusto's.

Oh, yes, by the way, there were two phone calls to my hotel room from a Mr. Quail.

Detective Wang looked slightly dazed.

"What about this Ferris-Flood? What's your connection?"

I filled him in on Mrs. Arbusto and the black marble clock. On Grace Upland and the Bio-Valerio memos, and why Homer might have been blackmailing Ferris-Flood. And that I certainly wasn't, although she thought I might be.

Confession made me thirsty, so I brought us another round of San Pellegrino. For a quick sugar fix, I ate one of Frankie's brownies.

Some of what I'd told Paul was already familiar to him. The detectives had taken statements from the Agrisure executives after Homer's murder. They were aware that Polley's job as spokesman was on shaky ground, and that he was prepared to sue Agrisure if he was fired. If his hot temper had led him to poison Perry Framboise, could he also have had a grudge against Ferris-Flood? Polley was still under heavy suspicion.

Paul had personally taken the statement from Ferris-Flood.

"A hard nut to crack," he said. "She was annoyed that Homer's death had delayed her marketing schedule. As if the guy planned to get murdered just to inconvenience her."

Paul was becoming easier with me. Even if I was (in his narrow view) muscling into police territory. Now that we were friendly again, I asked him for an update.

"Nothing new to tell you about the poisoned olive oils. No fingerprints on the bottles, and the oils are sold all over California, wherever classy people go to shop. A dead end."

"Any report from your lab? What was I poisoned with?"

Paul smiled. "It wasn't anything sinister cooked

up by a mad scientist. Turpentine, ordinary turpentine, is what it was."

I leaned back against the padded red banquette "No wonder it tasted so godawful!"

"A warning. Obviously not meant to be a fatal dose."

"To get Nick to fire Polley?"

"Or revenge," said Paul.

"Yes, revenge. By someone with a devious mind Why didn't this person simply kill *Polley?*"

"I believe," said Paul, "that the perp wanted to see Arbusto twisting in the wind, that's why."

So many slippery loose ends. Gathering them up was like trying to eat spaghetti with a toothpick. was relieved to turn it all over to Paul and the com bined expertise of the LAPD and the SFPD. On the other hand: "What about Laura? Any leads there?"

"We'd already interviewed all the Agrisure peo ple at the meeting after young Arbusto was killed San Francisco is talking to them again. We're also looking into Agrisure's corporate competitors and enemies. With all the research they do, there could be some biotech secrets involved that someone wants to buy or sell. We also have to check ou any disgruntled ex-employees."

"Is this privileged information?"

Paul shrugged. "Not really. It's the basic Homicide drill. Besides, Agrisure will probably offer a reward for information leading to the killer—or killers."

"Two different killers?"

"At this stage, we consider every angle."

"What about witnesses in Chinatown?"

"Another blank so far, although I know that the police up there have canvassed the neighborhood.

"The crime scene officers did find the bullet. It was lead, and pretty smashed up by the time it went through her head and into the wooden door frame of the noodle shop. Fired maybe thirty feet away, from a large caliber revolver. I talked to Inspector Hanlon. From your statement, and what forensics found, Hanlon believes someone called to her, she turned to see who it was, the killer stood in the middle of the street and fired. One shot, at night, in the rain. Bullseye."

We sat in thoughtful silence. Finally, I looked at my watch. "Got to check our supplies for the weekend. Have we finished?"

Paul rose, leaned over and solemnly shook my hand. "Thanks for your help, Cat. I'll call if something develops."

"Come by for lunch anytime," I said. "We don't need murders in order to be friends."

Funny. Nate had said something like that just the other night.

TWENTY-SEVEN

IT WAS SO FRUSTRATING, it made you want to scream. Tailing someone in San Francisco could turn a saint into a killer.

The narrow streets, cable car tracks, dawdling pedestrians, insane traffic. Not that the intruder was a saint, and killing was definitely on the agenda.

If only one could race up and down the hills, brakes squealing, car flying off the pavement, like Steve McQueen in Bullitt, gaining on the bad guys, letting them feel the terror before they crashed.

This was the reality, cursed the intruder. Stalled in traffic, losing sight of the grey Lincoln, having to do this over again the next night to see where and if the sonofabitch stopped on his way home. The intruder thought fondly about the boy. He had been an Eagle Scout, won medals in wilderness skills. Maybe he would have known how to track his prey over the San Francisco hills. The intruder smiled at the thought, shrugged wearily and gave up, just for this night.

CATERING TAKES ME all over partying L.A. Next up, a reception in a former beer bar and greasy spoon in a grungy part of Venice. The smell of stale beer and frying hamburgers had been covered up by fresh white paint. Storefront windows were newly washed, crummy floors replaced by sparkling blue vinyl tiles.

All to care for the beach cities' most helpless citizenry: homeless women and children.

Some Malibu and Santa Monica residents, including a couple of movie stars you'd know on sight, had hosted a series of pool parties and raised funds to buy and renovate the Women In Need Group (WING).

I'd personally called director Ronald Wesley, my most illustrious client. He'd agreed to pick up the tab for the pre-opening party.

All I had to do was gather enough staff to put on a good spread, with Nick out of town, Polley gone, and Bianca DeSavio not arriving until the next day. Frankie had brought in his brother and ex-partner, Benito, so the hors d'oeuvres had the light, flaky perfection that comes from a combined 70 years of baking Italian cakes and pastries.

We had Nick's signature pizzas, hearty fare for guests who'd be coming from work to the five-to-eight p.m. party. The homeless clients were not invited, but that's how it goes, folks. We'd leave the surplus food for the shelter's use.

THE MENU HAD BEEN planned weeks in advance of Polley's arrival and the horrendous events that followed. By late Thursday, when I surveyed the catering kitchen, Frankie and Benito were doing their advance preparations. Thank the Gods of Gastronomy, I'd set down the details before my mind wandered.

Crudities with Spinach and Crabmeat Dips
California Cheeses with Crackers
and Pita Toasts
Mushroom, Sauteed Onion and
Greek Olive Pizza
Brie and Blueberries Pizza
Baguette Slices with Thin-Sliced Turkey or
Roast Beef
Brownies and Lemon Bars
Decorated "Congratulations" Sheet Cake
Coffee Service

A nice balance, I thought, pleased because other parts of my life were so out of kilter. I'd wear my collarless blue crepe pantsuit and simple gold earrings. Balance in life and work, yes.

For an estimated ninety guests, there'd be three servers. Joe, the bartender, would have it easy. Only mineral waters and three popular California wines to pour: Sauvignon Blanc, Chardonnay and, with red wine trendy again, a fruity Pinot Noir.

Almost everyone showed up as promised: politicians, press, film and TV people. One grubby vagrant came to the back door. I gave him a couple of slices of pizza and told him the new shelter was for women and children only.

"Affirmative action. It's destroying America," he muttered as he clutched his pizza and turned away.

I'd even asked Aunt Sadie to help the homeless by checking out invitations at the door. A WING staffer would have done it, but Ricardo Winesap was visiting from San Diego, and Sadie wanted to show him movie stars.

He was as in-the-pink now as the first time I'd met him at the Farmer's Market. Impeccable tonight in a pin-striped navy suit, white shirt and a navy tie printed with tiny green avocados. I remembered that his son grew avocados in San Diego County.

Sadie, however, had the sniffles.

"I've been up at dawn and out jogging," sniffed Sadie.

"She overdid it," Ricardo told me. "After all, she's not in training for the Olympics. She caught cold."

"I'll get rid of it before next Sunday," said Sadie. "Don't forget, Cat, I expect you for Easter dinner. And Gil is looking forward to seeing you."

"Auntie, as you know, my ex-husband clings to the past. He needs to face the reality that I like him as a friend, but I'd never marry him again."

"With no disrespect, Cat," said Ricardo, "maybe

the fellow just wants a nice home-cooked dinner on Easter."

"That's right," said Sadie. "He loves my glazed ham and sweet potatoes." She sneezed, as if for emphasis.

Frankie was waving to me from across the room. I'd been heading to the small kitchen for half-and-half when Sadie had waylaid me. One last word for her.

"What happened to the tofu and the intense greens?" I asked.

"You will have a choice," said Sadie triumphantly. "Glazed ham or mixed beans stew. Or both, if you wish."

"Give me a week to make a decision," I said, planting a quick kiss on her cheek and dashing off.

IT WAS FIVE TO TEN when I arrived home, feet aching but happy. A damn fine party: caring people, pizza and wine, all the elements for success.

The answering machine was blinking.

Grace Upland had called at eight, knowing I wouldn't be home.

"Cat," she said, "I'm so sorry but I'm leaving town. For a long time."

A pause the length of a sigh. She said slowly and deliberately, "Mr. Doyle and Mr. Metcalf want to contribute *generously* to my pension. *Very generously*. Their idea, but I couldn't refuse. It will make my retirement so much more pleasant. I'm sure you'll understand. Oh, and good luck with your inquiries."

Disappointing. But Agrisure could offer Grace the Golden Gate Bridge and right now I was too tired, too euphoric to care. Off with my shoes, pantsuit with the crabmeat stain into the hamper. If anyone deserved a bubble bath, I did. The murder inquiry was withering like yesterday's parsley.

I slipped into the foaming bath and wiggled my grateful toes. I could give up playing detective anytime, I told myself. Almost everyone tells me I should. The scent of the newest antioxidant fragrance, green tea and mango, wafted up from the bath water. I felt a surge of wellbeing.

Okay, I give up, I said to the steam, but just for tonight.

TWENTY-EIGHT

THE CALL CAME two nights later, waking me from tranquil sleep. It was Sadie, gasping for breath, her voice faint and scared.

"I need help, Cat! Can't breathe."

Sleep leaped out the window.

"D'you think you're having a heart attack?" Sadie was, after all, 68 years old.

"No. A fever, maybe. I'm burning up. Come quick."

"It'll take too long. I'll call 911 and meet you at the hospital. Try to stay calm."

I called the paramedics then Fran Marcus, Sadie's next door neighbor, who had my aunt's spare key. Fran promised to stay with her until the paramedics came.

The ER section at Westvale Community Hospital. Sadie was already in a room, an IV drip in her arm. Her complexion was almost as red as the sweat-soaked curls that had matted on her forehead. She was alarmingly limp. Her eyelids fluttered in greeting as I rushed in.

"How is she? I'm her niece. What happened to her?"

The doctor scribbling in her chart looked up. Cropped pepper-and-salt hair, like those TV doctors; sadder eyes. Green scrubs heightened his pre-dawn pallor.

"An accidental overdose. We induced vomiting, but I want to keep her overnight, make sure she doesn't develop any respiratory or cardiac problems, though I doubt it. Your aunt is a healthy woman."

He patted her hand, smiling benignly. "Okay, Mrs. Haller?"

A feeble nod.

"How could this happen, Doctor—?"

"Benson. Dr. Benson." He shrugged. "We see this every now and then. She was doctoring her cold with comfrey tea. Ten cups in one day, she said. In large doses, comfrey can be toxic."

"But comfrey is a *natural* herb. I just saw it in a health food store."

"Natural does not mean safe," said the doctor emphatically. "And the labels usually don't give a clue. It's a self-regulated industry, these supplements. No one's forced to disclose any possible side effects."

"But aren't there laws? What about the FDA?"

"Vitamins and herbal remedies aren't considered drugs. There has to be proof of a health risk before the FDA can step in. So we need to be sharper consumers. I had an overdose case a couple of years ago, an eighty-year-old woman. She'd been drinking every granny's favorite, camomile tea. With older people especially, it's important to watch the dosage."

Sadie blinked. Her copper curls shook. I think the word *older* got to her. Sadie would like to believe she is invincible. Most of the time she is.

Dr. Benson laid practiced fingers on her pulse.

"Your aunt is coming along fine. Pulse is normal. Breathing's easier. She was a little confused at first, but that's expected."

He leaned over the bed.

"Mrs. Haller. Sadie. How's the dizziness?"

"My head is perfectly clear," said Sadie, sounding quavery but indignant. "How could it be the tea? It's one of the best natural cold remedies."

"Who said so?" asked Dr. Benson.

"Why, the nice young clerk at the health food store."

"Did this nice clerk tell you how often to drink it?"

"No. The ten cups were my idea. To sweat out this cold, fast."

"Were there any cautions on the label?"

"It said something about a pleasant experience."

The doctor chuckled. "Did it tell you about the potency of each tea bag?"

A tear trickled from Sadie's eye. "I was just trying to lead a more natural, healthier life."

"A fine goal," said Dr. Benson. "But not all herbs are harmless. So if you're taking one for a medicinal purpose, you should be as careful as if it were a medicine."

He patted her hand. "And, moderation helps."

She nodded, wide-eyed.

A TV doctor smile for me. Life imitating art. I wanted to ask for his autograph.

"I've called up to get your aunt a room," he said. "So you may as well go home now. Check with the hospital in the morning."

Don't upset this precious woman with your own anxiety.

"You look terrific," I lied. "See you in the morning."

Before you go," said Dr. Benson, "Please stop at the desk. They're waiting for you to fill out some forms."

In between life and death are insurance forms. But first, I had a thought. Had Dr. Benson ever heard of Bio-Valerio? I was about to ask when the ER's general clerk listened to a radio call and announced: ambulance on the way.

This wasn't the time for non-emergencies. My shoulders slumped as I shuffled to the desk, adrenaline rush giving way to fatigue.

So I dismissed Sadie's close call as a case of misguided enthusiasm. If I'd been more alert that night, made the connection to a larger issue, perhaps another murder could have been prevented. Who knows? We have set up learned Institutes to track earthquakes, but we still can't predict exact times and dates.

Ever since Ferris-Flood's death, I'd had a hunch about the murders, but it was too vague to be useful. And I totally missed the killer's need to murder again. So where's the blame?

Here's what went through my mind as I struggled through the paperwork: Some cosy cups of tea nearly did Sadie in, eh? Is nothing sacred? I guess not.

SHE'D RECOVERED in time to cook Easter dinner. The yeasty smell of hot breads greeted me at Sadie's door. As well as something delicious that was candied or glazed. Oh, yes, and a grace note, like perfume, of fruit pie warm from the oven.

My hostess hugged me, in a grip so firm I knew that she'd escaped any real damage. Bright hair freshly set, nails manicured, she glowed in yellow silk the color of a baby chick.

"Come in, come in, dear. The gang's here."

Sadie's gang consisted of two longtime gentlemen friends, Charles Oppenheim and John Kelsey. Sadie's chum, the birdlike Blanche. And my best friend, Marcy, with her current man, Phillip.

Yes, and Gil was seated in the living room, smiling, glass of white wine raised in a welcoming toast. Light brown hair getting thinner, trim as usual from his 5:30 a.m. jogging routine. He'd dressed to please me, I knew, in a navy blazer, grey pants and open-necked dress shirt, an outfit that was a tad more dashing than his best brown suit.

Gil designs computer programs for engineers. He is steady, smart, middle-of-the-road in his politics, considerate in bed, and enjoys hot oatmeal for breakfast every day. *Every day.* Much as I liked Gil even after the bliss of romantic love wore off, I could not see a long life, raising middle-of-the-road children, with him.

Though the divorce was amicable, I believe he now regretted not fighting harder to keep the marriage going. But Gil never desired anything or anyone with a terrible passion.

He brought me white wine, his fingers brushing mine as he handed me the glass. Leaning closer, he sniffed my neck.

"You're wearing *Rive Gauche* for me, aren't you?"

Lordy, it was going to be a long afternoon!

I'd heard that Gil was having trouble with re-entry into the singles world. Pursuing dates in L.A. involves freeway time, a working knowledge of astrology for icebreakers, a wardrobe that impresses doormen at the hot clubs, the aggressiveness of Attila the Hun. He had my sympathy, but I couldn't make him a contender.

I sat buffered between Charles and John at dinner. Sadie had scratched the mixed beans stew. She did, however, serve up whole grain buns as well as buttermilk biscuits; baked yams in their skins along with the scalloped sweet potatoes. She drew the line at tampering with her strawberry rhubarb pie and sherry cake.

"A yam, Gil?" she asked.

"The scalloped potatoes, please, Aunt Sadie. I'm a traditionalist, as Cat will tell you. Oh, and another delicious slice of ham."

"You're looking quite fit, Gil," I said, making conversation.

"My daily jog plus three nights a week at the gym. Treadmill, weights, all of it. You're looking tired, Cat."

"Well, I worked late last night. Getting into the wedding season, if you remember."

"You know, Cat, you're not getting younger. If you want children, you should start thinking about it now."

"Cranberry nut mold, Gil?" Marcy shoved the dish into his hand.

"None of us is getting any younger," warned Gil.

"Except Aunt Sadie," I said, lifting my glass of wine. "Here's to our hostess."

She beamed. "And to everyone's good health. You're all family to me, you know."

"Yes, family," echoed Gil, gazing into my suspicious eyes.

No question that Gil could provide the orderly life I'd been missing lately.

On the other hand, think about Joan of Arc.

First, please understand that I don't have delusions that I am the Maid of Orleans. For one thing, she never knew where to get a decent haircut. But I do identify with her determination to set things right.

What if Joan had stayed on her daddy's farm, milking cows?

The Dauphin would not have been crowned king at Rheims. The English would be running France. And the cafes would be serving bangers and mash and warm beer instead of pate and Beaujolais. *Quelle misere!*

No, Gil wasn't the one to set things right. Gil wasn't the rescuer in white armor, sitting astride a white horse. In spite of my protests, it was turning out to be me.

TWENTY-NINE

THE MONTH OF JUNE was approaching in a cloud of tulle and seed pearls. Five weddings to be planned, two baby showers, three graduation parties and two alumni brunches. All on June weekends.

For now there were the usual luncheons, teas and film premiere parties. The Dillenbeck wedding, coming up fast. A Tango Competition party at Carlos, The Tango Teacher's main studio.

Bianca DeSavio had arrived with her own set of chef's knives, rolled up her sleeves and taken over the catering kitchen. Nick began to visit, offering to knead dough or grate cheese. Bianca kept it professional, but Rosie began to worry.

"The wife of a chef," said Rosie, as we went over invoices in her office, "must face the fact that women will find him masterful. And attractive."

I scoffed. "He is also too busy juggling stockpots to pay much attention."

"You don't know, Cat," said Rosie mournfully. "Just look at Polley. He used to brag to Nick about his affairs. Poor Anna, what she suffered!"

"From what you told me, at least he behaved decently to her at the funeral."

"And ignored his poor girlfriend," said Rosie, setting down her pencil and folding her arms disdainfully. "Leaving her to drive home alone from the cemetery. She was crying, I saw her. Meanwhile, he's pretending to be such a good husband and father."

"Maybe Polley genuinely wanted to make amends to his family."

Rosie took off her reading glasses and regarded me with pity.

"Sometimes, Cat, you are such an innocent. I told you that Mr. Doyle and Mr. Metcalf were at the funeral."

"They seemed nervous, you said."

"Wouldn't you be if your staff was being killed off?"

Nick wandered in, chewing on a chunk of bread.

"Have you tasted Bianca's version of *bruschetta?* Even Frankie couldn't do it better."

"That's nice," said Rosie, busying herself with the invoices.

Nick swallowed. "Just talked to Polley. He called to say hello and let me know he's moving in with Anna."

"They're back together?" I asked.

"I'm not sure. Polley subleased his apartment for six months when he came here, so he needs a place to stay."

A worry removed. Polley wasn't returning to Dellacasa's.

"What about Lila?" I asked.

"Since the funeral she won't return Polley's calls."

"That's what happens when a man strays too often," said Rosie darkly.

"You're being unreasonable," Nick declared. "Anna was his wife. Their only son was murdered. For now, they need each other."

"Polley needs a cheap place to stay."

"That, too," Nick agreed. "He'll have to find a job soon. Especially if he has to hire lawyers to sue Agrisure."

"As long as he doesn't come back here," said Rosie. "Things have been nice and quiet since he left."

"As long as we have Bianca, we're in good shape," said Nick.

Luckily the phone rang, a supplier calling Rosie. Nick walked out, smiling like a man for whom suddenly birds sing.

I retreated to my office and called Nate, not only my lover but my source of information. There were sure to be stories on Bio-Valerio in the *Post-Ledger* library.

He was on deadline, so the conversation was brief and to the point, if lacking in sentiment.

"Sure I can get printouts and fax them, but it'd

be easier if you were here. Could be a big file, and I don't know exactly what you're looking for."

"About four years ago," I said, "there was an accident and Bio-Valerio got contaminated. I'd start with that."

"The details are on public record. So what's the mystery?"

"Still murky. But two murders are involved, and it's a given that Grace Upland was bought off."

"Then fly up here. I'll pull the stories, we can go over them at dinner. And we'll spend the night together. How about it?"

"I do have Monday off. And no appointments Tuesday morning."

"Then I'll see you Monday at my apartment, around six. Okay?"

"Okay."

THIRTY

I'D BOOKED A two o'clock flight to San Francisco, so there was time for an early bout with the Fencing Master.

At one end of the studio, Matt Maxwell, the most daring movie swordsman since Douglas Fairbanks, Sr., was fending off three athletic villains. Morning sun beamed through a high window onto the fencers, glints of light sparkled on the flashing epees. The lithe bodies in their white uniforms and masks advanced and retreated, leaped and lunged, and I stood entranced.

"Matt is preparing," said the Fencing Master, "for his role as Thomas Jefferson."

"Thomas Jefferson dueled?"

"Let's say he knew how. The script does take a few liberties. In this scene, Jefferson wins Louisiana by outfighting the French."

"I never knew that."

"It is diplomacy in its purest form. By striking first, you get your opponent off balance and win the advantage."

Like quicksilver, the Fencing Master moved his

body into the en garde position, pointed his foil at my unguarded heart and lunged.

"You see," he said calmly, "you would have been dead. You permitted me to outwit you."

"But we were just talking," I protested. "I wasn't ready."

"Obviously," said the Master. "You have the skills, Catherine, you need the cunning."

"Show me how," I said humbly, putting on my mask.

NATE AND I WERE drifting into sleep, arms and legs tangled, his breath warm on my cheek, when Inspector Hanlon called.

"It's for you," said Nate in surprise.

Propping myself up on one elbow, I took the phone.

"Thought I'd find you there," said Hanlon. "Paul Wang tracked you down, found out you were in San Francisco."

My life was an open book to the LAPD and the SFPD. In spite of myself, and glad the room was dark, I found myself blushing.

"What do you want?" The numbers on Nate's bedside clock glowed green. "It's nearly two in the morning."

"There's been another killing," said Hanlon. "Just thought I'd check on *your* whereabouts."

"Polley?" I gasped. "Was Polley murdered?"

"No. Mr. Arbusto is still very much with us. And at his ex-wife's house, though where he was earlier this evening is still in doubt."

"Who's murdered?" demanded Nate. "Damn it, find out who was murdered."

"Tell your reporter friend it was the Agrisure controller, Basil Doyle. The way things are going, they'll have to promote the janitor to run the company."

"I'm sorry he's dead, but what does it have to do with me?"

"Probably nothing, Miss Deean, but this is the third murder connected to Agrisure where you've been in the vicinity. We'd like a statement."

"About what?" I rubbed my sleep-filled eyes and tried to comprehend what Hanlon was saying. It seemed that I was under suspicion for murder. *Ridiculous!*

"For starters, where were you at six this evening?"

That was easy. "I took a taxi from the airport and got to Nate Greene's apartment at just about six o'clock."

"Well, that would clear you."

"Ask him where and how," Nate urged, practically leaning into the phone.

"You don't have to write this story, old buddy," said Hanlon. "Your paper sent a reporter to the crime scene. But I'll tell you anyway. Doyle and his wife have a restored Victorian in Pacific Heights. He had a habit of stopping after work at a neighborhood bar. We figure the killer followed him to the parking lot."

"He was shot?"

"At close range. No parking attendant. No witnesses. A couple leaving the bar found him."

Nate took the phone. "It could have been a robbery."

"He had over three hundred in cash on him, credit cards and a Rolex. It wasn't a robbery. Listen, I want a signed statement from Miss Deean before she leaves town."

I reclaimed the phone. "My plane to L.A. leaves at noon."

"Nine a.m. will be fine," said Hanlon, adding, "Same place, Hall of Justice, fourth floor."

"I'll be there."

Nate said, with indignation, "A waste of time, Hanlon. You know I can alibi her. Besides, she knows nothing about this."

"Miss Deean has a way of getting involved."

"Does she need a lawyer?"

"No. I'm just checking up on all the players. And there are many. Too many."

"Oh, for God's sake," said Nate, "the killer will probably turn out to be some little old lady who lost a bundle when Agrisure stock dropped."

"Anything's possible. I've got another call coming in. It's been swell talking to you." Hanlon hung up.

Nate had donned his blue-striped boxer shorts and hornrimmed glasses. He stood at the side of the bed blinking owlishly in the light of the bedside lamp. He regarded me with concern.

"Hanlon is getting desperate. Just go in there tomorrow morning, sign his damned statement, and don't volunteer anything."

I shrugged into my robe, wide awake now and annoyed. "There's nothing to volunteer. I never even said hello to Mr. Doyle. Honestly, Nate, I think everyone in San Francisco is paranoid. Including you."

A smile flickered at the corners of his mouth. "Sorry. I've been wanting to bed you for years, but I never expected the nights to be this exciting."

I started to huff and puff, then thought it over and laughed.

"Call me the Material Witness Girl."

"Well, what do you want to do now?" asked Nate. "I'm not sleepy."

"You don't want to—?"

"Nah," said Nate, "Not unless you—?"

"How about some hot cocoa? Do you have any cocoa?"

"I think so," said Nate, heading towards the small, spartan kitchen. I followed, feeling as jittery as if greyhounds were racing along my nerve paths. This latest murder was so remote from me, how could anyone think I was involved. Was I, and Hanlon knew but I didn't? Oh, nonsense.

"That remark you made to Hanlon," I said, "about the little old lady and her Agrisure stock. Why did you say that?"

Nate busied himself with a saucepan, cocoa and milk. I searched for two mugs.

"There was something in the stories about Bio-Valerio," he said. "Remember? It was one of the printouts we read over at dinner."

"Sorry. I didn't pick up on it."

"Well, Agrisure's stock dropped drastically when they started getting sued. Once the cases were settled, the stock went up, of course. Now, with the prospect of this AIDS test being approved by the FDA, Agrisure shares are hot again."

"So Bio-Valerio isn't an issue anymore."

"Seems that way," said Nate, pouring hot cocoa. We took the mugs over to the kitchen table, where Nate had left the printouts.

"Back to Homer's memos," I said, tapping my head in frustration. "There's something we've over-looked. Has to be."

Nate took the pile of computer printouts and handed a batch to me.

"Here, you look through your half. I'm going to reread mine."

Soon there was no sound but papers rustling.

Half an hour later I looked up. "There's a mention in one story about Germany."

"So?"

"Well, Homer's memos talked about this Bundesgesundesheitsant. Sure sounds German to me."

"Is it a word? A company?"

"I don't know. Could you call the *Post-Ledger* library? They'd have a German dictionary."

"Here's a better idea," said Nate, yawning. "In the morning I'll call the German language department at Berkeley. Someone there may know about Bundeswhatchamacallit."

I reread the story. "This is about how the doctors found a cluster of cases with these strange new symptoms. Muscle weakness. Lung problems. Rashes. Like nothing they'd ever seen before. And their patients were getting very sick."

"Yeah. There are several articles in my pile. How some doctors in Tucson got together and analyzed the data. And the one constant was that all of these patients had taken Bio-Valerio."

Nate stood and stretched. "Either I make some coffee, or we put this aside for the night and get some shuteye. What d'ya think?"

"I vote for shuteye. But let me read you this. It's just one line, and it says, 'Bio-Valerio was shipped to Germany, but the supplement was rejected and never sold there.' How about that?"

"Has possibilities. I can try another search from the office. Plug some new words into the computer and see what else comes up."

He came around behind my chair, and began to massage my weary neck and shoulders. "I promised you a back rub and I haven't delivered."

Nate had strong, capable fingers. Soon my tense muscles relaxed, and I felt that I could sleep without having nightmares about Hanlon and maximum security prisons in the Bay Area for women convicted of murder.

Only once did I wake during what remained of the night.

Laura Ferris-Flood, pulling her black curls over her bloody forehead, was complaining to me that I hadn't worked overtime.

Sit up, look around the dim, unfamiliar room. Realize I was safe. Nate was breathing easily at my side. I sighed, plumped my pillow and resumed the sleep of the innocent but nervous.

THIRTY-ONE

REMEMBERING BASIL P. DOYLE. The sorrowful, squashed-face pug dog look, in a three-piece banker's suit. Straight grey hair, rimless spectacles, self-effacing, he had walked in the shadow of his superior, the vigorous yachtsman Metcalf, at the Agrisure stockholder's meeting.

As I told Hanlon the next morning, I'd never met Mr. Doyle, just observed him at a distance. It was in my signed statement, along with the flight number of the plane I'd taken to San Francisco and a description of the taxi that took me to Nate's apartment, arriving there at six p.m.

"You can leave town, Miss Deean," said Inspector Hanlon. "This is just for the record. Anything else you want to tell me?"

He looked fresh and energetic, as if this new murder had psyched him up. I should have shared my growing interest in the Bio-Valerio cases but, frankly, I was too pissed off. And worried that he'd find another reason to detain me.

"Nothing else. Anything you want to tell *me*?"

He was amused. "Okay," he said. "I guess I owe you for calling last night. All I can tell you is that

Doyle was shot in the chest, close-up and messy, with a revolver. His jacket had powder residue, so the killer was standing less than two feet from him. Doyle may have known this person."

"A revolver. Like the one that killed Ms. Ferris-Flood?"

"We recovered the bullet. Could be from the same gun. Ballistics is running tests."

"What if—"

Hanlon stopped me. "That's really more than you need to know. But I'm hopeful. We are seeing a pattern."

"The next one up the ladder at Agrisure is the president, Mr. Foley."

The detective looked at me with new interest. "You've taken these murders to the next step, eh?"

Oh, Lord, why was I foolish enough to get chummy with this cop? He could keep me in San Francisco forever.

"It's logical, isn't it?" I said humbly.

"All right, Ms. Sherlock Holmes," said Hanlon standing up. "I'll tell my chief you said so. Thanks for coming in."

Was that a compliment, or a threat? I gathered up my purse and overnight case and left at warp speed.

A pay phone. There was a coffee shop around the corner where I could call Nate.

"Everything's okay," I told him. "They haven't snapped on the manacles, yet."

"Listen, I've got interesting news. One of the German professors at Berkeley, a specialist in medical and scientific language, knew about Bundesgesundesheitsant. Guess what?"

"What?"

"It's a government agency. The German equivalent of our FDA."

I felt a sudden chill. It was dangerous to have this information. Without knowing why, I was sure that this was a breakthrough.

"Cat? Are you there?"

"Yes, Nate. I'm just thinking. Wondering where this leads."

"I asked the professor if he knew about the Bio-Valerio cases. He didn't, but he did say that Germany has stiffer requirements on over-the-counter products than we do."

"I still don't understand why Homer kept those memos. As you've said, all of this is public record."

"Well, I'm off to a committee meeting at City Hall on hazardous waste. Can't stay on the phone any longer. Will you be at home tonight? I'll call."

"Sure, Nate. Thanks for your help. You've been wonderful with all of this."

"Tonight, it'll be back to take-out Chinese and *NYPD Blue*." His voice became terse and sexy. It was a pretty fair imitation of Bogie.

"But we'll always have memories, sweetheart. Maybe not Paris, yet. But we have Russian Hill."

"You may even have a full night's sleep."

"Take care, Cat. It's getting awfully scary out there."

THE BUSY Justice Coffee Shop had a 'fifties shininess to it. Chrome-legged tables and chairs, waitresses in pink uniforms with frilly white aprons, a fragrant mingled scent of fresh coffee and cinnamon. The clientele seemed to run to lawyers with briefcases and shirt-sleeved civil servants.

Although Nate had prepared toast and coffee early this morning, lack of sleep and sparring with Hanlon had left me starving. I bought a *Post-Ledger* and settled in with a thick mug of coffee and two cinnamon rolls topped with warm gooey icing.

The first news of Basil P. Doyle's murder was short and skimpy. The controller was 55 years old, had worked—and worked his way up—at Agrisure for 30 of those years. A real company man. He was married, no children. Doyle's grieving wife said he had no enemies.

Nothing to add to the details I'd already learned about his murder. A few lines in the article were worth noting: Ben C. Foley, President of Agrisure, was unavailable for comment about the shocking deaths of Agrisure executives. Mr. Foley was in the hospital recovering from bypass surgery. William

L. Metcalf, CEO, had issued a statement praising
the deceased Doyle, deploring the murders, and
urging the police to greater crime-solving effort.

I'd bet my first edition of *Joy of Cooking* that
Metcalf was behind locked doors, quaking in his
deck shoes.

It would soon be time to leave for the airport.
The cheerful pink-clad waitress refilled my coffee
mug as I pulled the printouts from my overnight
case. Was there anything more about Germany in
the *stories?* I skimmed through the sheaf of papers, found nothing but the one reference we already knew, and sat back baffled.

Think hard, Cat. Look for connections. I kept
coming back to Polley, who had to be involved
in all of this, starting with the poisoned quails.
Who had a compelling motive for ruining Polley
and closing down his restaurant? Was Perry Framboise's death an accident, and not a deliberate attack on gays? Was it Bio-Valerio that was the key,
and not Agrisure's AIDS research?

Had Homer saved the memos for Polley? As a
gift for his father, to protect him? It made more
sense than to think of shy, nervous Homer as a
blackmailer.

Too bad I'd already finished my second breakfast. The aroma of bacon and eggs wafted back to
me from the next table. Eggs, scrambled and hot.
Which came first, the chicken or the egg?

Which came first? Germany's rejection of the contaminated product, or the epidemic in the United States?

The memos were still in my purse. Hastily, I unfolded them and checked the dates. February and March. When had the epidemic been discovered here? Reread the printouts. The first reports from the Tucson doctors were in November of the same year. At which time the victims had been taking Bio-Valerio for about six months!

"Oh, God!" I groaned in horror, saying it so loudly the lawyers across the aisle stared at me.

No wonder the memos had to be hushed up. For four years they'd been hidden in Agrisure's files, overlooked, until Homer stumbled on them.

But study the timeline. The dates glared at me: Agrisure, knowing that their new formula was contaminated, had sold it anyway. Even if their own quality control had failed, they'd been warned by Germany. There'd been a rush to get the new version on the market. Laura Ferris-Flood had kept her department working day and night to revise the marketing plans.

So some top Agrisure executives knew they had a potentially dangerous product; they'd taken a chance. And Bio-Valerio had left victims all over the United States, some dead and others invalided for life. No way to excuse it, the executives were criminally liable. This was murder. At the hands of a corporation in a hurry.

How could it be double-checked? The only insiders I knew at Agrisure were dead or had disappeared. How about Polley? He'd been their spokesman for at least four years. I found the paper with Anna Arbusto's number and rushed to the pay phone.

"Anna? Hello, this is Cat Deean. I'm fine, just fine. Listen, I have to catch a plane soon. Yes, I know I always seem to be catching planes. But I must talk to Polley. Is he there? Good, I'll wait."

Fingers drumming against the wall phone. Finally, Polley's voice. Apologetic.

"Cat? I've been meaning to call you. To thank you for picking up Homer's stuff and bringing it here."

"Thanks aren't necessary. Listen, Polley, I have a question. In the box with Homer's things was an envelope with memos on Bio-Valerio. Dated four years back. Do you know anything about them?"

A deadly pause then an explosion. He was angry, shouting. "You have the memos? I've been searching for them everywhere. I always figured you for a bitch. Why didn't you give them to me?"

This man will always be a slob. Ignore the yelling. You need information from him.

"Cool it, Polley," I said crisply. "Grace Upland wanted me to have the memos. She told me so."

"Why? They were intended for me."

"Maybe Grace didn't know. She found them in Homer's desk, and obviously thought they were important."

"Of course they're important," roared Polley. "Homer said so. I don't even know what they're about. Just that they could blast Agrisure wide open."

"He was saving them for you?"

Polley had turned his voice down to a simmer. "My son was trying to help, in case Agrisure fired me. He told me the memos were a bargaining chip."

Homer was needier than I'd thought. Not blackmail for money, but to keep his father's love.

"Let me read them to you," I said, glancing at my watch, hoping I'd find a taxi, fast. I read through the memos.

"What do they mean?" asked Polley. "What's that foreign name?"

"Bundesgesundesheitsant." The word rolled around easily on my tongue now, like a dollop of whipped cream on the strudel.

"Never heard of it."

"You don't know? You honestly don't know? There's no time to explain now. I'm on my way to the airport. We'll keep in touch."

If Polley wasn't aware of Agrisure's shameful plan, why was he a target? I needed to talk to someone who knew him intimately. Maybe I was playing a hunch. Or, dragging out the hunch I'd had for some time and examining it in full daylight.

"Have you talked to Lila lately?" I asked.

Polley became defensive. "We broke up. Because I was comforting Anna at the funeral. Lila always was a little flighty."

"How would I get in touch? Can you give me her address?"

"You two did get on together, I remember. You can have her address, but it may be too late."

"Too late? Why?"

"Lila's taking a long trip. To forget me, she said." Macho pride bursting in my ear. "She's booked a tour to Australia and the South Pacific. I'm not sure when it leaves."

"Tell me where she lives anyway."

"It's an apartment house off Portola, nearly to the top of Twin Peaks. Very posh. On those streets, prices go higher as you go higher towards the peak." Polley was getting positively chatty. No longer a tiger, needing my help, he'd melted into tiger butter. He recited the address.

"If you know what those memos mean, Cat, don't hold back. This is very important to me. And, you'd be carrying out my son's last wishes."

Bleh! What a fraud. I said, "Sure, Polley. Gotta run." And hung up.

I could make my flight. Ticket in hand, no luggage to check. Sit back in the taxi and enjoy the charming variety of San Francisco. Clear the mind. Breathe deeply.

Australia! She was going to Australia.

I sat bolt upright, my heart pounding. Lila's address was scribbled on a paper napkin. I told the cabbie, "Forget the airport. We're going towards Twin Peaks. And, please, step on it!"

THE TAXI STOPPED on an awesome incline, squeaky wheels turned firmly into the curb. Telling the driver to wait, I got out and saw a 3-story arrangement of stark white cubes, like an architect's building blocks. "FULCHER 3-A" said the nameplate at the glass entry door. I buzzed and, to my relief, someone buzzed back.

Pristine entry hall, high-gloss white tiled floor, mirrors reflecting light off white walls. A waystation leading the good and the rich up to the Pearly Gates. I took the narrow elevator to the third floor.

The door to 3-A was open; a smell of fresh paint and the hum of a vacuum cleaner wafted into the entry hall.

I knocked and a slender grey-haired woman in a powder blue twin sweater set and pants emerged.

"Is Ms. Fulcher home?"

She was from the real estate management company; I could tell by her courteous smile and gimlet eye.

"Sorry, but you missed her. She vacated the apartment yesterday."

"Yesterday? You saw her? About what time was that?"

The agent looked at me with curiosity. "Are you her friend?"

I thought fast. "An old school chum, visiting from Cleveland. We were going to get together before she left on her trip. I must have gotten the dates mixed up. It took all morning to see the Giant Redwoods, then I called here but the phone was disconnected."

"What a shame. The movers came early yesterday morning. Everything went into storage. She stopped at our office and left the keys before she took off in her car."

Leaving this serene retreat high above the city. Even from where I stood, looking from the front door past off-white carpets through the glass-walled living room, there was a magnificent view.

"She was so excited about going to Australia," I said. "Do you know when Lila's tour leaves? Maybe she's still in town."

Checking out my Missoni mohair jacket (end-of-season triumph, drastically reduced), taking time to adjust the Hermes scarf tying her slicked-back hair, the agent decided that I was plausible.

"You really did miss signals, my dear. Ms.

Fulcher was going home first, to take care of some family business, she said."

"Home?" Plunging wildly, with a happy smile, I said, "Well, then I'll see her back in Cleveland. She was going to show me the Wine Country, but I can take pictures and share them with her."

"No, no. Not Cleveland. Miss Fulcher is returning to Borrego Springs. You know, near San Diego."

"Oh, *that* home. I guess Cleveland isn't home anymore."

A look at my watch. "My goodness, it's noon already. The boat to Alcatraz leaves in an hour. Thank you so much for your help."

"Not at all. Ms. Fulcher is such a fine person. We do hope she'll come back someday."

No more detours. I desperately wanted the next flight to L.A.

THIRTY-TWO

IT COSTS WHEN YOU miss the plane on these cheap commuter flights. I grumbled, paid the surcharge for a seat on the one o'clock to L.A., and booked a connecting flight to San Diego. There was just time after we'd landed at LAX to make three phone calls. To Nick, asking him to take over my five o'clock meeting with the Singles For A New Millennium planning committee.

"Where are you, Cat?"

"At the airport." Not mentioning which one. "Something came up. I'll be in tomorrow."

"You weren't at the Brittany last night. I tried to call you there. Detective Wang wanted to reach you."

"I stayed with a friend. Nick, the killings aren't over yet. Agrisure's controller was murdered yesterday."

A quick recap about Basil Doyle and my statement this morning to the SFPD.

"And you're handling this alone? I'll take the next plane to San Francisco and I won't leave your side till this is cleared up."

"Not necessary. You have a restaurant to run."

No need to upset him and Rosie with what I was planning now.

"See you tomorrow, Nick. Love to Rosie and everyone at Dellacasa's. Miss you all."

I hung up before he could protest. Next, a call to Paul Wang. Time for show-and-tell. If Paul believed my story, he could alert the police around San Diego.

It's a long ride south to Borrego Springs. Gil and I had passed through once on our way to the state park. Young lovers on a camping trip, the usual scene, sleeping out under the stars. Not exactly Times Square. Roads you wouldn't want to drive after dark. Lila may have stopped at a motel overnight, arrived today.

A detective at Robbery-Homicide said that Paul had the day off. I knew his pager number, but my plane was loading soon. Initiate alternate plan.

Ricardo Winesap's business card was still in my wallet. I left Paul a message and a phone number, asking him to call Ricardo in San Diego. Luckily, Sadie's beau was in his brokerage office. We exchanged fond greetings, I told him I was on my way to San Diego and asked for a favor.

"Do you know Borrego Springs, Ricardo?"

"Sure, we have a couple of accounts there. Small ones. It's a winter resort mainly. The desert is blistering in summer, so most visitors, and even the locals, get out."

Echoes of what Lila Fulcher had told me about her life, that night in Dellacasa's bar.

"Is there a newspaper in Borrego?"

"Yep. A little weekly, the *Borrego Banner*. Every now and then I place a few co-op ads in it as a service to my clients."

"Then you'd know someone to call at the *Banner*?"

Ricardo had a pleasantly deep, rumbly laugh. "It's a three-person operation. I know the entire staff. What do you need?"

"An obituary. For a man named Fulcher. First name Charlie, I think. Any mention of how he died."

"Fulcher?" said Ricardo, sounding surprised. "As in Fulcher's Health Foods? That's one of my accounts."

"Did you know him? Or Lila Fulcher?"

"No, I've never even visited the store. It's in my sales rep's territory. We sell them wheat germ, barley flour, sugarless jams, things like that. But the name on the invoices isn't Fulcher anymore. A new manager came in around the time they moved the store to the mall in town."

"Ricardo, my plane leaves soon. If I call you when I arrive in San Diego, in an hour, do you think you'd have some word?"

"I'll phone the *Banner* as soon as we hang up."

"You may get a call from an L.A. detective, Paul

Wang. Ask if there's a number where I can reach him."

One advantage of a phone call over a face-to-face conversation. You can avoid explanations by hanging up.

An hour later, on the ground again, I phoned Ricardo. He had news. He also had a question; it hit me like a lightning bolt hurled by an ancient and angry Olympian god.

"The *Banner* editor is a Borrego oldtimer. Didn't even have to look up the obituaries. He knew the people. My question is: which Fulcher did you want? The father or the son?"

A flash of lightning shaking up my head. Shaking loose the one essential word. Revenge.

"There were two deaths?"

"The father, Charlie, passed on ten years ago. A freak accident during a storm."

"And the other?" I asked slowly, dreading the answer that I knew would come.

"Dan, son of Lila and the late Charlie Fulcher, died three years ago. He was only twenty-three years old."

"And what caused his death?" My heart ached as I spoke.

"It was some strange illness that affected his lungs and muscles. My editor friend, Barney, says Lila was so broken up about Dan's death, she left town."

Yes, and went to San Francisco where she became part of Polley's life. And hard times.

"Well, Lila's returned to Borrego. I'm on my way to see her. Did Paul Wang call?"

Ricardo was embarrassed. "His call came when I was on the phone with the *Banner*. My secretary didn't know, she put him into my voice-mail. He said he'd call back."

Damn. This couldn't wait. Lila might be on her way to Australia within hours.

"Um, Catherine, please think of me as a good friend. Has this trip to Borrego anything to do with the trouble that Arbusto fellow caused at Dellacasa's?"

I figured that Sadie had called me recently at Dellacasa's, got Rosie in my absence, and heard an earful. It had happened before. We are a tight little extended family.

"Possibly, Ricardo."

"Then is it wise for you to go alone?"

"Right now it's the only way. But I need another favor."

"Ask it!"

"Call Paul back, tell him I've followed Lila Fulcher to Borrego Springs." I gave him Paul's phone and pager numbers.

Dear Ricardo. Before I hung up, he boosted my courage.

"You're a capable young woman. If this Lila

gives you any trouble, I'm sure you can deal with it. Good luck, and I'm here if you need me."

I'll confess, some of the things that could happen on this trip were as scary to me as scorpions:

Losing my way on lonely desert roads after dark.

Finding an address in a place where there were more coyotes than street lights.

Confronting a woman who might want to turn me into road kill.

I wasn't Trapper Catherine, the snag-toothed, sunbaked desert rat. My story was too long and vague to explain to Detective Swanson, Paul's partner. It was certainly not to share with Inspector Hanlon, the beady-eyed bobby of San Francisco. On the other hand, Ricardo had shown absolute faith in me, like no one else since my father died. A sudden tear rolled down my cheek.

If I hurried, I could reach Borrego Springs before nightfall. It was about a two-hour drive. I went in search of a car rental and a cheeseburger for the road.

THIRTY-THREE

ANZA-BORREGO DESERT STATE Park is one of the best kept secrets in the United States. Within its 600,000 wild and beautiful acres, Anza-Borrego has badlands as bad as Death Valley, wide sandy arroyos and deadly flash floods, hot dry lakes, Indian burial grounds, 268 kinds of birdlife, and more species of reptiles than you'd ever want to shake a stick at.

In its midst is the laid-back town of Borrego Springs, saved from becoming a smog-ridden, traffic-clogged replica of Palm Springs by its remoteness. Main access to the Park and the town is down a 12-mile eight percent grade into Borrego Valley, a long hot descent before you can reach the rewards of a swimming pool and a golf course in a green oasis.

The little Corolla's air-conditioning sighed *I think I can, I think I can* as the wheels took the final curve down to the desert floor. It had been a 90 degree day, cooling down now with the promise of a mild evening. Night would be dense and velvety, and come rapidly, but I still could count on half an hour of daylight.

A landscape of ocotillo and cactus, then I saw a lone gas station at a junction. A stop for a rest-room, an icy Coke and the thin local telephone directory. I copied Lila's address and phone number and showed them to the rumpled old-timer in the grease-streaked coveralls.

"Lila," he said, smiling. "I heard she just got back into town."

"How would I get to her house?"

"No problem. It's out in the middle of nowhere but so's almost everything else around here."

He pointed a grease-rimmed finger to the south. "Take Borrego Springs Road. There's a turnoff to Lila's house with a sign but you have to look sharp. It's just a dirt road, you'll see the house before you notice the road. Big white Spanish-style house with a red tile roof. You a friend of hers?"

"Why, yes. Yes, I am."

"That's nice. Awfully big house for a woman to live in by herself."

I looked toward the west. The sun was suspended low in the flawless blue sky, its flames as pure and intense as if this was still Day One in our galaxy.

"Thanks for the directions," I said. "I'd better go."

"Tell her Jim at the gas station said hello. And anytime she wants to come and work for me, to just show up. Ha, ha."

He let me in on the joke. "Lila and Charli
owned the other gas station in town. She's one o
the best mechanics in the County."

"I'll tell her."

Back in the Toyota as the sun slipped lowe
Driving south onto another paved road, then slowl
searching for the turnoff.

Through the dusk I saw the house: white with
red tile roof, about a quarter of a mile away. You'
have to like solitude to live here; the only neigh
bors making noise would be desert creatures wak
ing in the cool of evening and scurrying around.

I almost missed the sign and the turnoff. Ther
was a rutted path covered with drifting sand an
sagebrush, defined by caked tire tracks that coul
have been made yesterday or years ago. It ended a
a concrete apron that passed for a driveway.

Lila's grimy Volvo was parked there, lookin
as if it had recently been driven hard. I left my ca
on the dirt path and walked to the flagstoned fron
patio. She must have seen or heard the Corolla. A
light went on over the panelled front door, its dar
wood richly carved in the Spanish style. The doo
opened and Lila stood there, blond hair backlit by
the hall light.

She wore a black t-shirt and slim jeans, a leathe
belt with a chunky silver-and-turquoise buckle
Much more her style than a designer dress and
silk pumps.

I said, "Mr. Quail, I presume."

"I wasn't expecting you, but it's no big surprise." She shrugged. "Sooner or later you had to figure out my games."

"May I come in?"

"Why not?" She stood aside and I entered, wondering where she kept her gun.

THIRTY-FOUR

TWO SUITCASES and a flight bag sat next to the door; Lila ignored them and beckoned me to follow her.

Handmade Mexican tiles in the hallway led to a spacious living room. It was a page out of *Sunset*. Two large off-white sofas, overstuffed chairs, what looked like genuine Navajo rugs scattered on the tiled floor. From the full-size painting over the fireplace, an Indian shaman gazed at us with serene eyes; one hand held a wand of eagle feathers, the other a buckskin medicine pouch. A knowing collector had put together the display of Indian pottery that dominated one wall; scattered around, tall vases of desert grasses and dried flowers sent out a faint, spicy fragrance.

For all the gathering of Southwest treasures, the room seemed sterile. Of course, Lila had been living in San Francisco, but I had the sense that she'd never felt easy in this splendid house.

We sat on facing sofas. Without preamble she asked, "What tipped you off?"

"Not one thing. More an accumulation of hunches that finally led to you."

"The calls to your hotel room, I'll bet." Her

laugh could only be called merry. "I was getting very fond of Mr. Quail."

"Mr. Quail was one clue, yes. So many people involved in the poisonings at Arbusto's and the deaths at Agrisure, but only a few knew I stayed at the Brittany. Once I thought about it, the field got narrow."

"I told Polley to ask Nick for the name of your hotel. So I could call and thank you for picking up Homer's things. Polley, of course, would never bother with thanks."

Lila the Mild had disappeared.

"That was it?" she asked. "Thinking back, the calls weren't smart. But I wanted to keep you off balance. Polley told me you'd gone to San Francisco to track down the package of quails."

And to interview his replacement, but Polley didn't know that.

"The note inside said 'REVENGE.' It took me until today to figure out the reason why. Maybe I was slow. Something about your story always did bother me."

She raised an eyebrow. "That I cared about Polley, you mean?"

"No, you were convincing. It was your so-called 'insurance settlement' that was dubious."

I waved a hand toward the window. "Living is simple in a small desert town. What kind of insurance could a couple with a small business afford?

Or need? With a payoff after Charlie's accident that made you rich. Fancy clothes, an apartment on Twin Peaks, travel in Europe. Even an offer to bankroll Polley's restaurant."

"You're right. It was the wrongful death suit against Agrisure that made me a millionaire. Lucky me," she said savagely, and added, "Too bad you guessed."

My pride was wounded. "It was better than a guess."

"How did you find out?"

"A friend called the *Borrego Banner*. Charlie died ten years ago. You never told anyone that your son was dead. He was grown and gone, you said." I looked at her with pity. "I'm so sorry for you."

She shook her head vehemently. "Don't. I'm past sorrow. All I want to do now is avenge Danny's murder."

"Murder? Are you so sure it was murder that you've been willing to take three lives? Four, if you count Perry Framboise."

My words sounded sanctimonious, even to myself. Because Lila was right. Agrisure had deliberately marketed a tainted product. Still, we're past the days of an eye for an eye. Aren't we?

"Three lives so far," said Lila, She settled herself more comfortably on the sofa, crossing her legs, leaning back, as if we had all the time in the world for a pleasant chat. It seemed to me that she'd gone over the edge. Rage that became madness. Hiding under the cap of shining blond hair.

She frowned. "Framboise was an accident, his death wasn't intended. With all I know about herbs, the solution of jimson weed I used on the quails should have just made people sick. Who'd guess that Framboise had both a big appetite and a heart condition?"

"What about Homer? He wasn't at Agrisure when Bio-Valerio went on the market."

"Well, yes, I regret killing Homer." As if she'd added a row of figures wrong, and was admitting a slight error. "I wanted to destroy everything that Polley cherished. His reputation, his restaurant, and his son. Particularly his son. Let him know what it felt like to grieve."

"So you slashed Homer's brakes. Jim at the gas station here told me you were a good mechanic."

"Yes, I am. My husband and I had a service station next to our produce stand. Charlie taught me how to do repairs. The brakes were easy."

Her voice hardened. "Dear Lila, always so anxious to be useful. During the afternoon session I helped Homer load his car. No one noticed. But that's how I found his rental."

The scenario I'd written for Laura Ferris-Flood. Right script, wrong woman.

"Killing Homer was a mistake," said Lila. "So unfair to his mother. When I cried at the funeral it was because I'd made Anna so unhappy. You can't imagine how dark the world becomes when you lose a son. If I had to do it over again, I'd spare Homer."

"But what about me? After all, I ended up in the hospital after you spiked the olive oil."

"Oh, come now," she protested. "It was never personal, Cat. I like you, we had a good time together at your chef's farewell party. And who'd guess that *you'd* be the first to open that bottle? I was trying to make disasters for Polley wherever he went. So he'd lose his restaurant in San Francisco. Get fired in Los Angeles. Hound him, anything short of killing him. It would be better if he'd suffer. If I made this life into hell for him."

From the calm tone, you'd think we were discussing how high hemlines should go. Loony. Now where, do you suppose, she keeps her gun?

She must have seen my eyes searching for hiding places. Lila reached under a fat sofa pillow, and then there was a revolver in her hand.

"Just to keep this friendly, Cat. I don't want to kill you."

"That's a relief." A passable attempt at a chuckle.

"What I don't understand," I said, "is why you blame Polley for your son's death. Polley was never part of Agrisure's management."

"He was the spokesman. The great expert on

fresh, natural foods. The great con man," said Lila. "I'll explain it to you.

"My Danny grew up learning about the edible wild plants that are native around here. We helped him start an organic garden. Even in this sandy soil, everything grew for Danny. After Charlie died, Danny talked me into adding herbs and organic foods to our produce stand. We became Fulcher's Health Food Store. It was a smart idea, we did okay.

"But Danny wanted to be a chef. Once he'd seen Polley's cooking program on TV, he had a goal. He'd go to San Francisco and get a job at Arbusto's, learn how to prepare Polley's specialties. Did you ever see 'Northern California Chefs'?"

Yes, I'd seen the video. Complete with Polley's commercial for Agrisure. I nodded, but said nothing. Lila needed to unburden herself, and it was better for me if she kept talking.

So calm, such control. "The Bio-Valerio commercials. My son believed every word. After all, it was his hero talking. Danny fell and broke his ankle, it was a long time healing, the pain kept him awake at night. But Bio-Valerio helped you relax and sleep better. Polley said so. It was too expensive for us to carry in our store, so next time I went into San Diego, Danny asked me to bring him a three-month supply of Bio-Valerio. You could buy it anywhere. Health food stores, drug chains, supermarkets.

"I carried it home to him," she said. For the first time, the calm voice shattered, and tears rolled down her cheeks. *"I handed him his death."*

Her right hand held the gun. With the left hand she brushed away her tears. It was useless to be rational, but I tried.

"You couldn't know. Polley didn't know."

Lila shook her head. "If you're taking a sponsor's money, you should at least know the product. Polley told me once, he'd never used Bio-Valerio. Didn't believe in taking supplements if you ate right. The hypocrite. Where's the responsibility? No one takes responsibility. At least basketball stars wear the shoes they endorse."

She was becoming too stressed to sit. She walked over to the drapes. They were open and blackness pushed against the windows. With one hand, Lila worked the cords that closed the drapes. The gun in her other hand never wavered. She had a steady hand, that I could vouch for. I'd seen the direct hit on Laura Ferris-Flood.

"So Ferris-Flood was next," I said. Lila was pacing now, caught up in her story. I didn't want her to get too upset. Distract her with another topic.

"For the record, Lila," I said, "Ferris-Flood's shooting was another tipoff."

She was surprised. "Someone saw me?"

"No, only the victim. I was the first one to reach her after the shooting. She said, 'I would have paid you.' Accusing me, you see, of being a blackmailer. And believing I was her killer."

"So how did that point to me?"

"Remember, it was foggy that night. Hard to see clearly. Laura's dying words told me she'd seen a *woman* holding the gun. A woman she'd assumed was me. I thought about other women who'd had a grudge against Ferris-Flood. Anna or Cassie Arbusto? Only if Homer had been killed by a second person. Possible, but unlikely. There was Laura's secretary, Grace Upland. She had a motive, but she didn't know I was staying at the Brittany. I started thinking seriously about you, Lila. You stayed in the background, yet you always seemed to be around when something happened."

"You're right, Laura was next on my list. I was impatient. Pretending to care about Polley was such a strain. But, honest, Cat, I didn't know Laura was meeting you in Chinatown. What a surprise! I'd driven Polley to San Francisco after Homer's body was released. A whole day in the car with him in such a foul temper! I was ready to kill again. We were back early enough for me to track Laura when she left work. I just needed one clear shot."

She smiled proudly. "I used to practice shooting at empty cans in the desert. Charlie encouraged me to learn to use his gun. In case he wasn't around and I needed to protect myself.

"After Danny died, I was so angry I'd pretend that the cans were the executives at Agrisure. But blowing away tomato sauce cans with blanks wasn't healing enough.

"You can imagine, there were dozens of wrongful death suits against Agrisure. They'd been settled out of court. My lawyers urged me to settle. It meant faster payments for all of us, the victims and their families. For Agrisure, it put an end to bad publicity just when they'd made a breakthrough on their AIDS test.

"I'd signed a legal paper saying I wouldn't talk about the case publicly. That was a mistake, an insult to Danny's memory. By keeping quiet, I'd agreed to let them get away with murder. So I decided to use this blood money to hunt down Polley and the rest of the rat pack."

THIRTY-FIVE

LILA GLANCED at her watch. "We can leave soon. Now that the stores have closed and folks are settled in for the night."

"Where are we going?" Staring at the shiny black revolver.

"You'll see. I want to keep you away from a phone. Does anyone know you've come here?"

"A couple of people," I said, only slightly exaggerating. "The detective you met at Dellacasa's could be here any minute. Give it up, Lila. You've been found out. Let me take you to the police."

She regarded me with appropriate scorn. "After four dead bodies?" said Lila. "The story will get out to the media, and that's fine with me. Let the world know about Agrisure's criminal acts. But give up? I'd have to be crazy."

True. Her mind had snapped, but she was not that crazy.

"My plan was to drive to San Diego, I have a flight booked, but that's too risky now. So I'll drive into Mexico and work it out from there."

"They could stop you at the border."

"Not likely. You won't be around to give the

alarm. Besides, the border patrol knows me. Danny and I were always going across to buy herbs. The guards will just say hello, glad to see ya, and wave me on."

Pointing the gun. "Let's go now. We can leave through the kitchen. I have bottled water for you to take along."

Why was she looking over my clothes? I'd changed to sweatpants, a t-shirt and running shoes back at the San Diego airport. "You should be comfortable enough." Where? In some barn or stable? The rear of her health food store? Shouldn't be too hard to break free.

We were in the kitchen. Mexican tiles like folk art on the floors and counters. Doubtful that anything more elaborate than Wheaties and milk had been prepared here.

She opened a drawer, pulled out a pair of handcuffs and said, "Here, let's get these on you." At my look of horror she added, almost apologetically, "Left over from Charlie's days as a Park ranger. I'll take them off before I leave you. But I can't drive and hold a gun at the same time."

"You don't need them. I won't try to escape." I was friendly, reassuring. Lila studied me as if I were a Fringe-Toed Lizard, harmless but annoying, who'd come off the desert floor and invaded her kitchen.

"You're wasting time, Cat," she said impatiently.

"If you did tell that cop where I am, then I don't have all night. After dropping you off, I have to come back, get my luggage and close up the house. Thanks to you, I don't know how long I'll be gone."

Don't wait till she thinks about swatting me. I stuck out my hands and she clamped on the cuffs.

"Nearly forgot the water," she said, opening the pantry door. "Sorry it isn't Perrier." It was a bottle of generic mineral water that she tucked behind the handcuffs, so I could clutch it to my chest.

"Awfully nice of you," I said snidely.

"Yes, it is," she agreed. "Maybe this will give me good marks with God."

I stared at her, wondering if she was worrying about God's dismay now. Or in the hereafter. I hadn't seen the penitent side of Lila before but, then again, she was full of surprises.

Out a kitchen door into the garage. She switched on the light. I saw a red Jeep Cherokee; it was battered but clean.

"We'll take the Jeep. Four-wheel drive is easier on some of these roads." She opened the passenger door and I climbed in.

Lila chattered on as she strapped me in my seatbelt. "Diana Martinez, she was Danny's girlfriend, manages my store. She uses the Jeep, so there should be enough gas."

She clicked the garage door opener, backed the Jeep out into the night and maneuvered it onto the dirt road. "Diana's a lovely young woman. She and Danny were going to be married. If anything happens to me, Diana will get the store and the house. I have no one else." Lila, in profile, was stoic, eyes fixed on the road that dissolved into darkness past the beam of the headlights. Dark in spite of a three-quarter moon and so many stars they helped you believe in heaven.

She drove north and there were street lights not far away, coming from the town. A right turn and soon we passed the small airport, a half dozen private planes nesting for the night like a gathering of hawks. The first car I'd seen exited the airport and swung by us, heading towards town. We were going away from happy people on vacation; Lila was driving in the direction of the chillingly deep, wind-eroded canyons that make up the badlands. I began to worry, big time.

"We're driving away from town," I said, pointing out the obvious.

"I told you, don't worry. You'll be back in civilization by morning. I can't let you lead the police to me now, so close to the final revenge."

Ignore the fact that she was a liar and a murderer, and I could trust her not to harm me. To my mind, Lila was Annie Oakley cast by mistake in a Greek tragedy. But if I wasn't intended to be her final victim, I knew who was.

"I know what you plan to do in Australia," I

said. "That's why I came here today. To keep you away from William Metcalf. You told me yourself, that after the stockholder elections he'd be sailing his boat to Australia. But Lila, it's time to stop the killings."

It was so dark inside the Jeep, her voice seemed disembodied.

"Your final hunch, was it? And you're right. Everyone thinks I'm going to tour the South Pacific to forget that Polley broke my heart." Again, that merry laugh. "What a joke. I'd have gone after Ben Foley next, but he's too old and sick, and too protected in the hospital. Besides, it's Metcalf who made the final decision to market Bio-Valerio."

Suddenly, she veered the car onto a turnout and cut the engine. There was a scenic marker, impossible to read without a light. In daytime, we'd have been looking down into the primeval depths of the badlands. At night, these were nightmare chasms, inhabited by winds and wandering spirits.

"In case I never see you again," said Lila, "you should have the whole story."

I knew most of it, but I was willing to buy time. Not being a survivalist, the idea of finding my way out of the desert made me shiver, as if small stinging things were already crawling down my spine. When we stopped, I could hit her with the water bottle. Or, grab a rock and stun her. First, distract her some way. After all, you don't poison

a restaurant full of people, and kill three other
without having some problem with your attention
span. Or so I hoped.

"You asked me," said Lila, "how I could be sure
the Bio-Valerio deaths were murder, not an indus
trial accident. At first I wasn't sure.

"Danny died a terrible, lingering death. After
wards, I became deeply depressed. It was like fall
ing to the bottom of one of these canyons. With al
the millions from the settlement, nothing gave me
peace of mind. Even the new house, the one you
saw tonight. Such guilt, that my son's death had
paid for my luxuries. I moved the store to a busy
new location in the mall, and my mind still wen
round and round asking why Danny had to die."

"That's when you moved to San Francisco."

"After my trip to Europe. The turning point. I'c
spent days at the library in San Diego, researching
the newspaper stories on Bio-Valerio. It was just a
two-line mention, but one country wouldn't allow
Bio-Valerio to be sold."

"Germany," I said.

"You know?" She was surprised. "Agrisure was
able to hush it up because the wrongful death case
never went to court. Everyone forgot. Except Dan
ny's mother."

Looking down from this cliff, the world was cold
and lifeless. The earthquakes and erosion that had
formed the canyons had long ago lost their force

We sat and talked about human passions and folly, and I wondered if the restlessness in our own natures would destroy us over the next million years.

"I had to know," continued Lila. "The easiest way for a small town girl like me was to book a tour to Europe. I asked my congressman for a letter of introduction to our embassy in Berlin. An attache connected me to a government agency in Bonn."

"The Bundesgesundesheitsant."

"Cat, I underestimated you. Too bad, we could have gone after the bad guys together."

No chance, Lila. When it comes to shooting, my personal best is squirting whipped cream squiggles from a can. Much neater than murder.

She sighed. "Then, you know about the rest. When my tour group took a boat trip down the Rhine, I went to Bonn."

The voice in the darkness trembled, then turned as dry as an old document that had been filed and forgotten.

"It was true, oh my God, it was true! I talked one of the bureaucrats into showing me the rejection letter to Agrisure. The testing, it said, showed impurities in the formula. It was also stronger than the old product. Not acceptable on both counts. Warning: this Bio-Valerio formula could be dangerous. Reformulation is required before Germany will permit Bio-Valerio to be sold."

At Nate's apartment, I'd seen an article on the epidemic that reprinted the copy in one of the Bio-Valerio ads.

"New and improved formula. More essential ingredients to make you feel relaxed and fabulous even faster!"

According to the article, Agrisure had added about one percent more "essential ingredient," an amino acid, to Bio-Valerio. Paid for it by skimping on quality control. And raised the price of the finished product by ten per cent.

Metcalf, Ferris-Flood, and Doyle, the numbers cruncher, had made Bio-Valerio more profitable than ever. And, in their haste to put it on the market, taken a chance that the impurities were harmless.

"I was in a daze when I rejoined the tour," said Lila. "Knowing now for sure that Danny had been killed for a quick profit. By the time the trip was over, I knew how to avenge my child. By getting close to Polley—his restaurant made him approachable—I could learn more about the decision makers at Agrisure. Even meet them at some posh corporate parties.

"Metcalf," she said dreamily, "is quite fond of Beluga caviar and other executives' wives. Ferris-Flood was spartan, too busy hustling favors to indulge. Mineral water with a squeeze of lime. And tight skirts that barely covered her crotch. That was Laura, always taking care of business. Doyle drank too much. He should have died happy, he was on his way to a bar."

She started the engine, regained the main road and we went silently on into the night. A signpost loomed up, ghost-like, then disappeared as we sped by. If only I could scatter beans, like Hansel and Gretel, to guide my way back. My sense of direction, always iffy, had failed completely.

My heart bounced in my chest as the Jeep turned off the paved road, lumbered over a steep rise and then plunged down into an arroyo. We were on a wide, dry riverbed, a moon landscape.

"Not much farther," said Lila.

"Don't do this. I've never hurt you."

"Weren't you ever a Girl Scout?" she asked. "Didn't you get a Merit Badge in outdoor survival?"

"I flunked out," I said miserably. "Sat in a clump of poison oak and that was that."

"Ahead," said my captor. "See that grove of fan palm trees?"

The palms had tall, thick trunks, ringed near the top with what looked like shaggy beards. At the top, clusters of spiny green leaves fanned out against the night sky. In daylight, the palms would offer shelter from sun and glare.

"Our own oasis," said Lila, like a guide determined to impress a gaggle of tourists. "Used to be a stop on the stagecoach line. There's an opening in one of the trunks where folks could leave messages. No phones, though," she added with a laugh.

She drove nearer to the palms, the Jeep rocking over the sandy, boulder-strewn river bottom, then parked.

"It's a custom around here to leave water in the palm for any poor sons of bitches who've used up their supplies. Don't give up your bottle, though. Only about three miles back to the main road, but you might get confused. Just walk north and, sooner or later, you'll find the road. How long it takes before someone finds you, well, I don't know."

There'd be nothing but me and moonlight once I left the safety of the Jeep.

"Get out now, Cat," she said. "It's time to say goodbye."

The gun was in her hand again, just a few inches from my heart. Not much chance to get her off balance, but I'd try.

"How could you do it, Lila? How could you make love to Polley when you hated him so?"

She didn't even have to think about it.

"Just between us ladies," said Lila, "sometimes you have to act a little to get what you want. Haven't you ever faked it?"

There was that sweet, sunny grin. She lifted her hand and crashed the revolver down on my head. I slumped, heard her scramble out and come to my side of the Jeep. I was falling, hitting the ground hard, and soon even the stars faded to black.

THIRTY-SIX

IT WAS THE LONELIEST NIGHT of my life. My only companions were unseen, but I could imagine them slithering through the sand, or skittering towards me on webbed feet. There were rustlings in the dry fronds that fringed the palms: rats and mice that took shelter in the tree hollows and among the leaves. I was the intruder here, hugging my bottle of survival water.

Lila had removed the handcuffs and taken them away. I awoke with my face pressed in sand and a lump rising on my scalp. My head ached as if it was fun time on the San Andreas Fault. My watch, its numbers glowing pale green, read eight o'clock; I'd only been blacked out for a few minutes.

Staggering to my knees, I looked around. Sand, rocks, ancient rubble that formed the walls of the arroyo; the grove of palm trees was the only sign that this was not a dead moonscape.

Lila had said that the main road was about three miles north. I'd been hopeless as a Girl Scout. Put me in the middle of a wilderness, give me a knife, a rope and a compass, and I'd depend on the rest of my troop to lead me out. North was a mystery not to be solved tonight.

Tire tracks from off-road vehicles criss-crossed the river bed; impossible to decipher them by moonlight. The sun rises in the east, any fool knows that. After dawn, even I could find the elusive north and the path to the main road. It would exhaust my strength to go stumbling in circles tonight around this dry, dead land, risking a fall or a snake bite.

Soon after five a.m., the stars and moon would fade and a feeble light would show in the east. I'd walk out in the cool morning, find the road before the sun turned me to burnt toast. Only nine hours to kill. Best to stay away from the palm grove and its biting tenants. There was a large flat boulder a few yards away. I could sit on it, cross my legs and meditate. As long as I didn't have to share it with a rattler seeking the sunwarmed stone after a day's sleep. I armed myself with a rock, surveyed the top of the boulder, found it empty and clambered to the top.

That Lila. She was probably halfway to the Mexican border. If she eluded the police, if she hunted down and killed Billie Metcalf, would she be satisfied at last? She was mad, no doubt of it. *Could* she stop now? Considering:

She was one fajita short of a Mexican combo.

One spare rib short of a barbecue.

One eggroll short of a banquet.

God, I was hungry! Nothing for hours but a cheeseburger and fries devoured, one hand on the steering wheel, as I made my mad dash to Borrego. Remembering my survival handbook, in a pinch one could eat some insects. What was that childhood lament? "Everyone picks on me. I'll eat some worms and then I'll die."

A mournful bass sound nearby, it was a toad burping. Leave the insects to him, I could last until morning.

Mr. Toad was having a dialogue with Mr. Owl, who might have been poking around in the desert scrub looking for his own dinner.

Croak. Whooee. Croak Croak. Whooee. Croak Croak Croak Croak. The toad was winning the battle of words.

Even on this bleak terrain, there were winners and losers.

The gentle vegetarians would co-exist. The predators would bite or sting the smaller, weaker creatures and eat them. It was their nature, a matter of survival. No moral judgments in their universe.

The ache in my head had become a mild aftershock. If I could think clearly, maybe I could figure out who were the winners and losers in my own circle.

Polley was losing ground fast, but he might recover if Lila left for good.

Agrisure's stock was rising, but they had certain management problems.

On her terms, Lila was a winner, but she'd be a fugitive as soon as I could find a phone.

By all counts, I was a loser. Sure, I had done a fancy bit of deduction and identified the culprit. But how reckless I'd been, taking on a woman I knew was a killer, armed only with the fantasy that she'd listen to reason and surrender.

I mean, even Joan of Arc carried a heavy, no-nonsense sword for smiting.

I should have stayed in San Diego until I could contact Paul. Or his partner. Or even, as a fallback, Hanlon in San Francisco.

I shifted on my stone seat. The rock was still in my hand, just in case some irritable snake or iguana wanted to reclaim its territory.

Stars in the black sky were putting on a brilliant light show, just for me. Classier and cheaper than anything at Disneyland. The three-quarter moon was higher now, shining down a cold white light that drained the colors from sand and rocks and transformed them into a haunted desert.

What puzzled me was the haste with which I'd taken this trip that had ended with me as lizard bait. Usually, Cat Deean, Catering Manager, was a model of practical virtues. The grilled chicken or the baked salmon, the mousse versus the parfait;

these were menus I proposed with full attention to flavor, appearance and cost efficiency.

So strange. Of course, one reason I'd divorced Gil (not said openly, but deep inside I knew it was true) was my boredom at having *two* careful people in the same family.

As opposed to Lila, who'd destroyed so many lives, not least her own, in a passion for revenge. Mother love carried into madness. Yet I could almost admire her capacity to love and hate.

In between wars, which have more to do with greed than love or hate, we have become such a bloodless society. We take our violence on 24-inch screens, in the comfort of our living rooms. At a summer blockbuster in an air-conditioned movie house. When we've been wronged, we call in the lawyers.

What would happen to Lila once she was caught? California still had the death penalty. For multiple, premeditated murder, she'd qualify. With luck, she might end up in a hospital for the criminally insane.

Which brought me back to the question: why didn't I call in the cops?

There's this famous passage in the Sherlock Holmes canon. He talks about "the curious incident of the dog in the nighttime."

"The dog did nothing in the nighttime," says Watson.

"That was the curious incident," remarks Holmes.

There it was, I was the dog that did nothing. Me, whose favorite TV drama is *Law and Order.* Lila had avenged the dozens of deaths caused by the corruption at Agrisure. Should she suffer the fate of a killer who took lives because of money, sex or boredom?

I believed in the value of life, the necessity for law. But I couldn't quite grasp where justice fit in.

Somewhere in my subconscious, I'd pulled back. At least I think that's what happened. Tomorrow, at dawn, I might deny it, even to myself.

I might blank out about this long lonely night, recalling nothing but moonlight and stars, the sun-warmed rock, the sounds of small creatures making desert music.

Lila was still in pursuit of William Metcalf. I hoped that my warning would prevent his death. If the police could alert him, it would be one positive act that I'd accomplished.

Sometime later I fell asleep, still sitting crosslegged on the boulder. I remember clutching my rock and my water bottle and mumbling, leave her to heaven.

THE FIRST light of day was showing when I awoke, feeling the morning chill. I jumped to the ground, shook my cramped legs to get the circulation going. For breakfast, a cautious swig of water. Only half a bottle remained, after last night's bacchanalian sips.

It was time to leave, before the full sun rose. I

followed my nose north, stepping rapidly on the hard-packed sandy bottom.

Three miles, Lila had said. With luck and no dunes or cliffs in my path, I could reach the paved road in a couple of hours.

There was a Jeep route that seemed promising. It hadn't rained here in several months, so the tire tracks were clear and easy to follow.

Lila was somewhere in Mexico; I imagined her stopping in her flight to breakfast on a scrambled egg burrito and refried beans; the coffee would be dark and strong. Nick and Rosie would be rising around now; bowls of cereal on their kitchen table, toast and jam, the coffee French Roast and fragrant.

There were biting little sand flies to add to my discomfort. And I could use a shower and fresh underwear. I looked nervously at the sun. Oblivious to my comfort, it had every intention of rising again. The Corolla's radio yesterday had predicted ninety degree temperatures again for today, probably higher in this flat, unshaded terrain.

I slogged on, getting a little lightheaded as the morning brightened. Would I see mirages, I wondered? Waterfalls and date palms? Would I die out here if I'd mistaken south for north?

Ahead, I saw it, a black ribbon curling through the desert. It disappeared as I scrambled up over the last rise, dislodging rocks, scraping my ankles in my haste, then I was on the paved road. East, west? Which way?

East should lead back to town. The sun was hot now, and I drank up the last of my water. Where were the cars, the trucks? There should be signs that said FOOD. WATER. NEXT EXIT.

A speck appeared in the distance, growing larger as I walked towards it. A car, speeding my way. I stopped, raised my arms and waved frantically. Not that I could be missed in this solitude.

It was a white Jeep, coming closer. Two men in it, the driver wearing a Park ranger's Stetson, the other man a blue baseball cap. Something about the passenger was familiar.

I stood in the middle of the road, an apparition from the world before time: grubby t-shirt, torn pants, hair that hadn't seen a comb since the days of the woolly mammoths. In spite of myself, tears made furrows down my sandy cheeks.

The Jeep stopped and Paul Wang rushed to my side, grabbing me by the elbows as if I was about to fall over.

"Cat! Are you all right?"

"I was wondering when you'd come. Want to buy me breakfast?"

EPILOGUE

A YEAR PASSED before I heard from Lila. She sent a picture postcard of a quaint fishing village. The card had "Beautiful Baja" printed on it, but was postmarked Mexico City. I dutifully called Detective Wang, met him for lunch in Chinatown, and turned the card over to him. It said:

Dear Cat,
Enjoying Mexico. Next, I'll be off to the South Pacific. Sorry I had to run out on you in such a hurry. Too bad it's the innocent who have to suffer.
Lila

Well, I hadn't suffered too much. A few days of calamine lotion and moisturizer, and I was back to my usual dewy self.

Lila hadn't totally abandoned me that night. When Paul Wang arrived at her house, he'd found my rental car, my purse still on the front seat and a note stuck under the windshield. It said something like: *LAPD, try the 17 Palms Oasis.*

Soon after I returned home, I called Blaine Shepherd and Eddie Claire to inform them that Lila, not Polley, had poisoned the quails at Arbusto's restaurant.

Blaine said, "So it wasn't gay-bashing and that's a relief. I don't feel better about Perry's death, such a waste, but at least I don't feel worse." Eddie growled, "Too bad she didn't poison Polley, too." But he thanked me.

About the folks at Agrisure.

Ben Foley is an invalid, or so he said when he retired. He owns a big chunk of Agrisure stock. In spite of the negative stories after the murders, Agrisure is still considered one of the glamorous biotech companies; it is a hot stock. Foley leads a quiet life and is rarely seen in public.

William Metcalf and his wife have spent the last year sailing around the South Pacific. They never stay long in one port. Metcalf has hired a permanent bodyguard who also crews for him. The guard is big and blond, and favors short shorts that show off fabulous thigh muscles. I saw a picture of Metcalf, his boat, his wife and bodyguard in the Sports section of the *Times*. Billie looked nervous, but that may be because his wife was gazing fondly at his bodyguard.

Polley has relocated in Monterey, where he's become partners in a seafood restaurant. He's told Nick that he took Lila's betrayal very hard. He has no steady girlfriend for now. If Polley can manage

to be civil to the summer tourists, he may be abl
to rebuild his reputation.

Anna Arbusto has been receiving a check fo
two thousand dollars every month since Lila lef
the country. A cashier's check, no sender's nam
on it, drawn on a Barbados bank. The money ha
made life for Anna and Cassie much easier. They
still mourn Homer and always will.

Things are getting back to normal at Dellacasa's
Bianca DeSavio's husband returned from Argen
tina a few months ago; he's scouting a location fo
his new restaurant. Bianca will stay with Dellaca
sa's for the time being, as Mario is still in France
refining his new skills with bread and pastries
Nick has stopped visiting the catering kitchen.

Aunt Sadie has taken up tofu. She is collect
ing recipes for an all-tofu cookbook. Ricardo, who
drives up to L.A. regularly, tells me that she's come
close to perfecting a nutrient-rich cake that tastes
like coconut.

It's wedding season again and I've been too busy
to escape to San Francisco very often. Nate comes
to L.A. whenever he can. We're talking about going
to Paris together in August, before Dellacasa's clients start thinking about their holiday parties.

Today, I'm putting the final touches to wedding
plans for Carlos, The Tango Teacher's younges
sister, Mimi. She is marrying one of Carlos' top
pupils, Harv Ackerman, a thin, stooped balding

accountant with magic feet. The newlyweds will dance a tango exhibition at the wedding dinner to be held at Carlos' estate in Bel Air.

I'm still a pushover for weddings. The disappointments and losses come later. But for one glorious day, everyone celebrates the surprise of finding love. I'm happy with my single life but it's true that I've been restless lately. Maybe I'll ask Carlos about the cost of tango lessons.

* * * * *

AUTHOR'S NOTE

"WHERE DO YOU GET your ideas?"

Sooner or later, every author is cornered with that question. Often the answer is a simple, "Dunno. It just comes." *Chill Before Serving* was different: an idea that kept nagging at me until I knew I had to put it into words.

They are, however, inspired by two separate events in my life when I was witness to a friend's mystifying illness.

Several years back, a healthy young woman, the mother of two children, was rushed to the emergency hospital with heart palpitations. Later that day, after she was brought home, I stopped by. Her face was noticeably flushed, she still felt shaky. The cause of her sudden distress: eight cups of camomile tea that she'd sipped over a few hours to relieve the symptoms of a cold. Camomile, that cosy old remedy! Who'd dream that an herb tea, loved too well but not wisely, could produce such potentially dangerous side effects? A curious episode that I tucked away in the back of my mind.

The other impetus for my story was a tragic death. Robyn Gair was a brave and lovely young woman, whom I'd known from birth, the daughter of a close friend.

Robyn had taken a fall from a bike, breaking some small bones in her hand, and she was in constant pain. Her doctor suggested L-Tryptophan, not a drug but a nutritional supplement, to help her relax and sleep. Several months later, she developed muscle weakness, rashes, severe breathing problems. There was no cure for her; after a long, debilitating illness, she died.

Robyn was one of the victims of a strange new disease that eventually was traced to allegedly contaminated L-Tryptophan. The disease was given the name EMS, or eosinophilia-myalgia syndrome.

Since 1989, when the EMS nationwide epidemic began, it has claimed some 5,000 victims; at least 36 have died. Many survivors will never regain full health.

L-Tryptophan was sold as an over-the-counter food supplement, enabling the manufacturer to avoid testing and safety standards that the FDA requires of prescription drugs.

Of more than a thousand lawsuits filed, most were settled out-of-court, so there has been little public awareness of the disease and its cause.

To this day, there is no effective regulations of nutritional or dietary supplements, vitamins or minerals. No trustworthy standard of labeling.

Truth is, we know more about what goes into a potato chip than we do about over-the-counter products that promise to make us more energetic, sexier, eternally youthful, disease free.

The more I researched these supplements, the more I became convinced that the hazards are real.

No one wants to deprive us of our vitamins, minerals and energy boosters. The vitamin bottles are lined up on my own bathroom counter; I drink herb tea (in moderation!)

Innocently, I trust that the manufacturers of these products have tested them for uniform strength, for purity and safety, although I know in my heart it's not necessarily so. An expert on health fraud told me, "Reliable manufacturers observe the voluntary guidelines, the others know they don't have to and they don't."

As Americans turn to alternative medicines alone or in combination with traditional drugs, it is vital that we become more aware of what we take into our bodies. Uniform disclosure would help, such as the specifics now required on food product labels.

For starters, I'd recommend this reading:

The transcript of the NBC *Dateline* program on L-Tryptophan called "Bitter Pill," August 22, 1995, segment 246. At this writing, it can be ordered from Burrell's Information Service, 1-800-631-1160.

I don't believe that works of fiction must have a higher purpose. So I hope that Chill has entertained you. If you've been enlightened as well, please don't hold it against me.